Like Dust, I Rise

From award-winning author

Ginny Rorby

Black Rose Writing | Texas

ISBN: 978-1-68433-827-6
PUBLISHED BY BLACK ROSE WRITING
www.blackrosewriting.com

Printed in the United States of America
Suggested Retail Price (SRP) $19.95

Like Dust, I Rise is printed in Sabon

*As a planet-friendly publisher, Black Rose Writing does its best to eliminate
unnecessary waste to reduce paper usage and energy costs, while never
compromising the reading experience. As a result, the final word count vs. page count
may not meet common expectations.

Cover Image: Resettled farm child from Taos Junction to Bosque Farms
project. New Mexico. Photograph for the Farm Security Administration,
December 1935.
Dorothea Lange, Public domain, via Wikimedia Commons

Dedicated to my aunt,

Winona Rorbye Williams

And for Margaret Wallace
best wishes for a
Happy & healthy
2022

Jenny Roslyn

Also by Ginny Rorby

Freeing Finch

How to Speak Dolphin

Lost in the River of Grass

The Outside of a Horse

Hurt Go Happy

Dolphin Sky

Like Dust, I Rise

"But, still, like dust I rise."
–Maya Angelou, *Still I Rise*

"Where human arrogance meets the uncontrollable forces of nature."
–Eric Larson, *Isaac's Storm*

"When something bad happens, you have three choices. You can either let it define you, let it destroy you, or you can let it strengthen you."
–Dr. Seuss

1

Last night was so hot that, in spite of the stench from the stockyards, I left my window open. Between the heat and the smell, I tossed and turned for hours. I finally fell asleep as the sky begin to lighten, and then slept through the usual morning noises in our Back of the Yards neighborhood—the half dozen 6 a.m. factory whistles, train-wheels screeching at every bend in the tracks, terrified animals arriving, followed by the ringing of church and streetcar bells. We live with the constant lowing of thousands of cattle and the grunts of an equal number of pigs in pens that will empty and fill again in a single day. Animals killed, cut-up, packaged, and put on trains leaving Chicago for cities and towns all over the country.

This morning it takes the blast of a horn followed by the squeal of brakes, and a scream that sounds like Mama's to wake me. I untangle myself from my sweat-damp sheets, rush to the window, press my stomach to the sill, and lean out. A boy about my age lies in the road, the hoop he was rolling is still in motion. People stand stunned, watching as the automobile, tires spitting mud, fishtails away, skids around the corner, and disappears. Papa, who's just leaving for work, runs down the front steps. He kneels beside the boy and presses his fingers to his neck, then lowers his head and removes his hat, before turning to look at Mama, who's standing on the stoop, a hand at her heart. He shakes his head, sees me at the window, and motions for me not to look. "Turn away, Winona," he shouts.

I want to, but I can't.

Papa picks him up and carries him to our stoop. Even though most of his face is caked with mud, I recognize him as a boy from my school. Gangsters like Al Capone and Bugs Moran murder people here in Chicago every day, but I've never seen a real dead person before, especially someone my age.

"Nona?"

Owie, my three-year-old brother, is beside me. He tugs my nightdress. "I'm hungry."

I close the window before he notices the commotion on the street, pick him up, and hug him tightly. "You're my big boy," I say, and carry him to the kitchen.

I'm shelling peas when I hear Papa coming up the front steps from work. I know it's him by how heavy his footfall is, and how long it takes him to lift one foot, put it down and lift the other. I beat him to the front hall.

"Hello, Papa." I want to hug him but, as usual, he smells like rancid meat. Papa works at the Union Stock Yard where he slaughters hogs ten hours a day, six days a week—a job he hates. He wears rubber boots, coveralls, and a leather apron, and hoses himself down before leaving work, but he still comes home spotted with dried blood and carrying the stench.

Mama's in the doorway of our flat, hands on her hips. "Not another step."

She says the same thing every night and stands guard to make sure Papa remembers to leave his boots, muddy from the walk home, in the hall bench's storage box.

Papa takes off his raggedy hat and hangs it on one of the pegs. "I remember, Mother." To me he says, "How's my girl?"

I love both my parents but feel oddly shy about the depth of my devotion to my father. "Good."

He smiles, lowers himself stiffly onto the bench, leans his head back against the mirrored-center, and closes his eyes.

"Want me to pull your boots off for you?"

"No, honey." He doesn't open his eyes. "Your mama will butcher me if you get this muddy stink on you. Just give me a minute."

I lean against the opposite wall and watch the lines in his face gradually relax. A moment later, he starts to snore.

"Is he asleep?" Mama whispers from the doorway.

I nod.

"Let him be for a few minutes. I'm heating some water for him to wash up before supper."

I watch the hands on the hall clock click off ten minutes before touching his shoulder. "Papa, the water's hot."

He opens his eyes and smiles at me, puts his hands on his knees and pushes himself to standing. His still damp hair leaves a streaky circle on the mirror.

I hold his slippers and wait while he fits a heel at a time into the boot jack and pulls his feet free. "What's that?" I point to the rolled-up piece of paper sticking out of his pants' pocket.

He puts a finger to his lips. "Not anything I want your mama to see just yet."

"Is it a surprise?" I whisper.

"That all depends."

"On what?"

"I'll let you know. It's mighty quiet in here. Where's Owen Junior?"

"Mrs. Howard's got him. She took him and Win to the park."

"You and Kippy didn't want to go?"

Kippy's my best friend. "Not today. We played jacks." I duck my head. I'm not lying, but I'm not telling the whole truth either.

He probably knows Bubbly Creek, which is as sluggish as hot tar and black with blood and animal guts, caught fire again. I don't tell him Kippy and I went over to watch the fire department put it out, and I've never told him we once threw a lit match in to see if we could start a fire, too. It caught first try and scared us so bad we ran home like a pair of rabbits.

After watching Bubbly Creek burn, Kippy and I went to the city dump nearest our house. We go there to look for treasures, things rich people throw away. Professional scavengers wait for the garbage wagons, but once they've picked through, anyone who can brave the flies can look for what they've missed. Kippy found a gold ring once. I've collected twenty-five Lincoln wheat pennies and an 1864 Indian head penny. I took it to show Mr. Fischer, who lives by himself in the attic of our boardinghouse.

"Keep it in a tissue," he told me. "It may be verth something someday." Mr. Fischer's from Germany and still has an accent.

The paper he'd been reading and his magnifying glass were on the table beside his favorite chair. The front page had a picture of two men and a lady riding in an open car through what looked like a snowstorm. "Aren't those people freezing?"

He laughed. "That's not snow. It's ticker tape—a parade to honor Amelia Earhart, Wilmer Stultz and Lewis Gordon."

"What did they do?"

"They flew an aeroplane across the Atlantic last week."

I used his magnifying glass to look more closely at the picture. Miss Earhart was looking up and waving. If I angle the picture a bit, it looked like she was smiling and waving right at me. "Which man is she married to?"

"Neither. She's a lady-pilot, though this time she vas just along for the ride."

"Really?" I smiled back at her. *A lady pilot!* "How did she become a pilot?"

"Learned to fly and practiced, I suppose."

"Could I be a pilot?"

"I don't see vhy not."

"Can I have that picture when you're done with the paper?"

"You can have it right now." Mr. Fischer took out a pen knife, folded the paper to keep from cutting through to the table, and gave me the picture. I folded it carefully so there's no crease in her face and put it in my pocket. Once, when Kippy told me she wants to be a teacher when she's grown, she asked what I wanted to be, I said I didn't know. Now I do. I shall be a lady pilot.

Papa and I are still in the hall when the front door flies open and Owie charges in with Mrs. Howard, Kippy's mom, right behind him. "Fodder." Owie wraps his arms around Papa's knees. "Nona." He hugs my waist.

Owie's real name is Owen Williams Junior. My name is Winona, but Owie couldn't get it out, so I've been Nona since he learned to talk, except when Mama's mad at me, then I'm Winona Williams with an exclamation point.

"Hello, Owen," Kippy's mom says.

"Hi, Celia," Mama calls from the alcove we call our kitchen. "Was he a good boy?"

"Of course." Mrs. Howard musses Owie's blond hair.

"Nona," Mama says. "You've still got peas to shell in here." To Mrs. Howard she says, "I'll send Nona over with them when she's done. Do you want her to fetch coal from the basement?"

"Mr. Fischer brought some up earlier, but thanks." She pats my cheek and straightens the stupid bow in my hair that makes me look like I'm wearing a set of cow's ears.

Mrs. Howard is our landlady. She lives across the hall. Our rent of fifteen dollars a month includes evening suppers, which she cooks, and all the tenants eat together. Our kitchen has a sink, and a small table, no stove. Mama told me once to consider us lucky not to be eating her cooking. "My sisters were the cooks in the family. I was best at sewing."

Mrs. Howard glances at the clock. "Mercy me, I'm late getting supper started."

Mama takes her apron off the peg on the door. "Finish the peas, Nona, and make sure your brother washes his hands. I'll go help Mrs. Howard."

Mrs. Howard and Mama are best friends, too. They smile and hook arms as they cross the hall.

2

Papa sits at our little table waiting for Mama's answer. Overhead, the single incandescent bulb swings on its cord in time to the movements of the tenants who live in the flat above us. The ticking of the clock and the *drip, drip, drip* of the faucet are the only other sounds.

Mama stands at the sink with her back to us, her face reflected in the soot-encrusted window. I've given the empty pea pods to the chickens in our tiny back yard and am drying the bowl I brought back from supper.

The paper that was rolled up in Papa's coat pocket is on the table, the corners held down by the salt and pepper shakers, a kerosene lamp, and the hour-glass egg timer. It's a page from a Kansas City newspaper showing pictures of a watermelon the size of a wagon, another of corn so tall a man stands on a ladder to harvest it, and an angel wearing a beauty-queen banner like Miss Chicago wore, but hers reads: "Opportunity." The angel has an arm across a farmer's shoulders and she's pointing toward either a sunrise or a sunset; I can't tell which. Before I get a chance to read the caption, Papa puts on his glasses and says, "She's directing the patient toiler to the Health, Wealth, and Happiness on the beautiful south plains of Texas." He glances at me, then Mama's back, and waits. The faucet continues to drip.

"Wherever we end up, Glenny, won't be any farther from your family than we are now."

By family, he means Mama's sister, two aunts, and a passel of nieces and nephews, who all farm in Carthage, Missouri. Not that she's seen any of them since shortly after I was born. Her mother died of influenza in 1918. I don't know what happened to her father. When I've asked, she says she'll tell me someday.

"I know more about farming than you do, Owen." I recognize that smug tone of voice. I hear it a lot.

But I don't know what Papa means when he says, "That was eleven years ago, Glenny." He looks at his hands and turns them callused side up. "Besides, they're growing so much wheat on the prairie, a fellow doesn't need to know much to start. I'll learn what I need to know when I need to know it."

Mama turns and looks me. "Nona, go check on Owie."

She wants to talk to Papa without me listening. I go down the hall then creep back and stand where she can't see me. Papa glances in my direction but doesn't say anything.

"Look what it says." He taps the newspaper. "It's so easy to grow a crop, men travel down from big cities, plant wheat, and don't bother to return until it's time to harvest."

Mama leans against the sink and folds her arms. I've seen her do this many times, too. She's listening, but her mind is made up. Someone upstairs moves causing our bulb to sway, lightening and darkening Mama's expression. It makes her look bored then mean, then bored.

"Nothing is going to change for me at the Yards." There's an edge to Papa's voice that's a blend of desperation and determination. "Men willing to work for any amount they're offered, arrive daily. I can't spend the rest of my life hooking a chain around the hind leg of a hog, hoisting it, and listening to it shriek until I slit its throat, then chain and hoist the next one."

A vee forms in my mother's brow and her arms drop to her sides.

"I want to go see for myself if this—" He points to the article, "is for us. A homestead will give us a piece of something. Here we have nothing and never will."

Papa hates his work and I hate it for him. He's been talking about leaving Chicago since Owie was born three and a half years ago. He was a farrier in the Great War, but says there are now so many automobiles in Chicago, the only person left with a horse to shoe is the ragman. After the war, he went to work at the stockyards because he had Mama and me to support and the slaughterhouses paid the best.

When I asked Mama if she thought we would really move, she said no. "Your papa's been restless since the war ended, but he was born and raised in Chicago. He'll never leave."

But Papa started bringing it up again last month when the battles between Al Capone's South Side gang and Bugs Moran's North Side gang became headlines in nearly every edition of the paper. Back of the Yards is on the southwest side of the city. At night in the summer, when the windows are open, I sometimes hear the *rat-a-tat tat* of gunfire.

Mama knows this isn't the best place to raise children, but everywhere else, except Missouri, is unknown and unknowable. As always, she listens, then says, "Someday, dear."

I think the boy getting run over in front of our house has made Papa more determined. Death came to our doorstep. And now, for the first time, he knows where he wants to go. Texas. Mama looks worried.

Papa puts his head in his hands. Mama comes over and begins to rub his neck.

I feel safe going back into the kitchen. "Owie's asleep." It's not a lie. If he wasn't, he'd be in here with us.

"I've made up my mind," Papa says. "We are leaving Chicago."

"Are we going to Texas?"

"Go to bed, Winona." Mama says.

Papa looks at me. "Yes, siree." He smiles. "The southern Great Plains of Kansas, Oklahoma, and the Texas panhandle. Where exactly, I'm not sure."

"I'm going to be a pilot like Miss Earhart. Do all those states have planes?"

Papa doesn't get a chance to answer.

"Oh, Owen, what in the world would we do in any of those places? Where will the children go to school?"

"I'm sure they have schools, Glenny. I'll farm, and if farming is not in the cards, I heard tell of a cattle ranch in north Texas. I could go back to being a farrier."

"It sounds rash, Owen."

"Good God, Mother, you agree this is no place to raise children. It could have been one of ours mowed down by an automobile or caught in the crossfire of those gangsters. Remember Bobby Franks? What if that was Nona or Owie?"

Bobby Franks was a boy a little older than me. He was killed by two college students for the thrill of it.

Mama gives Papa her "little-pitchers-have-big-ears" look and says to me, "I told you to go to bed."

"I know who Bobby Franks is." I go to the door, turn and look back. "Was."

Mama's staring at the water stain on the ceiling. "When would we leave?"

I hold my breath.

Papa shrugs. "I'll go first and find us a place. You and the children can follow on the train."

Mama's eyes widen. "If we're going, we should all go together."

A train! Our neighborhood is bordered on three sides by railroad tracks. Kippy and I love to watch the trains and imagine the places the passengers are coming from or going to. If we take a train, I'll be one of those people.

"I'm not going to search for work with the children in tow," Papa says. "You have to wait here until I'm settled."

"How long will that take?"

Papa shakes his head. "A couple months, maybe."

Mama turns and stares at her reflection in the filthy, wavy glass. The light bulb sways. Then her shoulders sag and she bows her head.

Papa gets up and puts his arms around her. "I'm not your father, Glenny." He moves the hair that has escaped her bun and kisses the back of her neck.

"Okay," she says.

My breath catches. She said okay. We're going to ride a train, go live where there are planes. I can't wait to tell Kippy and Mr. Fischer. Then I realize moving means leaving the other people I love.

3

Papa's leaving July nineteenth, a month before my eleventh birthday. He bought two horses from the line headed for the glue factory, and an old prairie schooner like the covered wagons the early settlers used to move west. He parked it right over the spot where the boy got killed. When Kippy and I got home from school that first afternoon, it was already a hive of neighborhood kids playing cowboys and Indians.

I name the horses Ben and Sam. For the time being, they are in the shed behind our boardinghouse. Papa says when we come to join him, I'll likely have a horse of my own, so I might as well learn how to take care of them. It's my job to feed them and muck their stalls. Mama makes me wear my galoshes, so I don't ruin my school shoes. I pretend they are cowboy boots.

I'm partial to Sam. He has a sense of humor and snorts and paws the ground while I'm cleaning like I'm not moving fast enough to suit him. He lets the chickens roost on his back which is so broad and swayed that one laid an egg, and it didn't roll off.

The houses on our street are all the same: wooden, two-story, not counting the attics, and covered with a film of soot from the factory chimneys. The flats on either side of the central hallway are long and narrow. I sleep in the front room which is crowded with Mama's share of the furniture she inherited from her mother.

Papa thought everything we own would fit in the prairie schooner and that two horses would be enough to pull it. It didn't take him long to realize the schooner wasn't heavy enough to carry the weight of Mama's marble-topped furnishings: two parlor tables, a five-drawer dresser with mirror, her Singer sewing machine, two Oriental carpets, and the quilts she made for each of us, Owie's being her most recent. Papa swapped it for a heavier Conestoga which, when loaded, needed four horses to pull it.

A couple days before he leaves, Papa tries to show Mama his route map. She gets misty-eyed and she walks away, so he shows me. "Oh Papa, it's the Great Plains. I thought you meant P-L-A-N-E-S." Disappointment is clear in my voice.

"What made you think that?"

I shrug. "You told us we were moving there right after Miss Earhart flew the Atlantic Ocean. I thought it would be a place where I could learn to fly aeroplanes. I'm going to be a pilot like Miss Earhart."

Papa laughs—a laugh that is lighter and more frequent now that he's leaving. "Girls can't be pilots, Nona. It's too dangerous. Miss Earhart didn't fly the aeroplane herself. You're going to grow up to be as pretty as your mother, get married, and have a beautiful family."

I duck when he reaches to straighten the big bow in my hair. "No, I'm not. Kippy and I are never getting married, and I'm going to be a pilot." I hate all the clothing that keeps girls from doing what boys can do: bows, dresses, pinafores, and Mary Jane shoes. "Miss Earhart knows how to fly," I say. "And it was just as dangerous for her to ride with them."

"Yes, but I don't want my little girl risking life and limb." Papa sees the disappointment I feel. "I could be wrong." He folds his map.

Now I feel bad. At least one of us should act excited for him. "I want to see the map, Papa."

He smiles and spreads it out again. Chicago is circled, and he's drawn a line along new Route 66 to Saint Louis. The two cities look close. "How far *are* the Great Plains?"

"I don't know precisely, but from here—" He puts his thumb on Chicago and his index finger on Saint Louis. "is about three hundred miles."

"How long will that take?"

"I doubt more than a fortnight on that new road."

Two weeks! "It will take a year to get to the Great Plains." Tears threaten.

Papa tilts my head up by my chin. "What's this? Is my aeroplane-pilot daughter about to cry?" He wipes a tear with his thumb and hugs me. "Just a couple months and we'll be together again. Time will also fly."

It's the night before Papa is leaving. Mama and I are in the kitchen helping Mrs. Howard cook supper for the boarders. "I pray he finds ranch work so you don't end up living on the God-forsaken prairie," Mrs. Howard says. "Life out west is no cake-walk, but the loneliness of prairie life, my oh my." She rolls her eyes toward the ceiling.

"What is a prairie?" I'm peeling potatoes. Kippy's in the front room playing Pick-up-Sticks with Win and Owie.

"A wide-open, nearly treeless grassland," Mrs. Howard says. "The North American prairie, which stretches from Canada to Texas, is called the Great Plains."

"How do you know it's God-forsaken?" I ask.

"Winona Williams. Your language," Mama says.

Mrs. Howard smiles. "My mother grew up in South Dakota. She told how she wouldn't see another living soul, except kin, and the occasional Indian, for months at a time."

Between loving Papa and wanting him to be happy, and not wanting to leave my two best friends and the only home I can remember, I feel torn to pieces—for me and for Mama who's leaving her best friend, too.

Mama looks teary-eyed. Mrs. Howard pats her back and smiles at her. "And who's going to cook for you?"

That makes us all laugh.

I love eating at the long table in Mrs. Howard's kitchen with the rest of her renters. With no blood-relatives nearby, the other boarders have become family and I especially love Mr. Fischer in spite of Mama calling him "that old Jew" in the tone she uses when she doesn't like someone. He is old, but I don't know what a Jew is, or care.

Living backed up to the stockyards, you'd think we'd have meat with every meal, but what ends up on our table, if we can afford meat at all, is usually tough, tasteless, and, if not rancid, nearly so. But for Papa's last night, Mrs. Howard made a special supper—Papa's favorite: a Waldorf salad, roasted chicken with mashed potatoes and gravy, and the best part—a chocolate cake for dessert, which I loved, but don't think I'll ever taste again and not remember, in spite of the laughter all around and wishes for a safe journey, how sad we were at the end.

After Mrs. Howard talked about the hardships women face living on the Plains, Mama spent the rest of that evening trying to talk Papa out of going. With no success.

So here we are this hot July day—all the kissing, hugging, and tears are over. We stand on the steps waving a final goodbye. Papa studies us like he's memorizing the moment, then clicks to the four hot, tired-looking horses, and slaps the reins. The wagon, filled with Mama's prized furnishings, lurches forward. He's off.

"Hold your brother." Mama hands me Owie, lifts her skirts, and runs down the steps, calling to Papa.

"Whoa." He reins in the team and jumps down from the wagon. When Mama reaches him, he sweeps her into his arms and kisses her in front on the whole neighborhood.

"You'll keep your promise?"

"I will, Glenny. You can trust me."

An automobile rumbles up behind them spewing black smoke from its tailpipe. It has to wait for oncoming traffic to get around the wagon. The driver's horn quacks like a duck with a head cold. "Come on, Mack. Get that pile of junk out of the way."

The horses whinny and snort. Papa lets Mama go, puts his hat on, presses his hand to her cheek, and climbs back into the wagon. He waves a final time to Owie and me.

Tears roll down my cheeks. The arm I raise to wave weighs a hundred pounds.

It's the day after Papa left, and I'm helping Mama dust the front room. Without Mama's furniture, the room where I sleep seems much larger. I'm dusting and Mama is using lemon oil and beeswax to polish the furniture that came with the flat. It's been in the attic all this time, in a small space, behind a door opposite Mr. Fischer's room.

I shake the dust rag out the open window. "If you could pick between Papa working on a ranch or a farm, which would you choose?"

"A ranch, I suppose. Farming is going to be tougher than he thinks." She tucks loose strands of hair behind her ear.

"What did Papa mean when he asked you to trust him?"

She straightens and looks at me. "Trust him to send for us."

"I heard him say, 'I'm not your father.' Are you going to tell me what he meant?"

"I guess you're old enough to know." For a moment, she watches the dust motes dance in the hazy sunbeam coming through the open window. "My father deserted us when my sister and I were little. He went out West and we never saw him again."

My heart thumpity-thumps. "Papa would *never* do that."

She gives me the look I hate. The one that says, *You're such a baby. What do you know?* Then her eyes soften. "You're right. Papa is a good man."

4

A few days after Papa leaves, a brutal heat wave settles over Chicago. The foul air and smoke seal the neighborhood like a lid on a pot. Anyone who stands still for a few minutes collects a layer of ash from the factories. Through the haze, the sun is still baking hot, making the garbage in the alleys rot quicker and smell worse than usual. Flies by the millions swarm and fill any room with an open window.

Owie develops a cough that hangs on no matter how many nights Mama puts VapoRub on his feet and covers them with socks.

I write letters to Papa, but since I don't have an address, I keep them in a cigar box Mr. Fischer gave me. I'll wait until Owie is better before telling Papa he's been sick. When he does read my letters, he'll get the bad news and the good news at the same time.

Mama's been sick to her stomach, and some mornings I hear her in the bathroom, throwing up. Mrs. Howard tells me not to worry. It will pass. For a couple of weeks, until Mama feels better, Mrs. Howard has her drinking a disgusting sounding brew of warm cider vinegar and water in the mornings.

My eleventh birthday comes and goes with no word from Papa. Mrs. Howard bakes me a cake with pink icing and gives me a new bow for my hair. I try to sound pleased when I thank her. Mama made me a new pinafore that I'm to save to wear on the train. The boarders sing to me in their different languages, but it's not the same without Papa.

Since Papa's search for work and a place to live may take a long time, Mrs. Howard lowers our rent to ten dollars a month, insisting that Mama and me helping in the kitchen is worth the difference. After another month, with no word from Papa, Mama says we can't expect

Mrs. Howard to be charitable much longer. She applies for and gets a job at Swift trimming sausage ten hours a day.

Mama takes Owie and Win to the Guardian Angel Day Care in the mornings on her way to work. Kippy and I pick them up on our way home from school and babysit until Mama gets home.

A couple of weeks after Mama goes to work, three letters come all at once. The first is postmarked Dodge City, Kansas and dated July 29.

Dear Glenny, Winona, and Owen Junior,

Ah my girls and little man you'll not believe the air. Even in the heat there is sweetness in the morning like nothing you have ever smelt, and it's green as far as the eye can see.

Between the weight of the wagon, the heat, and the advanced age of these poor horses, I'm not making the progress I'd hoped. I travel in the mornings and evenings, resting the team during the heat of the day.

The paved section of Route 66 ended at the outskirts of Chicago. There the road narrowed, making it hard to find places to pull the team over when an automobile wants to pass. It's graded and graveled, which is good, but it means when I stop to rest the horses, I must pick small stones from their hooves. I've only covered about a hundred miles. At this rate I will not reach St. Louis for another week. I miss you all and will write again soon.

Your loving husband and father, Owen.

The second is dated August 18, a day before my birthday.

Dear Glenny, Winona, and Owen Junior,

Today I crossed the Mississippi river by ferry. Soon there will be a bridge, which has been started on both banks of the river with the hope that the Illinois side and the Missouri side will one day meet in the middle. Where I crossed is called Chain of Rocks. Water tumbled over and around them so loud the horses whinnied and rolled their eyes. The ferryman said many wagons and horses were swept away afore the ferry started its service.

The ferry itself wasn't more than a big, wide raft with a thick rope strung through a gas-engine pulley, one on either side of the river. Cost two bits, which I guess I can't accurately call highway robbery.

I love you and miss you, Owen.

P.S. I expect this will arrive after your big day, Winona, so a belated Happy Birthday. We'll celebrate when we're together again, wherever that turns out to be.

The third is dated September 29.

Dear Glenny, Winona, and Owie,

The heat took its toll on the horses. One has died—not Sam or Ben, Nona. I didn't dare spend the money I have left to replace him, so have kept going with three. I've been letting two pull and one rest and rotating them every couple of hours. I left Route 66 to join the Santa Fe Trail in Boonslick, Missouri. I picked up supplies in Arrow Rock and am aiming for the XIT ranch in Texas, where there will surely be work for a man like me. The most direct route has been across Kansas. At least it's flat and the weather has turned cool.

Winona, you will not believe the stars. On a moonless night they look near enough to touch and there are so many that if they fell, they would blanket the earth like a January snow.

Your loving husband and father, Owen

I read and reread Papa's letters and try to imagine him asleep in his bedroll on the ground near the horses, able to look straight up into the heavens and see stars instead of cinders rising into night sky.

I write Papa a letter telling him one of the boys down the street was bitten by a rat. He and other neighborhood kids were playing stick ball on 43rd Street and he chased the ball into an alley. It was dusk and the rats were pouring out of buildings headed for the meat warehouses. He stepped on one and it bit him on the toe. He had to have rabies shots in his stomach with a big needle. I'm not sure if I tell Papa this story as support for his decision, or as a reminder we're here waiting. Maybe both. I don't tell him Mama's been sick for a couple months, or that she took a job. I do mention how much I'm looking forward to seeing those stars. And to make Papa laugh, I tell him about the steer that got loose from one of the pens and ran amok through the streets until a cowboy on horseback lassoed him.

In mid-October, a letter arrives postmarked Dalhart, Texas.

My darling girls and little man,
Another horse died shortly after I crossed into Texas, but the only choice was to keep going south. Sam and Ben, though thin and tired, still show a determination to make it to the end—wherever that may be. The homesteaders have plowed the grass up, turning the prairie inside out. It's hard to find fodder for the horses or water since all the creeks and streams are bone dry. I'm forced to detour every time I see a windmill, and hope the farmer is friendly enough to let me refill my water barrels from his well and give the horses a drink.
October 25. I wrote the above last week, but there was no place to mail it. We—the horses and I—have made it to Dalhart, Texas. The bad news is there is no longer an XIT Ranch. Their cattle have been sold, along with a great deal of their land to people who wish to farm. But there is good news. I've found farm work, my love. Not just a job, but an opportunity we would never have in Chicago. Glenny, I think you will like Dalhart. There's a school, a movie theater, a couple of fine churches, a hotel, a restaurant, and even a sanatorium with a well-respected doctor. I'll explain it all when you get here. Enclosed are train tickets for you and the children. Wire me in care of the Dalhart postmistress when you're ready to leave. I will be waiting.
All my love, Owen

Kippy and I are in the kitchen peeling potatoes when Mama comes across the hall with Papa's letter. Mrs. Howard reads it, then puts her arms around Mama. "How soon?"

"I don't know," Mama says. Tears roll down her cheeks.

Kippy and I watch them, then look at each other. It's real now. Our lives are about to change. I realize that, until this minute, I thought there was a chance Papa would give up, turn around, and come home. Tears swim in Kippy's eyes. She gets up, comes over and hugs me. If I'm going to be a pilot, I will need to be brave like Papa. But tonight, I can't stop my tears and cling to her tightly.

5

Mama still isn't feeling well some mornings, which I thought was the reason she'd put off leaving twice. The Monday after Thanksgiving, a telegram arrives from Papa concerned about the delay and urging her to come soon.

"You should tell him," Mrs. Howard says that same night.

Kippy and I are playing tic tac toe in the flour on the bread board. When Mrs. Howard says that, I get a sinking feeling in my stomach. Maybe Mama has decided we're not going. "Tell him what?" I demand.

Mrs. Howard looks at my mother, who shrugs, then nods.

Kippy's mom smiles and says, "Your mama's going to have a baby."

"Really?" I turn to Kippy. "Did you hear that? A baby!"

Mama isn't smiling.

I want to hug her, but am not sure she'd want me to. "Aren't you happy?"

She nods. "Sure I am. It's just bad timing, that's all."

"Why haven't you told Papa?"

"I don't know. I guess I didn't want to worry him." She shakes a finger at me. "You're not to say a word to your father until I'm ready to tell him. Do you understand?"

"But—."

"Not a word."

"Yes, ma'am."

Mama first said we'd leave the day after my school let out for the Christmas holidays, then changed her mind and said she wanted to spend our last Christmas here with friends. Papa sent two more telegrams, the second worried that one of us was unwell. Mama finally answered and committed to leaving on Tuesday, January 1. It seems fitting to leave for a new life in a new year.

On the Wednesday before we leave, I find her in the bedroom. She's standing in front of the mirror in a long, old-fashioned sky-blue dress, humming *Blue Skies*. Her favorite cotton housedress and apron are on the floor at her feet. Two more fancy dresses lie across the bed. I've never seen any of them before.

The dress she's wearing has about a hundred buttons down the back, none of which she was able to fasten. She holds it closed with her hands on her waist, thumbs trying to press the two back halves together.

Mama's eyes are the same color as the dress and her glossy brown hair, usually worn in a bun, cascades down her back. In the light from the window the wisps around her face look feathery. I've never given a thought to how beautiful she must have been, and how beautiful she still is.

She tilts her head to admire herself and smiles a thin, sad smile.

"Are you taking all these dresses?"

She jumps. "You scared the life out of me."

"Sorry. Are you?"

"I don't think so. I was just trying them on." She turns to look at herself sideways. "I used to be so thin."

"You will be again."

"Not after yet another child, I won't." She laces her finger across her swollen tummy.

"What are you saving the dresses for if they don't fit anymore?"

"I don't know. Perhaps for the pleasure they bring when I remember wearing them. And I suppose I thought I *would* wear them again. We never know when we're doing something for the last time. If we knew, we might stop to appreciate the moment."

Kippy keeps saying the same thing, how this may be our last time foraging in the dump, skipping rope, or flirting with the boys shooting marbles in the alley. Her reminders of what might be our last times together makes us stop whatever we're doing and hug.

I rub the satiny material of one of the dresses between my fingers. "Were you rich before you married Papa?"

"We were comfortable."

I pick up the long dress in a shade of deep green, hold it at my chin, and look at myself in the mirror. "This one's pretty." It's sleeveless, low-cut in the front, with a deep vee in the back.

Mama's eyes soften. "I made that one to wear to a dance with your father shortly before he left for the war in France. I was seventeen. Can you imagine?" She gnaws a corner of her bottom lip as the memory plays out in her mind. She looks down at me standing reflected in the mirror, takes the dress, and folds it.

Mama's not a hand-holder or I would have taken hers right then. "Did you make all of these?"

"I did."

Mama's sewing machine went in the wagon with Papa, but I've never seen her make anything except dresses for herself and me, my pinafores, and a few aprons. These dresses are like the ones I see in her *Vogue* magazines.

"Were you and Papa married when you made the green one?"

She nods. "For a whole month." She holds her arms out and begins to sway, then smiles and flips her hands for me to dance with her. We do the box step around the room until the unfastened dress slips off her shoulders.

"What are you going to do with them?"

"I'm thinking of taking them to make school dresses for you."

"I hate dresses. Am I gonna have to wear them on the farm, too?"

Mama's right eyebrow goes up and I know what she's thinking. I'm more suited to having dresses made from Papa's work clothes. I'm never clean enough for her. I scrub my neck; she checks it and scrubs it harder. My collars are always grimy, and the sides of my pinafores are smudged where I clean the stink off the pennies I find at the dump.

"If that's how you feel, maybe I'll give them to Celia. She can use the material to make dresses for Kippy." Kippy loves nice dresses and is careful even when we sneak off to scavenge. Mama's trying to make me jealous enough to act more like girl and less like a tomboy. She can give them away if she wants to, but I don't believe she will. Like her marble top furniture, they have sentimental value.

"I think you should keep them and make something for our new house."

"Right. Might as well. Curtains or a quilt." Her voice is sneery and her eyes mist before she turns her back to me, folds the dress, and sets it aside.

Beneath it is a long-sleeved pair of faded blue denim coveralls, with a starched white collar. "Whose coveralls are these?"

She glances over her shoulder. "They were mine."

"Pants? When did you get to wear pants? I'd give anything to wear pants instead of dresses all the time."

"That was my Farmerette uniform when I was in the WLA." She grins. "The Women's Land Army." She clicks her heels and salutes me. "Don't be a slacker; be a picker or a packer."

I laugh. "What's a Farmerette?"

"A Soldier of the Soil."

It sounds silly. I giggle.

She takes the uniform from me, holds it under her chin and turns to look at herself in the mirror. "When your father and the other boys went off to war, there weren't enough able-bodied men left to grow the food. There were shortages and even a few riots. I was one of thousands of women who volunteered to work the farms."

Mama always looks bone tired—especially lately—but this memory makes her face glow.

"What job did you do?"

"I was trained to drive a tractor, but when I was assigned to my first farm, I found out you were on the way. I ended up being a packer. Canned corn."

"And they let you wear pants?"

"No one *let* us. We demanded pants." She juts her chin. "The work was impossible in a dress. We worked eight-hour days, and we were paid the same wages as any man. We lived together in a camp and had our meals cooked and served just like soldiers in the Army." She salutes me again. "I had the time of my life, Nona. You can't imagine what it's like to be valuable and valued—as a woman."

I'd never ever seen Mama's eyes sparkle like this. It's clear she's remembering a happier time and it makes me wonder if she yearns more for her life then than for her life now. I decide, no matter what happens, I'm going to be like Papa and look forward to the mystery and promise of the future over wishing to live in the past.

"The uniform gave us something to live up to," she says, "and wearing it made us all the same. It didn't matter how much education you had, or how far up the social ladder your family ranked, or your ethnic background. We were sisters. One of the posters is in the trunk your papa took. It read: "*The girl with the hoe behind the man with the gun.*"

"Is that why you said you knew more about farming than Papa?"

Mama refolds the coveralls. "I did learn to drive a tractor, but I shouldn't have said that. And he was right. If I could learn, so can he."

"Where did you live when you were a Farmerette?"

"Shenandoah, Iowa. First time I'd ever been away from home."

"Are you taking your uniform?"

"Should I?"

"We're going to be farmers, aren't we?"

"We are indeed," she says, but the twinkle in her eyes is gone.

"Maybe I'll grow into them and can wear them when I help Papa." As soon as I said this, I wished I hadn't. "Being a Farmerette was Mama's memory and I've reminded her that the last time she wore these coveralls was just as she said, the last time.

6

1929

As the time to leave looms, the more unhappy I become. Sometimes, a pain in my chest spreads to my throat and nearly strangles me. I sleep in a room I no longer recognize as my own, full of stored furniture and suitcases. Kippy and I were playing Jacks and I burst into tears. She did, too. She and I have shared all our secrets, all our adventures. And no one will ever care only about me like Mr. Fischer. He always wanted me to tell him about my discoveries, but we never talked about him. I only know that he came to America from Germany, but know nothing else about his life before I met him. After Papa's last telegram arrived, I found excuses to visit his hot, musty-smelling flat in the attic more often.

On yesterday's visit, he gave me a well-worn copy of *Heidi*. I sat on his sofa, thumbing through, looking at the pictures, while he served us tea. "How come you have a girl's book?"

"It vas my granddaughter's."

"I didn't know you had family. Where does she live?"

He closed his eyes and sent his bushy white eyebrows to meet his hairline. "She and my daughter died in 1918. My vife, too. Only I survive."

"Was it the war?"

"Influenza."

"Like my grandmother. Did you live in Missouri, too?"

"Vee vere in Germany. The influenza vas a pandemic."

"What's a pandemic?"

"Videspread. The 1918 influenza killed fifty million people, maybe more. I had no family left so I come to America. But I'm a Jew, and a German. Frau Howard vas the only person who vould give me a place to live. She is a kind voman."

My mind hears the snarly tone Mama uses when she calls him "that old Jew." "What does it mean to be a Jew?"

"Vee are an ancient tribe of people who believe that the Messiah has yet to come. Some Christians believe the Jews killed Christ."

Jesus died a long time ago and Mr. Fischer didn't have anything to do with it. I'm ashamed of my mother for holding a grudge, but curious, too. "Did they?"

"No, the Romans killed him, but Jews helped condemn him. Did you know Christ also vas a Jew?"

I shake my head, take his hand, and study the big, blue veins under paper-thin skin. I'm pretty sure I'm his only friend.

He pats my cheek.

This morning, when I go to the attic to tell him we're leaving tomorrow, he gives me a little coin purse of brown and white cowhide with bits of soft hair missing. Inside is a brand new 1929 buffalo nickel, which I think he must have overlooked when he emptied out his change. I hand it back to him.

"That's for you, Fraulein. You're a good little saver and I know you vill spend it visely."

Mr. Fischer is the only person I ever told about the money I collected over the months at the dump. If Mama ever found out Kippy and I regularly scoured the trash heaps alongside poorer children, who forage there for food and clothes, she'd have skinned me. We've yet to sink that low, she would say.

"I'll never spend it. I'll keep it to remember you by."

His already watery eyes fill with tears. He holds his bony arms out and flaps his hand for me to come sit beside him on the sofa.

"Will I ever see you again?" My head is against his shoulder. He smells musty like his apartment.

"The truth?"

It feels hard to breathe. I nod.

"Probably not. I'm an old man."

"I wish we weren't leaving." I choke back tears. "I wish Papa would come back so we could always live here."

"Stop your sniffling. Your Papa, he's vaiting for you and your life vill fill with new adventures and people. You'll forget me soon enough."

Tears roll down my cheeks. I want so much to say something important, something wise enough to show him what he means to me. Mr. Fischer is the only grandfather I'll ever have. Papa's father died when Papa was Owie's age and Mama's disappeared. But only dull little words get around the lump in my throat. "You're wrong. I'll remember you forever. Have you forgotten the people you loved when you were a boy?"

"No." His voice cracks. "I remember them."

I move in closer and he puts his chin on top of my head. "Be happy, Liebchen," he whispers.

◦～◦

I wake on our last day in Chicago to dirty sunlight slipping up the wall of my room. In a couple of days, I will be gone, and new people will move in. This must be what it's like to die. You're here then you're not. I lie watching the sun creep across the floor and realize I'll never ever again run up the front steps, shed my coat, smell Mrs. Howard's cooking, or climb the stairs to Mr. Fischer's apartment.

The taxicab waits at the curb. Mr. Fischer, Win, Kippy, and her mom are here to wave goodbye. Everyone is red-eyed from crying, even Owie, who isn't sure what's going on. "Don't go." He hugs Win, as if he's the one leaving.

I hug Win, Mr. Fischer, then Kippy, Mrs. Howard, and Mr. Fischer again. Mama shakes Mr. Fischer's hand. "I'm grateful for your kindness to Winona."

He clicks his heels and nods to my mother. "It is I who am grateful."

She pulls her hand away. "Yes. Well." She turns to hug Kippy, and kisses Win's cheek.

I wrestle Owie into the cab and crawl in beside him. Mama sits but doesn't swing her legs in. "God, this is breaking my heart." She rushes back into Mrs. Howard's arms. Kippy starts to cry again, but before I can climb out and hug her a last time. Mama's back and pulls the door closed. She stares straight ahead as the cab lurches away from the curb.

Kippy runs alongside, waving.

I love Papa almost more than my heart can hold, but at this moment I feel fear and dread like I've never known. What if Mama's right and it's all a big mistake? There will be no turning back. As the cab steps wheel by wheel over the ruts and potholes leading out of the Back of the Yards, I get on my knees to watch out the rear window as Kippy, Win, Mrs. Howard, and Mr. Fischer disappear from my life.

7

Even a short distance from the Back of the Yards, the air feels cleaner.
The train tickets Papa sent are for the *Scout,* which leaves Chicago's
Dearborn Station at ten in the morning and arrives in Kansas City,
Missouri, at nine-thirty at night. Our next train, the *Californian,* leaves
Kansas City that same day at five minutes before midnight and will
arrive in Dalhart tomorrow at 5:15, in time for supper with Papa.

The Dearborn Station is three stories tall with a twelve-story clock
tower, all made of pink granite and red bricks. It's the prettiest building
I've ever seen. Dozens of taxi cabs come and go, emptying passengers
and their luggage, which is taken by porters in red caps. Most of what
we'll need for our new lives in Texas went with Papa, so Mama makes
us carry our own bags because a porter would expect a nickel tip.

The terminal is cavernous and echoes with the noise of trains being
called, women corralling excited children, and hundreds of people
headed out to the tracks to board, and hundreds more coming off of the
incoming trains. There's a Fred Harvey restaurant, where pretty young
women in black and white uniforms serve customers. It smells
wonderful and my stomach growls.

Mrs. Howard made us cheese sandwiches, which we're saving for
supper in Kansas City. The *Scout* has a dining car, and, as a treat, Mama
says we'll eat lunch on the train. I'm willing to go hungry for however
long it takes, for the chance to eat on a train with the countryside
flashing past.

On board the *Scout,* a nice man gives Mama his seat so she and
Owie can sit together. I sit three rows behind them next to a man who
smells of cigar smoke and liquor in spite of Prohibition. He lets me have
the window. Our train pulls out on time, with a blast of steam that
obscures the people on the platform waving. I madly wave back as if
they are all there just to see us off. My real joy will come at the other

end where Papa is waiting. As happy as I'll be to see him, I want this ride to last. The more stops, the better.

After we leave Chicago, a boy comes through the car selling newspapers and apples. The man next to me buys one of each—eats the apple, core and all, covers his face with the paper, and falls asleep.

I want to take in everything there is to see, but my window is covered in a sooty film. When the man next to me starts to snore, I open it a crack, and scoot down in my seat to look out. I've lived my entire life on a gray street in a gray house, breathing gray air. The sun is out, and for the first time I'm not looking at the sky through a smoky haze. It's as blue as Mama's eyes, and in no time, tall buildings give way to flat, snow-covered fields that sparkle.

At noon, the conductor announces the dining car is open. My stomach rumbles in anticipation as I try to figure out how to get over the sleeping man's legs. When Mama taps his shoulder, he jerks awake, and stands to let me out.

The dining car is behind ours which means we have to cross the noisy, freezing cold space between cars as they pitch side to side. Mama and I each take Owie by a hand and make a game of jumping from one doorway to the next.

The dining car has white tablecloths, and waiters in white coats, like a fancy restaurant. We're given menus with dishes I've never heard of, like consommé en tasse and potatoes lyonnaise. The macaroni and cheese, topped with shredded ham, sounds wonderful, so Mama orders a plate for Owie and me to share. She has roast shoulder of lamb and gives us each a bite. I don't think I've ever eaten a meal so delicious in my life. It tastes even better than Mrs. Howard's cooking, but cost a whole dollar. Mama says to enjoy, we might never get another chance to eat this well again. She means her cooking. We laugh.

Our next train, the *Californian*, doesn't have a dining car. According to the schedule I keep folded in my pinafore pocket, the train will make two meal stops before we get to Dalhart, one in Pratt, Kansas, at 9:20 a.m. and another for lunch in Liberal, Kansas, at 1:25 p.m. then into Papa's arms at 5:15.

After night falls, a full moon, big as an orange, comes up over the farms in Missouri. It follows us, no matter how fast we travel, all the way to Kansas City. The coal-burning stove in the center of the car makes it hot and stuffy. I put my chin on the sill and breathe in the cold, delicious, clean-smelling air, and doze off to the steady clicking of the wheels.

In Kansas City, we sit on wooden benches worn to a slick shine to wait for the *Californian*. Owie sleeps with his head on Mama's arm. I put my head on her other shoulder but am too excited to sleep. Trains are called to destinations that run together over the loudspeaker and echo through the terminal. The doors to the platform open, letting in diesel fumes and clouds of steam. People arrive and depart, some dressed to the nines, as Mama would say, in clothes that look like they came straight from one of her *Vogue* magazines. Mama watches the women in their modern shorter skirts and fur coats, followed by porters pushing carts piled high with steamer trunks. Others look like us, carrying cardboard suitcases, and dressed in their least shabby clothes.

A group of children, all of different ages, huddle together on the far side of the room. I count nine of them: four boys, three girls, two babies. The two oldest girls, both about my age, jiggle the babies to keep them quiet. The group is minded by two adults—a man who looks like a preacher, and a tall, stern-looking woman. She keeps eying the boys and hushing their whispers. The girls, wearing wool dresses, black stockings, white pinafores, and what look like hand-me-down coats that are either too small or too large for them, are quiet and miserable looking. The boys are dressed neatly in ill-fitting clothes and wear newsboy caps.

At first, I think they must be one large family, but none of the children look like the adults, or each other. The babies are about the same size, but one is fair, the other dark. They remind me of the children from the Back of the Yards whose parents arrive almost daily and settle into Italian, Polish, Irish, and German neighborhoods.

Mama shifts her position.

I sit up. "Those children don't look like they belong together."

She yawns, pulls her arm from under Owie, rubs it to get the circulation going, and settles his head in her lap. "They're orphans."

"How can you tell?"

"I read about them. They came from New York, children of immigrants who died on the way to America, or who got here, found the streets aren't paved in gold, and now can't take care of them."

"Are they going to an orphanage?"

"No, they're traveling in the care of guardians to new homes in the West. People will come to the stations when the train stops, look them over, and pick one to take home."

"They have to go home with strangers?" I try to imagine how I would feel to arrive in an unknown place and be picked out like a horse with the best teeth. I study a sad-looking girl with bright red hair, wearing a dress that is too big for her. She looks about my age. "All of them?"

"Not necessarily. The ones who don't get chosen return to the Children's Aid Society in New York, to wait and try again."

The red-haired girl holds one of the babies. She turns away when she sees me watching. I'm embarrassed for staring but can't help myself. When I glance at her again, she's watching me. I smile and she smiles back.

The announcement for the *Californian* rings through the terminal. The voice reads a long blur of towns where it will stop. The station begins to buzz as passengers gather their belongings. The man and woman with the orphans spread their arms and herd them toward the door to the platform.

Mama hands our bags to me and hoists Owie so his head settles on her shoulder. The orphan girl glances back, sees we are on the same train, and smiles again.

On board, we find seats at the front of our car. So I can sit beside her and not with a stranger, Mama uses her hankie to clean a spot on the floor, and spreads her coat to make a bed at her feet for Owie. With a minimum of whispered instructions, the orphans settle into the back of the same car.

After the conductor collects our tickets, the lights in the wall sconces are turned down. I stay awake staring out the window. Once out of the city, we travel through a landscape of farms lit by the full moon, now high and small in the sky. I wonder if Papa is looking up, too, tracking us in his mind.

Sometime during the night, I wake with the side of my head against the window. I need to use the privy. Balancing myself with a hand on the wall in front of our seats, I step over Mama's legs and sleeping Owie. I hold onto the seat backs and make my way to the rear of the car, which lurches from side to side. There's a wooden railing around the coal stove, which saves me from getting burned when I'm pitched against it.

The orphans are asleep with their heads on each other's shoulders. The girl who smiled at me in the terminal sits on the aisle with a baby asleep across her lap. There's a heavy smell of dirty diaper rags, sour milk, and sweat in the hot car. Now, I do feel guilty that Kippy and I scavenged for pennies that might have meant so much to the really poor children.

A sign on the wall above the toilet forbids its use while the train is in a station. As soon as I lift the lid I see why. The toilet is over a hole in the floor. The noise of metal wheels clacking over steel rails is deafening, and there's an uncomfortable blast of cold air when I sit down.

On the way back to my seat, I nearly trip over the red-haired orphan-girl. She's on her hands and knees near the coal stove, searching for something.

"What's wrong?"

"The baby broke my chain." Her cheeks glisten with tears. "I've lost my locket." She whispers to keep from waking the others. "Will you help me?" She opens her hand. By the glow of the coals, I see a thin, broken strand of gold in her palm. I glance behind me. The baby is awake and watching us.

I join her and run my hands over the floor, under seats, and around sleeping passengers' feet.

"Maybe we should wait until it's light," I say.

"Please. I can't lose it." Her voice has a lilt I recognize as Irish.

"Okay." We crawl off in opposite directions.

"What's going on here?" a voice hisses.

I look up. It's the woman in charge of the orphans.

"We're looking for . . ." I don't know her name. "For her locket."

"Get up," the guardian says.

I stand and brush my hands together. They feel gritty and look filthy even in the pale glow of the coal stove.

The woman gives me a push toward the front of the car. "Go and sit down."

I decide she can't tell me what to do, and don't move.

She pulls the orphan-girl to her feet. "Look at your dress. Who is going to want a dirty child like you?"

The girl covers her eyes with an arm. "The locket is all I have."

The woman's voice softens. "Go into the toilet, take off that pinafore, wash it in the sink, and scrub your hands. We'll find the locket in the morning." She pats the girl's shoulder, turns, and goes back to her seat.

The conductor enters from the car in front of ours, letting in a gust of noise and cold air. "Herington. Next stop Herington. Better sit down, young lady," he says to me.

"This girl lost her locket. It's very important to her."

"I'll come back when we're out of Herington and help you look."

The man and woman seated behind Mama begin to gather their belongings.

"What's your name?" I whisper.

"Mary. What's yours?"

"Winona, but my family calls me Nona."

"My mother—" Her voice catches like mine does when I'm trying not to cry— "called me Mamie."

Brakes squeal, throwing us against the railing around the coal stove.

"The conductor says he'll come back to help us look for your locket. What's in it?"

"Pictures of my mother and father."

"Did they die?"

"Mama did—on the ship. Papa couldn't feed us all. I'm the youngest of five and the only girl, so he sent me to Children's Aid Society."

Sent her! "He must have thought you'd be better off," I say, but am shocked and grateful for the father I have instead of Mamie's, or Mama's, for that matter. "He couldn't know that they would send you so far away."

Mamie looks at me with a what-do-you-know expression "He knew. He signed the papers. He says the boys can earn their keep, but a girl who can't cook is useless."

I don't know what to say.

Two blasts of the train whistle sound, and we lurch out of Herington.

"Want me to watch him while you get washed up?" I nod toward the baby.

"I have to find my locket first."

"Shouldn't we wait for the conductor?"

Mamie shakes her head. "Someone might step on it."

I glance at the scary lady. She's got her head back against the rest and her mouth is open. Little sounds whistle from her nose. The baby has curled into a ball and is asleep, too. I join Mamie on the floor to begin the search anew.

8

The conductor doesn't forget us. He comes back carrying a kerosene lantern, which he lowers so we can see beneath the seats. By its light, I spot a glint of gold next to a passenger's foot two rows up.

"I see it," I whisper.

Mamie crawls up beside me, and I point. She gets on her stomach and tries to reach it, but it's too far. She inches her way under the seat like a caterpillar but her arm accidentally brushes a woman's leg. The woman shrieks.

"What?" Her startled husband jerks awake and steps on the locket. I hear it crack. "What's the matter?" he says.

"Something touched my leg."

Mamie backs out from under the seat with the broken locket in her hand. She opens her palm and shows me the two halves.

"I'm so sorry, Mamie." I take both pieces and study the two young faces in the light of the conductor's lantern. The side with her mother's picture is pancake-flat and no longer fits the side holding her father's stern face. "I'm sure it can be repaired." I'm trying to make her feel better.

Two legs in brown, thick-soled shoes appear beside us. I scramble to my feet, but Mamie doesn't move.

I show the lady-guardian the broken locket. She shakes her head, lips tight like there's a battle going on behind them between showing kindness and demanding obedience. The steely side wins. "I told you to wash up. Go now, both of you."

Mamie's hands are open in her lap. I place the pieces in her left palm, but she doesn't seem to notice. "Mamie?" I touch her shoulder.

"What does it matter?" Her voice is barely a whisper. She looks up at me. "Mama left us behind and Papa gave me away." She closes her fist over the locket halves.

"Your mother would have stayed if she could, and I'm sure you father hopes you will have a better life." I don't believe the last part. I think her father must be a terrible person. Papa would never give me away.

Mamie's eyes search my face for a moment. She sees the lie, raises her arm, and throws the locket pieces up the aisle as hard as she can, then buries her face in filthy hands and sobs, shoulders shaking.

I watch where the pieces land and go collect them. One is against the door and the other lands near my brother's feet where he sleeps on the floor. Mama's eyes open. She looks up, sees me, and smiles, then notices the smears of grit on my pinafore and dirty knees. "What in heaven's name have you been doing?"

"Helping the Irish girl find her locket." I open my hand.

"Oh, that's too bad." She looks down the aisle at Mamie sitting on the floor, sobbing. The guardian stands over her, waiting.

"She threw the pieces away."

"She'll change her mind and want them back," Mama says.

"I think so, too." I look at the broken locket. "Being loved is everything, isn't it?

"Pretty much, yes." Mama's eyes soften. "Are her parents dead?"

I shake my head. "Only her mother. Her father gave her to that orphan Society."

"That's terrible." Mama leans and strokes Owie's hair, damp from sweat.

"Maybe *we* could adopt her?" I rush to add. "She's very nice, and she's small. I doubt she eats much."

Mama pats my chest. "You have a good heart, Nona, but we don't know what our own lives are going to be like or what hardships we'll face. We can't add another person to your father's burden. I'm sure she'll be chosen by a nice family."

I watch Mamie pick herself up and walk with the woman to the privy. When they come out again, the woman hangs Mamie's wet pinafore on the railing near the coal stove. Mamie lifts the sleeping baby and sits down. When she sees me watching, she looks away.

While I'm in the privy washing my own pinafore, I hear the conductor announce Canton, the next station. It's getting light out. According to the schedule, we'll stop in Pratt for breakfast in a couple of hours. I hang my pinafore beside Mamie's and go back to sit next to Mama. When I pass her seat, Mamie's asleep. I'm exhausted, too.

I open my eyes when Mama whispers my name. Mamie's standing in the aisle holding the baby. "In case I get chosen, I came to say goodbye." She stares past me, out the window.

I look where she's looking. We're in Pratt. Nailed to a post is a broadside: *Wanted: Homes for Orphan Children* with today's date— January 2. The other orphans are already being corralled on the platform. The man-guardian makes them stand in a straight line with the tallest boy in the center. A couple dozen adults mill around.

The woman guardian taps my window. "Mary. Come out here."

"Goodbye," Mamie says.

"Wait." I jump up and step across Mama's legs. Mamie's locket is in my pinafore pocket.

"I'll meet you in the café." Mama says, picking up a sleepy Owie. "Don't be long. We only have twenty minutes."

I walk with Mamie toward the rear of the car. "I have your locket."

"I don't want it."

"You will." I pull my pinafore off the railing and search the pockets for the sharp-sided pieces. "It has your mother's picture. Don't leave it behind."

Her pinafore still shows smudges of ash. I drop the two halves in one of her pockets. The baby smiles at me. He's got a clump of Mamie's bushy red hair in his fist.

"I hope we meet again," Mamie says.

"Me, too. My name is Winona Williams, and we're moving to Dalhart, Texas."

"Mine's Mary Grace McNair."

"Now, Mary." The guardian sticks her head in the door. "There are people out here looking for a baby."

Mamie presses the baby's cheek to her own. "I don't even know his name," she tells me. Her green eyes search mine before she turns and steps down into the cold wind.

I follow her out.

Mama waves to me from a café window.

I hug Mamie. "Good luck." I don't know what else to say.

Mamie joins the other orphans. Two women immediately step forward and ask to see the baby. The lady-guardian pries the baby's fist loose from Mamie's hair and hands him to the youngest woman. He begins to wail. The other woman throws up her hands and turns away. She shakes her head at her husband. "A crier," I see her say. The young woman jiggles him, cooing with her lips near his ear, but he continues to cry, holding his arms out to Mamie who locks her hands behind her back and stares at her feet.

The young woman's husband joins her. They smile and nod to each other, then to the guardian, whose stern face cracks in the first smile I've seen. When Mama, Owie, and I come out of the café, the young couple is signing the adoption papers. I hear the woman guardian tell them they must promise to send him to school and take him to church on Sundays. They promise.

"We'll be back in six months to check on him."

Mama and Owie get back on the train, but I stay to watch with my fingers crossed that someone nice chooses Mamie.

An old man in coveralls points to the tallest boy. "I wanna see that one." His voice is gruff and raspy.

The male guardian makes the boy step forward. The old man looks him up and down, asks him to turn all the way around, then tests the muscles in his arms. "Open your mouth."

The boy takes a step back. "What for?"

"I wanna see your teeth."

"I ain't a horse." The boy stomps back toward the train.

"Come back here," the woman guardian says. "You don't get to walk away."

"I ain't letting that smelly old man make me his slave."

"You don't have to go with anyone you don't want to, but you *will* stand here with the others."

He shuffles back to the line.

The old man asks to see the next tallest boy, but to their credit, the guardians refuse.

My heart leaps in my chest when I hear a man say to his wife, "How about the red-haired girl? She's skinny, but she looks like a good worker."

"Absolutely, not," snaps the woman. "Can't you see she's shanty Irish. Do you want to be robbed blind?"

I gasp and slap my hand over my mouth.

Mamie stares straight ahead, but I see her left hand close around the pocket with the picture of her mother.

9

Mamie is one of three orphans to get back on the train. Six were chosen: both of the babies, two of the older boys, and the two youngest girls. The remaining boys are a scrawny kid with bad skin and a hacking cough, and the tall one who refused the man who asked to see his teeth. He helps Mamie, the only girl not chosen, climb aboard. Mama gives me permission to sit with her as far as the town of Liberal, where the leftover orphans will again be offered up.

Mamie doesn't look at me when I take the seat beside her. "Maybe you weren't meant to be chosen. You'll end up back in New York where your father will have realized his mistake."

"I don't want to go back there." She turns to look out the window at the flat, brown landscape.

I can't think of anything to say to a girl who's been given away by her father and rejected by strangers. I want to say something to make things better, but I can't think what would make that kind of hurt, hurt less. I put my head back and close my eyes.

After every stop, a boy comes through selling things we can't afford: newspapers, maps, magazines, fruit, coffee, tea, candy, soap, towels, and cigars.

Mama wakes me. "Watch Owen." She gags, covers her mouth, and dashes for the privy. The car is filled with bitter cigar smoke from a man sitting two rows behind us. It's freezing outside, but fresh air is better than cigar smoke. I move up to sit in Mama's still warm seat, and crack the window.

Mama comes back looking pale. The open window has cleared the air around our seats, but the man behind us still puffs out clouds of yellow smoke. Mama walks past him, squares her shoulders, and turns.

He glances up and away. "If I'm sick again, I won't bother trying for the privy." She glares at him.

He must hear her, in spite of the clatter of wheels on steel rails and the wind whistling through our window. He puts his cigar out without looking at her again.

She and I exchange smiles when she reaches across me to close my window.

We pull into Liberal, Kansas for lunch a few minutes late. Liberal also has a sign advertising orphans for adoption, and a number of people wait. Mamie and the two boys gather their satchels. On the platform, I hug her goodbye for the second time and go into the station's eating house for lunch. I nibble at my liverice sandwich and watch from the window for Mamie to get chosen.

When people see there are no babies left, most climb back into their wagons. A few farmers remain behind to inspect the boys. This time both are chosen, first the tall one, then the skinny sick one. Mamie walks back to the train alone.

When Mama, Owie and I reboard, Mamie is sitting a row in front of the two guardians. I take the seat beside her. I have a *Baby Ruth* Mama bought me. I offer it to Mamie.

"I don't want your candy." She doesn't look at me.

"I already ate mine. This one's for you."

"You're not a very good liar, Nona." She continues to stare out the window.

"I'm not ly— ." I stop. A tear forms in the corner of her right eye but stays clinging to her pale lashes. "I saved it to share with you."

"I don't want your pity or your candy," she says.

"It's not pity, Mamie. I care what happens to you. I wish you were my sister."

She turns in her seat. "Do you mean that?" The tear dislodges and slides down her cheek.

"You said yourself, I'm not a good liar."

"Thank you." We wrap our arms around each other, me holding the candy bar away from her wild, red hair.

In Texhoma, Oklahoma, a smaller crowd waits to adopt and all but one couple leave when they see the single leftover girl. Mamie stands for inspection with her eyes downcast. I go stand near her and she smiles at me. I take her hand.

"The pretty blonde one looks healthy enough," a man says.

I'm thinking I've made a big mistake standing by her, when his wife says. "My mother had hair exactly that color red." She smiles at Mamie.

I squeeze Mamie's hand and her chin comes up.

"Must be something wrong with her to have made it this far."

"Or maybe she was meant for us," the woman says.

"I don't know," the husband says.

"Well, I do." To the guardian, she says, "We'll take the one with the red hair. She looks Irish."

"She is Irish." The guardian says, smiling warmly.

"I hope the other one finds a good home."

The guardian winks at me. "I'm sure she will."

While the couple sign the papers, promising to send Mamie to school and take her to church, Mamie and I say goodbye for real this time.

"I think that lady's right. You were meant to be get this far. Dalhart is only fifty miles away. We're sure to see each other again."

Steam spews in big wet clouds followed by two blasts of the train's whistle. I hug her, then run and jump aboard. Instead of joining Mama, I run from car to car until I reach the rear of the train. A door opens onto a narrow platform with a railing to keep people from falling off onto the tracks.

Mamie, carrying her satchel, follows the couple to the rusting hulk of a Model T.

"Goodbye, Mamie," I shout. "Goodbye."

She drops her satchel and waves with both hands. The woman walks back to stand beside her. She smiles and waves, too. Before I lose sight of them, I see her call her husband. He turns. His wife puts a hand on her hip and points to Mamie's bag. He picks it up and the woman takes Mamie's hand.

I stay at the back of the train, thinking about how the two tracks are the width of the train's wheels, but, when I raise my eyes, they narrow until they appear to merge and form a silver line to the horizon. Before we left Chicago, I thought the train ride would be the event to remember, but I'll bet, long years from now, my sharpest memory will be of Mamie waving, her red hair lit like a match by the sun.

10

I've lived my entire life at the edge of a big city with no view of a horizon. Now I've seen farmland in Illinois and crossed Mark Twain's Mississippi river. I liked how the railroad cut through the hills of Missouri, exposing the creamy white layers of shale, streaked with rust and stacked on top of each other like the work of a sloppy bricklayer. Kansas was flat. So was Oklahoma and now Texas is more of the same. In some places it looks as if all the land has been plowed, and only windmills and round, metal corn cribs break the monotony of an endless horizon. It feels big and empty.

Owie is restless and squirmy. But Mama keeps him penned in by sitting on the aisle with a foot against the front wall. I sit behind them and play peek-a-boo with him over the seatback. Since leaving Kansas City last night, the *Californian* has made forty-two stops—I counted—but, except for meals, none have been long enough for anyone to spend time off the train.

The towns look the same with wooden buildings, none above two stories: saloons, a mercantile, a hotel or two, dusty, rutted streets. Model Ts park alongside wagons and horses tied to hitching posts. Women, dressed in long dresses rather than the shorter, flapper-fashion of the day in Chicago, stroll wooden sidewalks. People walk, hands holding hats, bent into the wind. The farms outside the towns, just brown stubble. Since Liberal, Kansas, passengers have left the train, but no new people have boarded.

After we leave Stevens, Texas, I slide forward and hook my arms over Mama's seatback. "Three more stops, then Dalhart!"

"Thank heavens," Mama says.

"Do you think Dalhart will be as ugly as these towns?"

"I'm sure Papa has found a nice town. Certainly, cleaner than the Back of the Yards."

"What kind of job did he find?"

"He didn't say. I think he wants to surprise us."

Ahead, on the horizon, a white cloud rises into the sky. "I wonder what that is?" I want it to be the dust from a herd of buffalo being chased by Indians.

"Looks like smoke." Mama stares.

The row across the aisle from Mama is now empty. I move up and take the seat by the window to watch. Owie crawls under Mama's legs, climbs up beside me, and puts his head on my lap. He likes to have his ears tickled. If there's no one to do that, he'll suck his thumb and hold his own earlobe until he falls asleep. I run my finger around the outside of his ear and watch the white smoke curl into the clear blue sky.

I'm the one who falls asleep but wake again when the train slows. I think it's a station, but there are no buildings. We must be stopping for water, or coal from one of the hulking black chutes, but we don't actually stop. The door between cars opens and the conductor comes through. Cold air and the smell of smoke trail him.

Our car is broiling hot from the woodstove, and many of the windows are cracked, including mine. "Close all windows, please." He goes from row to empty row latching the windows. "There's a small prairie fire ahead. Nothing to worry about. Happens often enough."

"How did it start?" A man from the back of the car asks.

"Lightning usually. Then the wind spreads it." He reaches over, closes and latches my window.

"Oh my." Mama reaches for me to pass her Owie. "Should we be frightened?"

"Not at all. They move quickly and aren't very hot—as fires go." He smiles.

The train suddenly picks up speed, throwing the unprepared conductor against the side of a seat. He flinches, steadies himself, and rubs his hip.

Mama hugs Owie tightly. "What's happening?"

"We're making a run for it. Not to worry." The conductor takes the seat next to me. He glances at the card he stuck in the rim of the overhead rack with our destination code on it. "Is Dalhart home?"

Mama's eyes are squeezed shut. "It will be." Her voice ends on a shrill note.

"Nice town," The conductor says soothingly.

I have a moment to wonder if he says that about every town before the smoke thickens and swirls past our sealed windows. I put my hand against the glass. It feels icy cold, even though yellow flames burn the grass right up to the rail-bed. We're going thrillingly fast. Flames lick the side of the train. I glance at the conductor for reassurance. He's looking at his watch. "Only six minutes late," he says to himself, as we rumble out of the smoke into clear air and blue skies.

11

Dalhart, Texas
January 1929

At 5:25, the conductor comes through the car calling, "Dalhart. Next stop Dalhart." Mama gathers our belongings and gets Owie into his coat. I'm glued to the window, and don't care that the approach to Dalhart looks like every town since we left Liberal—dry and brown—Papa is waiting for us in this one.

Brakes squeal and my heart begins to ricochet in my chest. Papa sees me waving with both hands. He sweeps off his hat and runs alongside the train until we stop. His dark hair has grown long and there's a white line across his forehead where his hat blocks the sun.

I carry Owie off the train. When I put him down, he runs at Papa shouting, "Fodder, Fodder." Elbows plowing the air. Papa scoops him up and lifts him high, then frees an arm to wrap me in a hug. He kisses the top of my head. "My babies."

I hug him back as hard as I can and am looking up at him when Mama steps off the train. His lined, sun-browned face softens. He releases me and puts Owie down. The conductor places our bags on the platform and tips his cap to Mama. A moment later, the train, snorting and puffing like a bull, pulls out of the station.

Mama seems to glide into Papa's arms. They close their eyes and cling to each other. "I've missed you so." His voice chokes with emotion.

Mama breaks the spell first and steps back. Her eyes take in what can be seen of the town, and Papa gets an uneasy look, as if he's expecting her to be disappointed. From her frown, she is. I, too, wish it was a nicer place and not some scrappy town with no character of its own—nothing to set it apart from all the other small towns on this flat brown prairie.

At the end of the station platform is a Conestoga, stacked high with lumber and a roll of tarpaper. "Papa, is that our wagon?"

"It is."

"What's the lumber for?" Mama asks at the same time I ask, "Where are Ben and Sam?" I'm afraid he's going to tell they have died, too.

"They're fine, Nona. They're one street over at the livery stable."

"Can I go see them?"

"The lumber?" Mama says.

Papa acts like he doesn't hear Mama's question. "Sure, let's go see them." He picks up Owie. "Want to see the horses?" And tickles his ribs, which makes Owie giggle.

"Owen," Mama says. "What is all that lumber for?"

"Can't it be a surprise, Mother?"

"I'd like to see our house first, Owen. The children are exhausted and we all need a bath."

Papa brushes something off his coat, and says, "We live a ways outside of town, so—" he smiles at me, musses Owie's hair, and avoids looking at Mama. "I've booked us a room at the DeSoto Hotel for tonight. We'll see the horses later. You get cleaned up, and then we'll have a nice supper to celebrate."

A hotel and supper! Papa must have found a gold mine.

Dalhart is at least the largest of the towns since Liberal. There's the movie theater Papa promised. It's showing *The Jazz Singer*—a movie where you can hear the actors' voices. It showed in Chicago a year ago— not that we could afford to see it.

Papa walks us down Denrock Street to the DeSoto Hotel. He points out the two-story Trans-Canadian Sanitarium, one entire wall of which is painted with a red and white snorting bull advertising tobacco. There's the Felton Opera House, a mercantile, and a jewelry store with a big clock. Both have flower boxes in front, ready for planting in the spring. There are three banks, and Herzstein's, a clothing store. Papa points each one out like he's trying to sell Mama a horse with worn teeth.

Mama holds her hat on her head against the cold wind, and keeps saying, "Uh huh" and "Nice," but the suspicious edge to her voice stays.

He hustles us across the street to avoid a rough-looking group of men staring at Mama from the windows of Dinwiddie's pool hall. One of them snarls, "Sodbusters" and spits out the door as we pass.

"It's so dry and dusty," Mama says. "Do they get much rain?"

"About twenty inches a year."

"Papa," I tug on his sleeve. "What's a sodbuster?"

Mama stops and looks at him. "Owen, that's not enough to grow a crop of anything."

"Sure, it is. You need to read Campbell's "Soil Culture Manual." And the Department of Agriculture guidelines for dry-farming. Rain follows the plow; the government says so."

"Humph. Dry-farming? There's a contradiction in terms if I ever heard one."

"Might sound like it, but men are getting rich using that technique. You plant Turkey Red wheat seed in the fall, when there's still moisture in the soil from the summer rains. It sprouts but stays dormant all winter. We harvest the next summer. There's plenty of water down a hundred feet or so. Windmills pump all we'll need for a garden and the animals."

"We'll see." Mama sounds doubtful.

"Papa, what's a sodbuster?"

His brow creases. "Where'd you hear that word?"

"One of the men in the pool hall said it. And spit!"

"It's what some people call the farmers who homestead the prairie."

"We're going to be sodbusters, right?"

Papa smiles. "That's right."

"It sounded like a bad thing the way that man said it. Is it?"

Papa glances at Mama. "Any way a man can make a living and a home for his family can't be a bad thing. The land has many uses. The Indians had their buffalo here, then the cattlemen their herds, now it's the farmers' turn."

I glance at Mama. She doesn't look convinced.

The DeSoto Hotel is a new looking yellow brick building with beautiful walnut doors. It has a coffee shop. The smell of fried chicken makes my stomach growl. Our last meal was lunch five hours ago in Liberal.

Our room has its own bathroom and a telephone. Mama lets me bathe first, then Owie. It's hard to imagine, but we each get clean hot water instead of using the same tub, with the water getting colder and dirtier with each person. Mama bathes last and comes out smelling of talcum dust and the light orange scent of her Florida Water, which is not lost on Papa when we join him in the hotel coffee shop. He puts his nose against her hair, closes his eyes, and breathes deeply.

A large, well-fed man sits at a table in the back of the restaurant playing cards with three other men. He looks up when Papa seats us.

"That's Uncle Dick Coon," Papa whispers. "He owns most of the town including this hotel and the drugstore."

Uncle Dick tips his hat to Mama and smiles at me. "Finally arrived, huh, Williams?"

"Yes, sir."

"Mighty pretty girls and a handsome little man."

"Thank you. This is Owen Junior." He gives Owie a little shove in the direction of Mr. Coon. Owie walks over, shakes his hand, runs back, and hides his face in Mama's skirt. "My wife, Glenny, and my daughter, Winona."

"Mrs. Williams." Uncle Dick tips his hat again. "This man of yours is going to do well. He has plenty of ambition and he's a hard worker. Won't be long 'fore he's got a pocket full of these." He takes a bill out of his watch pocket, and crooks a finger at me.

"Go look," Papa says. "In spite of Mr. Coon's predictions, it may be the only one you'll ever see."

I walk over and stand with my hands clasped behind my back. Mr. Coon unfolds the bill, places it on the table, and flattens it with the side of his hand. The men he's playing cards with watch for my reaction.

I gasp. It's a hundred-dollar bill. "Is it real?"

"The gen-u-ine article."

"Wow." I lean over to read the printing. *This Certifies That* is at the top. Beneath that it says, *there have been deposited in,* then in big fancy letters, *the Treasury of the United States, One Hundred Dollars in GOLD COIN payable to the bearer on demand.* A red seal adds authority. "Are you going there to demand your gold?"

Mr. Uncle Coon laughs. "It will be there if I need it and paper is easier to carry."

This is the first rich person I've ever met. "Did you make it growing wheat?"

"No, ma'am. I made it giving wheat farmers plenty of ways to spend their money."

All the men laugh, including Papa. But not Mama.

12

At breakfast the next morning, I see a framed magazine ad for Postum on the wall of the coffee shop. It says, '*children brought up on Postum will be free from the evil effects of* caffeine—*the habit-forming drug— in coffee and tea.*'

Papa sees me reading it and says Postum is made from wheat and sweet molasses and that it tastes like the coffee he and Mama drink.

"May I try it?"

"Don't see why not. Wheat will be supporting us." He orders a cup each for Owie and me. When Owie makes a face, Mama lets us add sugar that's free for the taking in a bowl on the table, and a bit of milk. I don't know what coffee tastes like, but Postum tastes good.

While we wait for our meals, and because my printing is better than his, I help Papa make a list of necessary staples he needs to get from the mercantile: a barrel of kerosene, tins of tea and coffee, yeast, baking soda, baking powder, spices, and a gunny sack each full of pinto beans, flour, corn meal, plus fifty pounds of sugar. He must think Mama learned to cook while he was gone.

There are postcards in a rack on the counter by the cash register. Papa lets me pick out one with a picture of the Dalhart high school to send to Kippy. It looks much nicer than our school in the Back of the Yards. I write her a note saying we've arrived; that I saw a million stars last night from the train, and that I miss her.

Papa gives me another penny for the stamp, and lets me run down the street to the post office to mail it. On my way back, I see Papa, who's got Mama bundled up in his heavy coat, walking toward me. Owie's got her skirt wrapped in his fist and marches a few paces ahead, trying to pull her along.

"What's wrong?"

Papa says, "Something she ate. We're going to the doctor."

Mama says, "It was the cigar smoke."

"It never bothered you before." Papa loves a cigar now and then.

She hasn't told Papa about the baby. "She was sick on the train, too."

Mama gives me a squinty-eyed, *keep-your-mouth-shut* look.

"That's odd." Papa feels her forehead with the back of his hand.

"It's nothing," Mama says. "I'll be fine." She's pale and leans heavily on his arm, but she puts her hand against Papa's chest when he starts up the stairs to the sanitarium. "Nona will help me." She shrugs his coat off and hands it to him.

Papa places his hand on Owie's head and smiles down at him. "Well, then we men-folk will head to the barber for haircuts and a shave."

"Can I have a shave, too?" Owie rubs his cheek.

"Maybe when you turn five."

Mama kisses Papa's cheek, then she and I climb the dark, narrow stairs to the doctor's office.

Doctor Dawson is tall with a bushy black beard. He's wearing a big, black Stetson hat, which he tips when Mama takes a seat. I stand behind her.

Doctor Dawson's got a plug of tobacco in his cheek. "What seems to be the trouble," he says, then turns his head and spits a stream of tobacco juice into a brass spittoon next to his chair.

Mama gags.

"Sorry about that ma'am. It's a hideous habit."

"No, I'm sorry. My stomach is a little upset."

"Willie," Doctor Dawson shouts.

A dark, exotic-looking woman about Mama's age comes through a door from another room.

Doctor Dawson's face lights up the way Papa's did at the sight of Mama getting off the train. "This is Willie, my wife." He beams at her. "She'll take you to the examination room."

There's a grinning human skeleton in the corner of the office. When Doctor Dawson rolls his chair back and stands up, it sways, and picks up speed as he crosses the uneven floor to spit his plug of tobacco into the sink. He waits by the closed door until his wife opens it and beckons him in.

I wait until Doctor Dawson shuts the door behind him before starting to inspect the specimen jars on top of a glass-fronted bookcase. Each is labeled. I carefully study the tumors, goiters, and organs, including a heart, a shriveled pair of black lungs: *The effects of smoking*, and a huge, gray-green liver: *Cirrhosis, the effects of drink*.

"What did he say?" Papa asks, when we come out.

"Something I ate."

Of course, that's not what he said at all. My eye was to the keyhole when Doctor Dawson put his hand on Mama's shoulder and said, "Congratulations, Mrs. Williams. I'd say you're 'bout six months along." Mrs. Dawson hugged her and said, "April is a lovely time to have a baby."

Papa's got our luggage and all the supplies loaded on the wagon when we come down for breakfast the next morning. I run to hug Sam's neck, then Ben's. They are still thin from the trip, and their eyes look as dull as the bottom of an old pot, but Sam nickers and lets me stroke his silky, soft nose.

Papa and Mama, with me seated between them holding Owie on my lap, leave Dalhart a little after eleven. We're wrapped in horsehair blankets and clutch our coat collars to our throats against the wind and biting cold. Even with the sun high in the sky, the ground is still frosty and crunches beneath the metal rims of the wagon wheels. I turn to watch the town melt into the horizon, shimmering until it disappears and we're left bouncing and dipping in unison along an empty road past plowed fields and wheat sprouts sugar-coated with frost.

Owie's lulled to sleep by the rhythmic clop of the horses' hooves and the creaking of the wagon seat springs. My parents are quietly lost in their own thoughts. Papa stares past the horses' bobbing heads at the road that stretches to the horizon. Mama keeps her head turned to face the barren landscape passing on her side. I don't think she wants Papa to see the occasional tear that forms and clings to her bottom lashes.

Before Papa left Chicago, we all played cowboys and Indians on the Conestoga, but the hard wooden bench has lost its appeal. We're about an hour into the trip. "How far is it to our place?"

"About twelve miles."

"How long will it take us to get there?"

"The rest of the day."

I smile, like he's joking, then realize he's not. Mama closes her eyes.

An hour later we pass a man plowing. The plow is attached to the back of a Model T Ford. Mama and I stare. I laugh, then look at Papa.

"Men are desperate to get wheat seed in the ground. By any means. Noel says if you've got a pulse and a plow, you can't help but make money."

"I can't wait to meet this man," Mama says. It doesn't sound like she means it, but I'm not sure why. If Papa likes him, I'm sure he's nice. And he's old, Papa said, like Mr. Fischer.

Papa looks at her. "We're lucky, Glenny. Noel settled here before all the good land was taken. He has six-hundred and forty acres of prime farmland."

"What does that have to do with us?" Her tone is snippy.

"I wanted to explain our arrangement yesterday, but with you falling ill, I didn't get to it." Papa clears his throat like this is going to take a while. "Noel's getting on in years, and the work's hard on his rheumatism. He's got no wife or kids, so he and I struck a deal. I'll work his land and he'll live out his days with us. When he dies, the land will be ours free and clear."

A picture forms in my mind of a little white house, and Mr. Noel living in the attic like Mr. Fischer.

"How do you know he'll keep his word?"

"He's an honorable man. We shook hands on it."

"Oh, Owen, you're always overestimating people. You'll be nothing but a sharecropper."

"What's that?" I ask.

"Living and laboring on someone else's farm for a piddling share of the profits," Mama says.

"Stop it, Glenny. Uncle Coon introduced Noel to me and took us to his lawyer. Noel's already deeded me the land, and I've given him a life estate. It's all legal and sealed with red wax."

"And who's going to take care of this old man if he gets sick?"

"That's a long way off," Papa says. "Right now, he's healthy and strong as an ox."

Papa wanted a piece of land of his own, and he got it. I'm happy for him but sorry for Mama. It looks like Mrs. Howard was right about the desolation.

13

The sun is close to setting when we crest a dip in the road and see, off in the distance, a windmill and a barn. "There she is." Papa reins in the horses to give us a chance to appreciate how beautiful and golden the fields are in this light. "Our land," Papa says.

His dream fulfilled. I glance at Mama. Her eyes are horrified spheres. I know Papa wants us to feel what he's feeling. I'm trying, but all I see is nicely lit nothingness. I want to take his hand, but instead, I find Mama's clenched fist under the horse blanket and squeeze it. It relaxes enough to fold around my fingers, and her chin comes up. "The children are cold, Owen."

A crease forms between Papa's brows, then he nods, and clicks to the horses. As we get nearer, he clicks again, urging the horses to pick up the pace. A short distance further, without any signal from Papa, they trot through two gateposts even though any sign of the fencing ended miles ago.

The windmill clickety-clacks in the cold wind. Chickens, dusting themselves in an ash pile, scatter. An old dog lifts his head and thumps his tail.

Papa reins in the horses, jumps down, takes Owie from me, and sets him down. The dog scrambles to his feet, rushes over and licks Owie's face, which makes him giggle.

"Shoo." Mama leans over and swings her hat at the dog.

"That's Karlo, Noel's dog," Papa says. "He's mostly German Shepherd and gentle as a lamb."

Mama isn't listening. She and I are looking for a house. Except for a hill about the size of a railway car, the barn, and a shed, all that can be seen in any direction are plowed fields.

"Owen?" Mama says.

Papa pointedly avoids looking at her as he lifts me off the wagon.

That mound of dirt in the middle of the yard holds my attention. There's a door in the side of it that looks like the one to the cellar back home. I walk toward it. The hill has a dried-grass-covered roof—long and low, with a wide-angled peak in the center. One edge of the roof sticks out over a wall of square blocks of sod. There's a narrow window beneath the overhang cut right through the dirt wall. A stove pipe pokes through on the far side. A line of gray smoke appears from it and is whisked away by the wind.

"What's inside that hill, Papa?"

"That's a dugout." Papa places his hand on the lumber stacked in the back of the wagon. "It's where we'll live while I build us a real house."

Mama, whose hands cup her stomach protectively, gasps.

Oh Papa. I'm horrified, sorry for him, sorry for Mama, and can't wait to see inside.

My mother's eyes flick toward the tired-looking barn, then the rackety windmill, the shed, the horizon, and back to the dugout. I'm pretty sure if she'd known we would be living like termites, we would never have left Chicago. Even now, I think she might take up the reins, whip the horses, and make a run for it.

"It's homey inside." Papa draws a line in the dust with the toe of boot. "Noel's lived in there for years."

I can't imagine one person making do in there, much less the four of us, and him. "Will we all fit?" I ask.

Papa smiles at me. "Noel moved to the shed. The dugout is ours until the house is finished. We've nearly got the cellar dug." He nods toward a hole in the ground, which I hadn't noticed. "With the wheat already planted, Noel and I will have the house built in no time."

Papa offers his hand to Mama. She leans away from it. "Why didn't you wait to send for us?"

"It's been six months, Glenny. I missed you."

Mama's focus shifts to the side of the shed, where the packing crates her furniture was in are now nest boxes for the chickens. Her face pales. "Where's my mother's furniture?"

"Perfectly safe in the shed."

The outhouse door slams and a raisin-faced old man comes up the path between the shed and the dugout.

"That's Noel," Papa says, unnecessarily. He beckons to him. "Come meet the family."

Noel's a stooped, slow-moving, raggedy-looking man dressed in bib-overalls and an old blue shirt.

Owie's squatted beside Karlo with an arm slung over the dog's shoulders. When Karlo sees Noel, he runs to greet him. Noel scratches the dog's ear and smiles at us, but when his eyes rest on Owie, an odd look crosses his face, like he's received a painful shock. He walks over and offers his hand to Owie. "I'm Noel."

Owie darts behind Papa, who drags him around and makes him stand in front of him. "What do you say?" He holds him in place with his hands on Owie's shoulders.

"Nice to meet you, sir."

Noel turns to me and he sweeps off a battered brown hat with a sweat blackened ribbon. His face is two-toned, rust-colored from the sun below and white from his bushy eyebrows to his hairline. He holds his hat in one hand like a bowl of water and offers to shake my hand.

I've never shaken an adult's hand, but I put mine out and he takes it. His palm feels like the rasp Papa uses to file a horse's hoof. "It's nice to meet you, sir."

"And this here's the missus," Papa says. "Glenny, this is Noel Andersen."

Mr. Andersen holds his hat in front of his chest and bows to Mama. "I'm mighty proud to make your acquaintance, Mrs. Williams." An accented voice whistles through ill-fitting dentures. "I'm terrible sorry me and this place ain't more presentable."

Mama only nods.

"Noel is originally from Denmark," Papa says to me.

I think of Mamie. "Is that near Ireland? I have a friend from Ireland."

"It's on the same side of the globe," he says. "About as far from here as a body can get." He puts his hat on and glances up at Mama.

I do, too, and see the look that crosses her face. An unmistakable wish to be as far from here as she could get. Then it's gone. Her shoulders sag. "It's nice to meet you, too, Mr. Andersen." She leans forward and lets Papa lift her from the wagon.

14

Papa holds the dugout's wooden door open for Mama, who stands with her arms at her sides like someone about to step off the plank of a pirate's ship. I can't wait to see what's inside. I squeeze past Mama, duck under Papa's arm, and go down the three steps.

As my eyes adjust to the dimness, it becomes clear why it's called a dugout. The room has been hollowed out of a hill. I can't tell the measurements, but the whole thing is no bigger than my room in our Chicago flat. The only light comes from the window in the sod wall. The earth floor is swept to a hard, smooth finish. Beams laid from wall to wall support the peaked board roof. Mr. Andersen has covered the walls with newspapers, some dating back to the Great War. One faded headline reads: "Food will win the War. Grow Wheat."

Mama's rocking chair sits next to a fat, cast-iron, two-burner stove. Beside it is a tall stack of newspapers, a box of full twigs, and a pile of round, dry disks. Mr. Andersen must have built us a fire, because the room is warm, but it smells awful—like burning dirt.

There's a rope bed and a wire cot, both with horsehair mattresses. They are pushed against two of the walls. Both beds are covered with the quilts my mother made. The table is a pickle barrel with a marble top from one of Mama's parlor tables. Papa has put one of my grandmother's tatted doilies in the center and a kerosene lamp on it. The seats are two nail kegs and two lard cans. Poor Papa, he's done all he can to make things look nice.

Behind me, I hear Mama gasp. "Oh my God, Owen. It's a coffin. I can't have a child born here."

"A child?" Papa turns Mama to face him. "Are you—?"

Mama nods. Tears spill down her cheeks.

"Oh, Glenny, that's wonderful." He takes her hand, leads her to the rocking chair and helps her to sit. "The baby won't be born here." He kneels in front of her. "I promise. I'll have the house built in a month, maybe less."

Owie appears at the dugout door and hops down the steps. Karlo's right behind him. Papa shoos the dog out and closes the door.

Mama wrinkles her nose. "What *is* that awful smell?"

"Cow chips. We burn them for heat. I don't notice the odor anymore."

"What's a cow chip?" I ask.

Papa looks to the ceiling for the right words. "Dried cow droppings."

Owie claps his hands and shouts, "Poop."

Papa smiles. "For the benefit of your sister and mother, let's call them cow chips or cow patties, shall we?" He stirs Owie's hair. "They come out in nice round disks and collecting them will be your job."

"Can I go do it now?"

"Later. I'll show you where to find the dry ones."

Owie grabs his crotch and starts to dance in place. "I need to use Mr. Noel's little house."

Papa and I laugh. "I'll take him," I say. It will give our parents a moment alone.

Outside, Owie runs down the path to the outhouse, pulls open the door, and lets it bang shut behind him.

"Eewww," he shouts, bursts out again, turns his back to me, and piddles on the side of the outhouse.

I go in. It's icy cold inside, and drafty, with only a sliver of light coming through the quarter moon slit in the door. A black toilet seat is attached to a rough wooden bench above a smelly hole. Strips of newspaper flutter from a nail in the wall. A Sears and Roebuck catalog with a lot of missing pages is on the bench, and there's a basket full of dried corncobs on the floor. I sit on the cold black seat and think of the lovely bathroom at the DeSoto Hotel, do my business, pull up my knickers, and flee.

The first night in the dugout, Mama and Papa take the rope bed, which is high enough off the earthen floor for Owie to sleep beneath it in a packing crate. For warmth, Papa gives him his old bedroll. He tucks him in, telling him this is how he slept every night under the wagon.

I'm disappointed. His letters made his trip sound so much more exciting. "You said you slept looking up at the stars."

Papa puts a finger to his lips. "Not when it rained."

My bed is the wire cot with a lumpy horsehair mattress. Papa tucks me in under two of the blankets Mama's furniture was wrapped in. I watch as he loads the woodstove with cow chips, then reaches above my bed, and cracks open the only window.

"Owen, it's awfully cold out," Mama says.

"You'll be glad it's open if the wind kicks up during the night. It blows so hard across the top of the stove pipe the smoke can't escape. Can fill the room in no time." He blows out the kerosene lamp and joins Mama. "I'll keep you warm," I hear him whisper.

I fall asleep listening to the coyotes yipping and howling and Mr. Andersen yipping and howling back at them. I guess he's lived alone out here for so long, he probably knows all the animal calls and considers them good company.

Sometime during the night, I hear Mama say, "What's the matter?"

"It's nothing."

"It must be something. It's freezing in here and you're soaked with sweat."

Papa doesn't answer.

"Is it the war again?" Mama says.

He doesn't answer.

Later I wake again to scratching on the walls. "Papa," I whisper. There's no answer, and after a while, I fall back to sleep. Until something bites me. "Papa," louder this time. "Something's crawling on me."

The rope bed creaks.

"What's wrong?" Mama whispers.

Papa answers, "I'm not sure." He lights the lamp and holds it above my bed.

The blanket is a swarm of tiny brown insects, no larger than apple seeds. "Papa!" I try to brush them off my arms, throw off the covers, and jump up. I shake my nightgown and stamp my bare feet.

"What?" Mama sounds strangled.

"Bedbugs."

"Oh my God. We're sleeping in a hole in the ground and the children are being eaten by insects."

I claw at the bites on my arms and legs. Scratchy sounds come from the walls. "Are there bedbugs in the walls, too?"

"No. Those are centipedes moving around under the newspapers."

Papa takes a box of baking soda from a shelf holding some canned goods, opens it and pours it over me. He sprinkles it in my hair, pushes up the nightdress sleeves and rubs it down my arms, and pours some in my cupped hands for me to rub on my legs. When I look thoroughly floured, he sends me to get in bed with Mama, then rolls up my blankets, opens the dugout door, which lets in a blast of cold air, and throws them outside. He adds more cow chips to the stove, turns my mattress over, sprinkles it with the rest of the baking soda, and lies down. His feet stick off the end of the cot.

When I wake again, it's morning. A rectangle of dull light comes through the window, which is now closed. I peer over the edge of the bed. Owie's still asleep on the floor underneath, but Mama's not beside me. I hear sniffling.

"Where's Papa?"

"Out working on the house."

"Are you crying?"

"No." She's in the rocking chair by the woodstove.

"Sounds like you are."

The rocking chair whooshes back and forth when she gets up. "The fire's going out." I hear her lift one of the two cast iron covers.

"I'll do it." I swing my legs over the edge of the bed and put my bare feet on the cold, hard ground.

From the stack of the Dalhart *Texan* newspapers beside the box of kindling, I crinkle a few sheets, stuff them into the chamber, and add some twigs. There's smoke, then the fire flares. I throw cow chips on the blaze.

"Light the lamp, too, will you?"

I strike another match, lift the chimney and light the wick. Mama's face glistens. "You were crying." I claw at the bites on my arm.

"Let me see those." She pushes the sleeve of my nightgown up to my elbow. "I think Celia used to make a paste of baking soda and water, or maybe it was vinegar for bites."

There's a pitcher of water from the well and a basin on a small handmade table. A few pots and pans hang on nails driven into one of the rafters holding up the roof of the dugout. A crudely made set of wooden shelves holds tin plates, bowls, a tin each of sugar, salt, lard, flour, three cans of beans, and the empty box of baking soda.

"They only itch a little. Don't worry."

Owie giggles in his sleep and turns over.

I lower my voice. "Why are you crying?"

"Look at this place," she snaps. "Your father promised me a home of our own."

"He's going to build us a house." It comes out sounding defensive.

"I don't think a house will make much difference. We'll still be living in the middle of a God-forsaken prairie. Exactly where I prayed we wouldn't end up."

"Would you rather be back in Chicago?"

"There must be somewhere between empty land and a big city, somewhere clean with a little company."

"You said you liked farming."

"I liked being a Farmerette. This place is your father's dream, not mine." She sighs.

"Did you have one?" I've never thought to ask.

"Once you marry, you don't get to have dreams of your own."

I think of my dream to be a pilot like Miss Earhart. "What did you want to be before you got married?"

Mama puts her hand on her stomach. "Don't laugh."

"I won't."

"I wanted to be a dress designer like Coco Chanel. I had a creative eye. Everyone said so."

"Why'd you stop?" The stove ticks as it reheats. I turn my back to it and hold my hands out to the warmth.

"I married your father."

"Wouldn't Papa let you keep sewing?"

"It's not just sewing. I wanted to go to design school." She waves away the thought. "That's what happens when you marry, Nona. You turn your life over to your husband."

"I'm going to be an aeroplane pilot."

Mama smiles. "That dream may be a little too big. At least dress designers are girls. Flying is a man's job."

"So is farming, but you were a Farmerette."

"I wasn't likely to get killed canning corn."

Owie rolls over and sees us. "I'm hungry."

"Aren't we all." Mama holds her arms open to him. "Let's find Papa."

I don't say so to Mama, but I'm not giving up my dream. And if getting married means it has to end, then I'm never doing that either.

Outside, the day is cold and windy with no sign of Papa until a shovel-full of dirt sails up and out of the cellar hole. "Good morning, sleepy heads." He smiles up at the line we form along the rim. "Bet you're all hungry."

"Starving." Mama tries to sound happy even though her nose is stuffy from crying. "Where's the nearest restaurant?"

Papa grins. "'Bout twelve miles. We can be there by supper."

The door to the shed bangs and Mr. Andersen comes across the yard, scattering the chickens, Karlo at his heels. When the dog spots Owie, he races to greet him, nearly knocking him into the hole.

"Sit." Mr. Andersen pushes down on Karlo's rear end. "Sorry. He's taken a shine to your son."

"It's good for a boy to have a dog," Papa says. He's looking at Mama, who is wrapped in one of the horsehair blankets from the wagon. She's staring at the landscape, now a much bleaker shade of brown in the light of day.

Papa climbs the ladder. "Might as well start divvying up the tasks," he says. "Nona, your morning job is to collect the eggs—if there are any. It's winter after all. Later, Noel will show you how to milk Miss Langtry—the cow."

Mr. Andersen smiles at me.

I look away. It's his fault I'm covered in bed bug bites and Mama is miserable. If Papa hadn't met him, he might have found a job somewhere in a town with real houses. "Where do I start?" I say to Papa.

"If you're really hungry, start with the eggs. There's a basket hanging on the wall inside the chicken coop. You'll also be in charge of mucking the horses' stalls." He glances at Mama, then back at me. "Once your mother decides where she wants her vegetable garden, that's where you'll put the horse manure."

Owie, with Karlo at his heels, runs down the path to the outhouse, but isn't brave enough to go inside by himself. He lifts his nightshirt, arches his back, and piddles on the outside wall, then slaps his thigh like a cowboy encouraging his horse to pick up the pace, and gallops back toward us.

"Want to help me find eggs?" I say to him when he reins up beside me.

"Yes." He takes my hand. "And the cow's poop."

15

Owie and I find only two eggs, which he carries in to show Mama. I follow Mr. Andersen into the barn where he shows me how to milk the cow he calls Miss Lily Langtry. He washes her teats to "let the milk down," then tugs firmly, alternating between the first two. Streams of warm milk ping against the sides of the pail. When I try it, Miss Lily turns to look at me. Her expression, as she chews her cud, reminds me of Mama's when I ask her something she thinks I should know the answer to.

By the time the milk pail is full, Papa has my board-thin, horse-hair mattress boiling in a cast iron wash boiler. When he's satisfied the bedbugs are cooked, he lifts out the sodden wad, and drapes it over the side of the wagon to dry.

Our quilts and blankets go in next. Mama stirs them with a broom handle while Papa strings a clothesline behind the outhouse, between the only two trees for as far as I can see in any direction. It makes me wonder why there are no other trees and who planted these, but no one wants to hear my "how come" questions right now.

Mr. Andersen helps Papa drag the rope bed and my cot out into the sun. They scrub them with rags dipped in kerosene. I muck the horses' stalls, then clean both sides of the dugout's window with vinegar and a sheet of newspaper, to let in more light.

For breakfast, Mr. Andersen brings us a basket full of eggs. I'm not sure how Owie and I missed this many, but they are the best eggs I've ever tasted. The eggs Mrs. Howard's chickens laid tasted like the ash from the slaughterhouses. With the eggs is a thick, pretty awful-tasting biscuit that Mr. Andersen made out of flour and water and fried in lard.

After we eat, Mama and I pull off the old newspapers that cover the sod walls of the dugout. We burn them in the woodstove, enjoying the sound of insects popping and sizzling in the fire. With gusto, Owie takes to his job of stepping on the live bugs as they wiggle out of the sod wall and fall to the floor. I sweep them up and add them to the fire.

When the sod is bare, Mr. Andersen shows us how to make paste out of flour and water, only slightly thinner than what we ate for breakfast. Mama and I use it to re-paper the wall with sheets of the *Texan* from the stack of newspapers next to the woodstove. We put them on in neat horizontal rows, so we can later read the articles all the way through.

I find a story about Amelia Earhart placing third in the Women's Air Derby from Santa Monica in California to Cleveland, Ohio. I paste it on the wall beside my cot so when I turn on my side, a picture of her standing next to her plane will be eye-level.

For lunch, Mr. Andersen brings us more of his thick, dry biscuits. This time he covers them with sorghum molasses, so they taste a little better. We have it again for supper. It's now clear why it's called hardtack.

None of the mattresses dry before dark, so Papa fills the wagon with hay and our blankets. I'm excited. I've never slept under the stars.

It was windy all day, but that night in the wagon, and after the wind dies, a rumbling sound drifts across the prairie and lights to the west are so bright it's impossible to see any stars.

I can't hide my disappointment. "Where are those lights coming from, Papa?"

"Tractors. They plow night and day to get more seed in the ground."

"Do we have a tractor?"

"Not yet. We rented a neighbor's to plow our fields."

"I wanted to see the stars like you did."

"You'll see them plenty. Just maybe not tonight."

⁓

My ability to sleep through the clanging, banging, honking, shouting, factory whistles, and church bells in the Back of the Yards makes me immune to the rooster crowing, horses neighing, and the grunts of my father and Mr. Andersen at work digging the cellar. I sleep in the wagon until the sun warms my blanket.

I crawl out of the wagon and, with the blanket around my shoulders, walk over to watch.

"Hey there, sleepy head." Papa smiles up at me.

"What time is it?" I yawn.

Papa reaches for his pocket watch; Mr. Andersen rests on his shovel and looks at the height of the sun. "About ten-thirty," he says.

Papa checks his watch and smiles at Mr. Andersen. "Ten-twenty."

"Where are Mama and Owie?"

"In the dugout. She's keeping eggs warm for you. Owie was carrying a chicken around, but I don't know where he is now."

It's toasty and warm in the dugout, and as clean inside as something underground can be. The air smells of vinegar, flour, and Mama's Florida Water. The mattresses are back on the beds where the heat from the stove can finish drying them.

Mama's in her rocking chair knitting. She smiles at me. "You're up."

She looks comfortable and not so unhappy. "I'm sorry. You should have awakened me."

"There's still plenty to do, but eat first."

The eggs were probably good when Mama first cooked them, but now they're dry and rubbery. I eat them without complaining because I'm the one who overslept and woke hungry. The hardtack we had for supper was not good or filling. I'm not sure how long we can wait for Mama to learn to cook.

"Where's Owie?"

"He's with your dad, isn't he?"

"No."

"Oh my." Mama drops her knitting, rushes up the steps and flings open the door with me right behind her.

"Owen Junior?" She shouts, then runs down the path to the outhouse. "Owie?"

Papa comes up the cellar ladder like a gopher out of its hole. "What's the matter?"

"We don't know where Owie is."

"Owen," Papa yells.

Mr. Andersen comes up the ladder, perspiring like it's a hundred degrees out instead of forty-something.

I spot Owie trudging across the plowed field across the road. Karlo is with him. When Papa shouts, he turns, and marches towards to us.

We wait for him lined up with our hands on our hips. "What are you doing?" Mama scolds.

Owie knows the difference between mad and worried. He smiles and hugs her. "Looking for cows."

Mr. Andersen laughs, looks at his feet, and jams his hands in his pockets when Mama glances at him.

"There's a cow in the barn," Mama says.

"Her patties are too wet to burn."

We all laugh.

"Come on." Mr. Andersen holds out his hand. "I'll show you where to look for dry ones."

"Nona, go with them," Mama says.

Either Mr. Andersen doesn't hear the concern for Owie in Mama's voice, or he ignores it. "We'll need the little wagon from the barn," he tells Owie.

On the way to the barn, I glance back at my parents. Papa's face is close to Mama's. I think they're kissing, until I over hear him say "He's a fine man," in a low voice.

"We don't know a thing about him." Mama walks away.

There's a wooden Liberty Coaster wagon hanging by its handle from a peg on a post in the barn. Mr. Andersen gets it down and puts it in front of Owie. "Consider this yours from now on."

I wonder why Mr. Andersen has a child's wagon, but I don't ask. I nudge Owie. "What do you say?"

"Thank you, Mr. Noel."

His eyes soften. "You're very welcome, son."

There's a large, handmade wheelbarrow leaning against the wall just inside the barn. Mr. Andersen rights it. "We'll need more than a little wagon full of chips, if we're to keep you folks warm for any stretch of time."

We cross the yard to a sagging fence line. On the other side is unplowed land. "Who owns that?" I ask.

"It's mine. Ours," he corrects. "I ain't never plowed this section."

"How come?"

"I think farmers are doing wrong turning this prairie inside out. I don't think it was meant to be covered in wheat." Mr. Andersen lifts Owie's wagon over the fence and reaches for Owie. Again, he gets that sad, soft look in his eyes, before patting Owie's back and putting him down on the other side.

Karlo whines and paces.

Mr. Andersen walks to the nearest fence post, rocks it back and forth until it snaps off at ground level. Karlo leaps over the downed barbed wire, finds a twig, and runs to catch up with Owie.

"That boy has given my old dog a new lease on life."

Mr. Andersen rotates the broken post which twists the three strands of barbed wire into a single braid. He rolls the wheelbarrow across, returns, and stands on the wire to make sure I don't trip.

"Papa said there used to be buffalo right here."

"That's true. Buffalo is what this land was meant for." He stops and runs his boot over the dry, brown grass we're walking through. "This here grass and the buffalo evolved together. They could tolerate temperatures to thirty below, and as high as 110. Them and Indians are who should live here."

"Then why do you grow wheat?"

"A man's gotta survive and wheat's what's feeding us." Mr. Andersen's breathing hard and sweating. We stop to rest and stand side by side to watch Owie test cow patties with the stick he took from Karlo.

"All this was grazed pretty much down to bare soil when the XIT ran cattle here, but the grass takes the land back if you leave it alone. Come spring this field will be soft and green."

We start moving again.

"Will the buffalo come back then, too?" I'm picking up cow patties and putting them in the wheelbarrow.

"No. They're gone for good."

"What tribe lived here?"

"Mostly Comanche. Some Apache."

"And all they ate were buffalo?"

Owie's got a full wagon and is dragging it back toward us, stopping every couple feet to replace the ones that fall off.

"They didn't just eat them, they used every part. Nothing went to waste. They even made soup out of the dried skin. Cut it thin as newsprint, and ground it to a meal that would keep." He wipes his brow with a red and black bandana. "Whites drove the Indians off their lands and killed all the buffalo to starve out the ones who held on. I once seen a pile of buffalo skulls ten stories high. Without the buffalo, the Indians was finished."

I think he's making that up about the skulls and smile at him like I get he's joking.

He raises his right hand. "It's the God's truth."

"How long have you lived here?"

"Nearly thirty years. Afore that, I drove cattle for the XIT ranch. You know what that was?"

"The biggest cattle ranch ever. Papa came here hoping to be a farrier again. What did XIT stand for?"

"There's no agreement on that. Some say it means Ten in Texas, referring to the number of counties it covered. Others think it was a straight-line brand applied five different directions to make it harder for rustlers to steal their cattle."

Owie's reached us and stands on his tiptoes to watch Mr. Andersen empty his wagon into the wheelbarrow. He smiles proudly, and marches off again.

"Papa was disappointed when he found out the XIT had gone out of business?"

"The blizzards of '88 and '89 killed off most of their cattle. I had a couple friends freeze to death in their saddles. I was nearly one of them. The herd I was helping to move froze on the trail in snow drifts belly deep. Most died stacked against a drift fence."

"What's that?"

"One long unbroken fence strung clean across the Panhandle. It was meant to keep the XIT cattle from drifting south in the winter where they'd have to be rounded up again. It worked, but so many head died stacked against it a man could walk on their back the width of the Panhandle without ever touching the ground."

"That's so sad," I say, and hope he's pulling my leg.

"When the XIT finally shut down, I bought a section—six hundred and forty acres—of the old ranch. Been here ever since."

In the distance, I see what looks like a line of bare branches snaking along the horizon. I shade my eyes. "What's growing out there?"

Mr. Andersen sees where I'm looking. "Cottonwoods."

"How come they're so short?"

"They ain't. They're growing in a ravine. There's a creek for swimming in the summer if we get rain. Too far to walk today, but you can ride one of the horses over in no time."

"I don't know how to ride a horse."

"I'll teach you."

"Thank you." I think Papa's right. Mr. Andersen *is* a nice man.

Mr. Andersen rests again. I circle him, picking up cow patties and putting them in the wheelbarrow. They seem to be everywhere—hundreds of them.

Owie's wagon is full again and he's trying to control the load, but a few slide off at every bump he hits. He picks them up and adds them back on the pile. Mr. Andersen smiles as he watches, then his gaze shifts to the line of cottonwoods in the distance, and his expression changes. He looks at the heavens, then walks out to meet Owie.

16

In the two weeks we've been here, progress on the house seems both slow and fast; fast because Mr. Andersen and Papa are at it every day; slow because we can't wait to move in. I'm sure Mr. Andersen is just as eager to see it finished so he can move out of the cold, drafty shed and back into his dugout.

I don't keep a diary, but I do have a pad where I jot notes to remind myself of things to tell Kippy, Mamie, and Mr. Fischer when I write again. Most have to do with the constant wind and my chores, which are heavily weighted with uses for manure—mucking the horse stalls and cleaning the chicken coop. Mr. Andersen says horse manure is the best fertilizer there is and, to quote him, "It don't need to age like chicken manure."

Now that the cellar is finished and the floor of the house is in place, it's easier to imagine a garden. The ground's too hard to plant, but Papa stakes it out on the east side of the house, where it will get the most sun and be protected from the wind. I haven't seen a direction the wind doesn't come from, but don't say so. I've already emptied many wheelbarrows full of horse manure inside those lines. Mr. Andersen says we'll work the manure into the soil when we're able to plow the rows.

Mr. Andersen seems to be looking forward to spring and getting the garden started. Twice he's shown me his list of the seeds we'll need. Today, when he comes into the barn, I lean on the muckrake and ask, "Why don't you already have a garden?"

"I did when the wife was hereabouts. Takes a woman to make a success out of a garden."

That statement opens up a million questions in my mind, but I don't want to be too nosy all at once.

This afternoon, I come out of the barn with the milk and see Mr. Andersen standing by the stock tank. He's watching Owie pulling his little wagon down a row between the wheat sprouts, headed for the unplowed acreage. I walk over and stand beside him. He's so lost in watching Owie he doesn't know I'm at his elbow. The wind sometimes bothers all our eyes, so I don't know if the tear that finds a gully in his face, and takes some dirt with it, is because of the wind or something else.

I back away to pretend I'm just walking up. "He sure loves that job."

I startle Mr. Andersen. He jumps, takes out his bandana and wipes his face. He turns to me. "I got time to give you a riding lesson this afternoon. You ready?"

"I can't wait." Butterflies erupt in my stomach.

There's no saddle and only what Mr. Andersen calls a hackamore bridle, made from an old rope. I choose Sam, who likes me better than Ben does.

I climb into the Conestoga and stand on the seat. Mr. Andersen leads Sam alongside and holds the rope. I'm glad Mama's not there to watch me hike my skirt, swing an unladylike leg over his broad back, and shift until I'm centered.

Sam's spent his life hitched to a wagon. Having someone on his back is a shock. He rolls his eyes to look at me and pins his ears.

"Talk to him," Mr. Andersen says. "If he's ever been rid, he probably don't remember."

I lean forward and stroke his neck. "It's me, Sam."

Sam skitters sideways. I grab a handful of mane and would have fallen off if Mr. Andersen hadn't been there to shove me upright.

"You gotta pay attention to your backside, feel which way he's headed with your, you know, your bum."

"Okay," I say, though I'm not sure what he means.

Mr. Andersen holds the reins loosely and starts walking Sam around the yard. "Don't sit up there like a feather. Make your backside heavy and keep your belly muscles in charge of the rest of you."

"I weigh what I weigh."

"Push down. Glue your bottom to his back.'

"How do I steer him?"

"You got nothing to do right now but stay on board. If he ain't never been rid we'll have to teach him how to bend from the ribcage. When that time comes, you'll turn him with the reins and pressure from your legs. Capisce?"

Mr. Fischer used to say *capisce*. It means "understand?" I smile at Mr. Andersen, but in my mind, I'm racing to the attic to share this new experience with Mr. Fischer.

Mr. Andersen continues to lead Sam around the yard. "Watch his ears. Pinned ain't good, but see how his right is turned toward me? He's listening. Hanging on every word." He smiles up at me. "How's it feel?"

"It's fun." It is. I do what Mr. Andersen says and try to make my bottom heavy, hugging Sam's sides with my knees. I start to feel the rhythm of Sam's pace and let my body move only from my waist up, and tighten my stomach muscles to control my balance. After a few minutes, I relax my knees a little and let my legs dangle. I still keep a fist knotted in Sam's mane.

The next day, Mr. Andersen hands me the rope reins.

"Go." Full of confidence, I wiggle my rear end.

Sam doesn't move.

"Do I have to kick him to make him go?"

"He ain't had much practice, but try wiggling your feet against his sides, and give a couple of clicks with your mouth. He'll get the idea soon enough."

I do that and Sam starts to walk toward the gate. I pull on the left rein, lean too far in the direction I want him to go, and fall off, landing hard enough on the cold ground to knock the wind out of me. Sam stops and puts his warm muzzle against my ear, then butts me with his head trying to make me get up.

Mr. Andersen squats beside me. "You okay?"

I nod because I can't talk.

"Lesson learned, right?" Mr. Andersen holds a callused hand out to me. "You shouldn't have to do more than press his side and turn your body from the waist up in the direction you want him to go. May take some time, but he'll figure it out and so will you."

Mr. Andersen says from the looks of the sky it's fixing to snow by morning. Papa takes his word for it and decides the trip to town he was going to make later in the week is better made today. Mama's going with him and will see the doctor while she's there. I want to go, but she doesn't want to have to keep track of Owie, so I have to stay home and watch him.

Owie whines about getting left behind until Papa makes it sound as if our lives depend on him collecting enough kindling and cow patties to last until spring. He kneels in front of Owie. "There's no telling how long the snow will last, so it's up to you."

"Okay, Papa," Owie sniffles. He turns and marches toward the barn to get his wagon. I take the big wheelbarrow.

After our parents leave with Ben pulling Mr. Andersen's buckboard, he begins getting things battened down. Without him along to slow us down, Owie and I walk, with Karlo trotting ahead, all the way to the creek and the cottonwoods. I'm surprised at how steep the sides of the ravine are. That's why, from a distance, I only saw the bare tops of the cottonwoods. Owie and I climb down to the sandy creek bed and walk in opposite directions, collecting twigs and fallen limbs small enough to carry back. Owie comes back carrying two short white boards nailed together in the shape of a lopsided X. "Show me where you found this."

He takes my hand and tugs me along the creek bed for a few yards. "Here, I think."

The ground all looks the same as it slopes up through the trees. There are small rocks everywhere, but under the carpet of leaves a clearly man-made pile catches my eye. I brush away the leaves. It's almost certainly a grave; a small grave. Someone or something is buried here. A child or a pet maybe. I spread the boards apart. It's a cross. I place it on top of the stones.

"Why are you leaving them?" Owie's got his hands on his hips like Papa does when he's peeved.

"Because it belongs with this grave."

"Whose grave?"

"I don't know," I say, but think I do know. This is where Mr. Andersen's son is buried. It must be, and he must have been the same age as Owie is now. That explains why Karlo was so happy to see him and the first sight of Owie seemed to shock Mr. Andersen.

"Okay. Can we collect cow patties now?"

"Do you still have room in your wagon?"

"Yup." He's starting to sound like Mr. Andersen.

We make two trips between the house and the field for cow patties. By the time we get back with the second wagon and wheelbarrow loads, it's starting to snow. Flakes swirl in the wind. Mama and Papa aren't home. Before we left to hunt for wood, I lit a fire in the stove and put on a pot of beans with onions and potatoes. The dugout is warm and smells good.

Mr. Andersen fed and watered Lily and Sam, and he has feed and water ready for Ben when my parents get back. The chickens are locked in their coop.

Owie's pulling the wagon to the barn when Mr. Andersen comes down the path from the outhouse.

"How'd you do?"

"I got a million."

Mr. Andersen smiles. "By golly, a million should get you through this winter and next. You're the best durn patty-collector of all time." He musses Owie's hair. "You're a fine lad." There's that sad look again.

"Mr. Andersen, we found—" I hear a horse whinny and we all turn.

Not a bad day, I think. Mama and Papa are home. We'll have warm stew with tonight's hardtack, and the dugout is warm. Let it snow.

17

By the time Papa and Mr. Andersen unload the buckboard and unhitch the Ben, the snowfall is heavy. Mama, Owie, and I retreat to the warmth of the dugout. I'm getting used to the odor of cow patties burning, the same way we got used to the rotting-meat stink of our neighborhood in Chicago. Today, simmering soup covers the earthy scent of manure and reminds me of home. If I close my eyes, I can see Mama and Mrs. Howard laughing as they set the kitchen table for supper, and later, all the tenants sitting over hot soup and warm bread. Mr. Fischer is in his seat at the head of the table, full of compliments for the meal, no matter how meager.

I lift the lid to stir my soup and realize I should have waited to add the potatoes. They've turned to mush.

Mama pats my cheek. "It smells wonderful, honey. Thank you." She crosses to the bed and lies down.

"Are you okay?"

"Just tired."

"What did Doctor Dawson say?"

"The baby's fine. He gave me iron pills, which should give me more energy." She closes her eyes. "I wish it was April and this was over with."

Once again, I vow not to marry and be forced to bear children. I don't want to wish something was over that I didn't want in the first place.

Papa comes in, followed by Mr. Andersen, Karlo, and a gust of cold wind.

"Can Karlo stay?" Owie asks.

"No." Mama doesn't open her eyes.

"I'll take him home," Mr. Andersen says.

Mama realizes Mr. Andersen's in the dugout, sits up, and tucks a loose strand of hair back in her bun.

Mr. Andersen puts a basket covered with a dish towel on the table and a dish of butter beside it, then pats his hip for Karlo to follow.

Papa stands with his hands to the heat from the stove and stamps the snow off his boots. He lifts the lid and sniffs the soup. "Smells good, Nona." He waits until Mr. Andersen closes the door behind himself and Karlo. "It was nice of you to invite Noel," he says to me. "It must have meant a lot to him. He's baked a loaf of sourdough bread for us and churned some butter."

I glance at Mama, who doesn't seem to be listening. "He's nice and I think he's been lonely here all by himself." I want to ask if Papa knows if he had a son who died, but don't think in front of Mama and Owie is the right time.

I'm putting spoons and knives on the table when Mr. Andersen comes back without Karlo. I'm a little suspicious of bread made with sour dough. Sounds as if it's gone bad, like most of the meat we used to get from the butcher on the corner. We always hoped if we cooked it long enough, it wouldn't kill us. I don't want to be rude, but I have to ask. "Is bread made out of *sour* dough okay to eat?"

Mr. Andersen smiles. "Sure is. I've had this starter for fifty years. Since I was a wet-behind-the-ears kid in Alaska."

Fifty-year-old dough! My face must show what I'm thinking.

Mr. Andersen explains, "Starter is just fermented yeast and water. I've kept it alive by feeding it flour and water once a week or so. When I get ready to bake a loaf of bread, I use starter as leavening to make the bread rise while it's baking."

"How do you make butter?"

"Churn it from the cream I separate from Miss Lily's milk. I'll teach you. And teach you how to bake bread, if you like. Give you some starter of your own."

"Thank you," I say, but think I'll wait to accept until I see how sour dough tastes.

Papa takes off his coat and hangs it by the door. "I've got something for you." he says to me.

"What?" I try to sound excited. Mama quit making me wear ribbons, but I'm afraid Papa noticed my bare hair and that's his surprise.

If only I could wear a newsboy cap and coveralls instead of this dress and pinafore, I'd be happy.

He pats his coat pockets. "Hope I didn't lose 'em."

Two ribbons!

He grins and pulls two letters from the front pocket of his coveralls and hands them to me. One is from Kippy. I recognize her hand-writing. I'm not sure about the other one which is addressed to Winona Williams, General Delivery, Dalhart, Texas. I tear open Kippy's first.

Dear Nona,
I MISS YOU!!!
Your postcard arrived yesterday—

I turn the envelope over to look at the date. It was mailed on January 8. It's now January 29. Her letter's been at the post office three weeks. I read on.

I miss you because there's no one else I can beat at Jacks. I miss you because there's no one to sneak off to the dump with or tell secrets to. I hope you are happy in Texas. Please write and tell me what it's like. Do you have a yard? A pony? Have you started school yet? Does Texas smell wonderful? Tell me everything.

Mr. Fischer's been sick but is better now. We have new boarders from Germany. I thought that would please Mr. Fischer but they don't seem to care too much for each other. The husband is working the killing beds and the wife is sewing bags for hams. Nothing else has changed here.

Write soon. I miss you. Your friend forever,
Kippy Howard

I fold the letter and put it in my pocket until I find a safe place to keep it.

Mama watches me with sadder than usual eyes. "What did Kippy have to say?" She gets up, takes five bowls from the shelf, and puts them on the table.

"Mr. Fischer's been sick, and Germans have moved into our old flat."

"Her mother told me."

"You got a letter, too?"

"I did."

That explains Mama's mood. Missing people you love is harder when you've got a reminder in your pocket.

I start to open the other letter and see it's from Mamie, but Mama says to wait until after supper to read it.

Papa pulls a lard bucket over for Mr. Andersen, who doesn't sit until Mama does.

Most of the time Mama's nice to Mr. Andersen, in her own way. Tonight is one of those nights. She thanks him for the bread and has a second piece. The bread is not sour at all—different tasting, but, with butter, it's delicious. By the time supper is over, there's nothing left but crumbs for the chickens.

Mama gets up. "You cooked, Nona, I'll do the dishes."

Mr. Andersen must think this is a hint. He stands to leave.

"You should stay in here with us," Papa says.

Mama says nothing as she collects the bowls from the table.

"Karlo and I have survived worse. Good soup, Nona." At the door, he tips his hat to me and Mama's back. The snow tops his boots before he disappears into the white night.

I stay at the table near the lamp and open the letter from Mamie.

Dear Nona,

I want to thank you for befriending me on the train. I felt so lost and alone. Turns out, I'm one of the lucky ones. Texhoma is nice enough. We live on a small wheat farm about ten miles north of town. The Johnsons are very nice to me. I have a room of my own and my chores are light.

I don't know how any of the others fared except Tim. He's the one who wouldn't let that old man inspect his teeth. Not sure how his letter found me, but he wrote to say that he ended up with a cot in the barn and is a slave for the family that took him. They say he can go to school if he finds a way to get there, but they won't let him use one of their horses and it's a five mile walk one way. He hopes when the chaperones come in six months to check on all of us, they will let him go back to New York with them. I'm not sure that's a good idea. At least he's got

*a roof over his head and they are feeding him. In New York, he lived on
the streets.*

*I hope you are happy in Texas. At least you are with your family
and your father. I looked on a map and Dalhart isn't too far away. I
hope we see each other again one day. You are my only friend. Please
write back.*

   Sincerely,
   Mary 'Mamie' McNair

I put her letter in my pocket with Kippy's.

Outside, the wind howls, blowing smoke back down the stove pipe.
Owie begins to cough and Papa opens the window. It doesn't help much.

18

It's still dark when I wake the next morning under a damp blanket. Snow has drifted in through the open window and melted from the heat.

Mama and Papa sit drinking coffee; Mama in her rocking chair, Papa on a pickle barrel. The only light is from the kerosene lamp on the table. More unnerving is the absolute silence. Usually, I hear the rooster crowing, Lily mooing, and the clackety clack of the windmill turning.

"What time is it?"

"Good morning," Papa says, and takes out his watch. "Eight-thirty."

"How come it's still dark?"

"We're snowed in. I'm hoping Noel isn't and is digging us out."

We fall silent, listening for the scrape of a shovel or Mr. Andersen's voice calling to us. I glance at the window. There's no way to tell how much snow covers the dugout, but it's enough to block out any light from the outside. At least the wind has died, so Papa could close the window. There's a smoky haze near the ceiling. I glance over at Owie and am not surprised he's still asleep. He coughed most of the night.

"Well." Mama sighs and gets up. "At least we have eggs for breakfast."

The day we moved in, Papa hung a sheet from two nails in the rafters in a dark corner of the dugout. There's a galvanized tub behind it where we bathe. Now the sheet also hides a chamber pot since we can't get to the outhouse.

Hours pass with no sound. I worry more and more about the animals. They are safe in the barn, but if Mr. Andersen is snowed in, too, there's no one to feed them or to milk poor Lily.

When we're quiet, we're alert and listening. If Papa glances at the door or the window, we all look, hoping he hears something.

We wait as late as we can for lunch—a fried egg each—and wish we'd saved some of Mr. Andersen's sourdough bread. For supper,

Mama waters down the bean and potato soup by adding ice Papa scrapes out of the window with spoon. If we're still here in tomorrow morning, we'll be having bean and potato-flavored water for breakfast.

I've read *Heidi*, the book Mr. Fischer gave me, twice. After we eat, I start reading it to Owie. He is immediately taken with the story of Heidi and her cranky grandfather.

We go to bed early and hope to sleep through our hunger. In the morning, we're still buried. The air inside the dugout is rank from the chamber pot, and so warm, it's hard to breathe. I roll over and go back to sleep.

I wake the second time to the sound of ice splintering. The light from the lamp throws Papa's shadow up the wall and across the ceiling, as he chips at the snow blocking the window.

The door to the dugout opens out, which I thought was a stupid plan until Papa told me that if it opened in, the snow packed against it would cave in on us. The window opens in and is sheltered by the overhang of the roof. Papa's arm is out the window to his shoulder. He's whacking at the ice with a pick and scooping the chips and snow into a bucket with a big spoon.

"What are you doing?" I yawn.

He puts a finger to his lips and whispers, "Trying to tunnel through to the outside to get some air."

I get up to use the chamber pot, and wash my face and hands in the basin.

Papa has a pot on the stove to melt the ice in. I put the leftover stew water on the other burner to heat for Owie when he wakes. Even the smell of it warming makes my stomach ache from hunger.

By late afternoon we hear water dripping. Sunlight through the snow causes the window to glow. Encouraged, Papa attacks the snow-pack again, chipping away with the ice pick, and digging out what he breaks loose with the spoon. Twice he glances at me and back at the tunnel. He holds his hands on either side of my shoulders, then holding them steady, turns and measures the width of the window. "Turn sideways." He draws a circle in the air with a finger, then cocks his head trying to decide if I'm thinner than the window is deep. "I think you can fit in here. Want to try to dig the rest of the way out?"

"Sure."

Mama's knitting by the light of the kerosene lamp. "You can't send her out there by herself," she says.

"We don't have a choice, Glenny. We're out of food, and there will soon be nothing left to burn except the furniture."

"Whose fault it that?" Mama stands. The rocking chair whooshes.

Papa's head snaps back as if she'd slapped him. "Glenny?"

I want to say he couldn't have known how much it was going to snow, but I keep my head down and my arms at my sides. Mama needs me, too.

Papa looks at me. "Put your coat on." He takes the oilcloth off the table, folds it, and lays it the length of the tunnel, then puts a pickle barrel against the wall for me to stand on.

Papa has dug to the point where the roof ends. He lifts me to stand on the barrel and I fit myself into the tunnel with about an inch all around to spare. There's no way to tell how deep the snow is covering the dugout, or how far I will have to tunnel to reach the outside. The only encouragement we have is the brightness of the snow and the sound of dripping.

I stab at the snow with the pick, but in this tight space I can't move my arm with enough force to do it any damage. Cold water drips on my head and down the back of my neck.

Between the hunger and the cold, I tire quickly. "I can't do it, Papa."

He helps me back out, reaches in with the spoon, and scrapes out what little I chipped free.

I stand next to the stove to warm up, then walk to the cabinet and open the only drawer. "How about this, Papa?" I hold up the butcher knife. It's twice as long as the ice pick.

"Good girl." He takes it, turns sideways, presses his right side against the sod walls, and stabs at the ice. "We're almost there. Want to try again?" He pulls his arm out, rubs, and rotates his shoulder.

I nod.

Papa slides the sheet of oilcloth back into the tunnel, and makes sure my coat is buttoned snugly. Once I'm in the tunnel, it takes some wiggling on my part, fitting one shoulder through at a time with Papa pushing against the soles of my feet. Using the butcher knife, I break through in just a few minutes. Cold fresh air whooshes in. I stab harder, enlarging the hole. Using my mitten-covered hands to push free of the tunnel, I slide face first down the side of the knoll and come to a stop buried to my elbows in snow. I roll over, stand up, brush myself off, turn and smile. Papa, framed in the window, gives me a thumbs-up.

"There's a shovel in the barn," he says. "Do you think you can dig Noel out?"

I'm not at all sure, but I say yes.

The sun on the snow is blinding, and the buried dugout looks like a giant scoop of ice cream. I glance toward the shed and the barn. Snow has drifted nearly to the hay doors and covers the shed as well. The only signs of life are the coyote footprints to and from the chicken coop, which is also buried.

"Nona?" Papa's calls from the window. "Can you get in the barn?"

"No. Snow's blocking the doors."

"How about the shed?"

"It's buried, too."

"See if you can find something to dig with."

"Okay."

The snow is melting where the sun hits it. My feet sink in to slush. Water puddles in my footprints.

The snow is nearly to the shed's roof line, but I know Noel's okay inside because smoke curls from the chimney. I reach up as high as I can, to wear the drift is the thinnest and scrape away enough snow to expose the wood siding. "Mr. Andersen, can you hear me?"

Karlo barks. "I can," comes a muffled reply. "Where's your father?"

"In the dugout. I crawled out through the window."

"Can you get in the barn?"

"The snow's too deep. It's over the doors."

"You need to try. Poor Lily's bawling. Can you fetch the ladder from the cellar and climb in through the hay doors?"

I look over my shoulder. The floor of the house is buried under snow. I feel the sting of tears, wipe my nose with the back of my hand, and look again. Two brown knobs poke out of snow. It's the ladder Papa left in the cellar because he hasn't built stairs yet, or the doors. I slog across the yard in my heavy, wet boots, sink to my knees, and dig around the posts deep enough to get a grip on the top rung of the ladder. I pull. It doesn't budge. I wiggle it back and forth and sideways to loosen it, then stand up and pull as hard as I can. The next step is exposed. I pull again and again until it slides free.

The ladder's wet and so heavy I can barely drag it across the yard to lay it against the snow drift. If the barn were tall like most barns are, the ladder wouldn't reach the hayloft doors, but this barn is low and wide. The top of the ladder ends just short of the loft. I climb up, lie across the snow, and stretch to reach the hay doors. I fling one side open. The horses whinny and snort; Lily bawls pitifully. I grab the ledge, pull myself across the snow, and tumble over the edge onto the loft floor.

I scramble to my feet, drag a bale of hay to the edge of the loft, and push it over the side. I climb down the inside ladder to the barn floor. My feet ache with the cold as I limp over and open the stall doors so the horses can get to the hay. I grab the bucket and the milking stool. Lily's udders are gigantic, but when I try to milk her, nothing comes out.

I remember Mr. Andersen's instructions: Calves nudge their mothers' udders with their noses. To imitate that, I stroke and press my fist against her bulging udder gently to let the milk down. She turns to look at me with her sad brown eyes, lifts her head, and moos.

"I know it hurts, Lily."

Even though my hands are numb, I pinch two teats snugly against her udder and squeeze. The stream is weak at first, then heavier. I fill the first bucket, then another. The horses finish the hay. To take a rest from milking, I climb the ladder and use the pitchfork to throw more hay down to them and enough to fill Lily's trough. I give each horse a bucket of oats.

All their water troughs are empty. I take a bucket up the ladder to the hay doors, lean out and scoop snow to fill it. My feet hurt so badly, I'm in tears by the time I've climbed up and down enough times to fill the troughs for Ben and Sam, and for Lily.

The back of Mr. Andersen's shed is the west wall of the barn. I rap on it and call his name.

"I'm here." His voice is muffled.

"I've milked Lily and fed the horses. They all needed water. I filled their troughs with snow. Will it hurt to add some of Lily's milk to make it melt? It's as cold in here as it is outside."

"No, it won't. Great idea."

When I finish dividing one bucket of Lily's milk between the troughs, I knock on the barn wall again. "I've got the shovel, but I'm not sure where your door is."

"You get started and I'll knock to guide you."

I get the shovel, climb the ladder to the hayloft, and throw the shovel to the ground. I lean out the loft door, grab the top of the ladder and pull myself across the snow.

The sun is going down. The snow had started to melt but is now refrozen. It cracks and crunches under my throbbing feet as I walk to Mr. Andersen's shed.

19

It's dark by the time I clear a path to Mr. Andersen's door. He takes one look at my wet boots and pulls me inside. He places his only chair next to the woodstove and makes me sit. Karlo comes over, puts his head on my lap, and looks at me with eyes so sad it feels like sympathy.

"When did you eat last?"

"Last night."

"We're going to take care of your feet first." He pulls my boots off, then my socks, and examines my toes. The tips are a grayish-white.

"That color is from ice crystals. You've got frostbite."

I always thought Mama's winter warnings about frostbite were to get me to wear my galoshes. My bottom lip quivers. "Are they gonna turn black and fall off?"

"No." He pats my shoulder. "But they're libel to blister and hurt pretty bad for a time." He pulls a box over, puts his pillow on it, and props my feet up close to the fire.

This is the first time I've been inside his shed. The woodstove's in a corner near the door. Mr. Andersen's wire cot, covered with a saggy horsehair mattress, is pushed against the wall the shed shares with the barn. Mama's furniture is stacked neatly in one corner. I can hear chickens clucking in their coop on the other side of the wall they share with Mama's furniture. A few pots and pans hang from hooks in the ceiling. There's a washbasin with a jagged shard of a mirror resting against a post behind it. Beneath the washbasin table is the reeking chamber pot. The floor, like the dugout's, is packed dirt, swept to a shine.

"I'll be right back." He leaves the shed and a minute later I hear him shout to my parents. "She's okay. I'm going to fix her something to eat, then dig you out."

I can't hear Papa's response.

Minutes pass before Mr. Andersen reappears carrying a pail of milk. He's breathing hard from the effort it took to climb the outside ladder then the inside ladder, carrying the pail. He pours some in a pot and puts it on the woodstove. "How're your feet feeling?"

"Better." Actually, they hurt worse. They were numb before, but now the feeling is coming back, and they throb.

Mr. Andersen looks at me. "You're a brave young lady, Nona."

I'm feeling a little proud of myself, too. It was hard, but I did a good job. As well as any boy could do.

Mr. Andersen lifts a corner of the one blanket still covering Mama's furniture, opens a drawer in one of the parlor pieces, and takes out a loaf of bread. "Figured there was no sense being sealed in here with the heat going to waste, so I baked more bread."

It's been twenty-six hours since yesterday's watery lunch. My stomach growls at the sight of the bread.

Mr. Andersen takes a tin cup from a nail on the wall, holds it to the lantern to look inside, and wipes it out with his shirt tail. He tears a chunk of bread off the loaf, then rips it into smaller pieces and drops them in the cup. He pours warmed milk over the top, sprinkles it with a little sugar and a brown powder.

"What's that?"

"Nutmeg." He hands me the cup and a spoon. "Eat slowly, or you'll give yourself a bellyache."

In my mind, I hear my mother's once-nightly reminder to eat like a lady. I take a small first bite. The second bite is as much as I can get on the spoon.

Mr. Andersen laughs. "Good, huh?"

I can only nod.

"You saw how I made it, so help yourself to more. I'm going to start digging your folks out." He takes a lantern from a nail in the wall, lights it, and calls to Karlo, who doesn't budge. Mr. Andersen smiles at him. "Don't blame you, old man. Good company and a warm room." He closes the shed door behind him.

The next thing I know Papa is shaking me. "Nona. Come on, honey, let's go home."

I'm curled up on Mr. Andersen's cot. I sit up and rub my eyes. "What time is it?"

"A little after ten." He picks my boots off the floor, ties their laces together, and drapes them over his shoulder, one boot on either side. He picks me up, kisses my cheek, and carries me out of the shed, through the snow to the dugout.

The roof is leaking. *Drip, drip.* Water filters through the sod, finds cracks in the board ceiling and falls into the pots Mama has put around the room. The *ring, bing, plop* of water dripping, on any other night might have kept me awake. But not this night.

20

Owie and I were supposed to start school on the Monday following the blizzard, but, because of the frostbite, I spent a month with cotton between my toes until the blisters healed. Tomorrow, March 4, we start. To celebrate, Mr. Andersen comes to supper with a plate of fried chicken. He knows Owie and I have gotten attached to the chickens and assures us this one had a full, egg-laying life, and was tired. After supper, Mr. Andersen opens the satchel he carried over from the shed. "I found a few things that might come in handy for tomorrow."

For me, he has a slate and chalk. For Owie, a barely used set of eight Crayola crayons. He strokes the box with his thumb for a moment before handing it to my brother.

"What do you say?" Mama instructs, smiling at Mr. Andersen. Fried chicken has finished melting her heart toward him.

Owie scoots off his chair, walks over, and puts his hand on Mr. Andersen's arm. "Thank you, Mr. Noel."

Mr. Andersen nods. Again, I see that pained look. He clears his throat. "That ain't all." He pulls out a strap for carrying books and an empty *Sure Shot* Chewing Tobacco tin with a picture of an Indian aiming his bow and arrow. "Thought you could use this to keep them letters in."

"This is exactly what I need." I kiss his cheek and open it to find a little batch of stationery tied with a pink ribbon. I show Mama.

"Pretty," she says, and gives Mr. Andersen the second warm smile of the night.

Mr. Andersen's face is dark and ruddy except the white skin of his forehead, which is usually covered by his hat. "Weren't much use to me." He blushes from his eyebrows to his hairline.

The schoolhouse is two miles east on the road to Hartley. I'm nervous and excited. I've missed school mostly because I miss Kippy. I hope to meet someone nice and make a friend, though out here the farms are miles apart, so a friendship will be hard to keep up.

Local farmers have cleared the road, but the snowbanks on either side are still too high to see over. Papa says we'll walk when the weather is nice, but until the snow melts, he'll take us in the buckboard.

I'm not sure how Karlo knows we're going to school, but when Owie and I climb up, he jumps in the back. Papa calls for him to get down, but he whines, and puts his head on his paws.

Karlo gets out at school and makes himself comfortable in the doorway. If I'm right about Mr. Andersen's son, then as old and gray as Karlo is, he must have been here many times before.

The schoolhouse is a one room wooden building painted white. There's a large bell by the front door and a merry-go-round made from a wagon wheel on a post in the front yard. Miss Brown, our teacher, is at the door to welcome us. She's very young—seventeen or eighteen—and pretty like Mama, only blond. She smells of chalk and lavender water.

After we stomp our feet to get the snow off, Miss Brown shows us the cloakroom where we leave our boots and hang our coats and mufflers. She takes our sack lunches and places them on the shelf above our coats, then leads us to the front of the room, where the other kids stare at us, and whisper to each other. I've never been the new person in school, much less an outsider. Now I know how the newly arrived children of foreigners felt coming to school in the Back of the Yards. Owie tightens his grip on my hand.

Posters decorate the walls—one of the alphabet, another of the multiplication tables, and a map of the United States. There's a world globe on Miss Brown's desk.

Four-year-old Owie is the only kindergartner. There are eight grades. Miss Brown says she'll give me a test to see what grade I'll be in after she gets everyone else started on their assignments for the day. In Chicago, I was in fifth grade with nineteen other students. Kippy and I went to Hedges School with a different classroom for each grade. Most kids in the Back of the Yards, once they graduated from grammar school, went to work since their parents couldn't afford for them not to.

After Miss Brown introduces us, she picks up a piece of chalk and writes Owen and Winona Williams on the slate board, then asks each student to stand up and give their name and what grade they're in. There are nine of them.

"Winona, do you want to tell the class where you and your brother are from?"

"Two miles down the road."

The students laugh.

"I mean where you moved here from."

"Chicago."

"Do any of you know where Chicago is?"

No one raises their hand.

"Winona, would you show us Chicago on the map?"

I cross the room, Owie on my heels, holding the edge of my pinafore.

Miss Brown has a pin stuck approximately where Dalhart is located in Texas, though it's not named. This is the first time I've seen where we live and how terribly far we are from Chicago.

Lake Michigan is higher on the map than I am tall. I'm using the pointer Miss Brown handed me to show that Chicago is near the tip of the lake when something lands in my hair. I feel the back of my head and remove a spitball.

"Who did that?" Miss Brown says.

No one answers, but I can tell by the smirk on the face of one of the seventh-grade boys, that he did it.

"If no one owns up, we'll all stay after school, except Owen and Winona, of course."

"Joshua did it," the eighth-grade girl says.

"Squealer," Joshua sneers.

"Joshua will stay after school and write 'I will not misbehave in class' one hundred times on the board."

"I got chores to do at home."

"Now you have another."

The only empty seat among the older kids is next to the spit-ball boy. Miss Brown sends me to share a desk with him. Owie follows.

"How come I have to sit next to her?" he says.

Miss Brown doesn't bother to answer.

"Owen, you come sit up here near me." Miss Brown points to a small table at the front of the room.

"I want to sit with my sister." Owie puts his fists in his eyes and starts to cry.

"What a baby," sneers the boy next to me. He smells stale, his hair is uncombed and oily, and there's a caramel-color plug of wax in his ear.

"Okay," Miss Brown says to Owie. "Just for today."

I don't give her time to change her mind. I get up and take an empty bench at the back of the room near the coal stove. Owie runs to join me and crawls into my lap. He clamps a hand on either side of my face to make me look at him and puts his face close to mine. "I don't like it here. When is Fodder coming to get us?"

"Hours from now, so you have to be a good boy."

The room is stuffy and smells of coal smoke and unwashed children. I gaze out the windows at the snow which is level with the sill, then at the backs of these strangers. I wish Kippy was here. Or I was there.

For lunch, Owie and I each have a sourdough sandwich with butter and apple jelly. I look for Denmark on the globe and show Owie where Mr. Andersen is from. A pinky-finger length west of Denmark is Ireland, Mamie's home.

The first-graders are reading *McGuffey's Readers*. Second-graders are doing arithmetic. While I take the placement test, Owie sits beside me and colors. He gets up and follows me to the front of the room when I deliver the test to Miss Brown. She smiles after she grades it. "Class, we now have ourselves a sixth-grader," she announces.

In the afternoon, I have writing, spelling, and grammar. The seventh and eighth grades are studying Texas history, geography and agriculture.

By the time school ends at three, the snow is slush. Miss Brown stands at the door waving goodbye. When Karlo sees her, his tail thumps the ground, and he struggles to his feet.

"Well, my goodness." She leans and cups Karlo's face. "This is the Andersens' dog. I haven't seen him—" She looks up at Papa. "In years."

I knew it. Karlo used to come to school with Mr. Andersen's son. Miss Brown must have been a classmate. She's too young to have been his teacher.

When Owie climbs up beside Papa, Karlo runs and tries to jump in, but he must have gotten stiff lying in the cold doorway all day. He falls back. Papa jumps down and lifts him into the wagon. Owie crawls over the seat to lie beside him, puts his arm around Karlo's neck, and is soon asleep with his head against Karlo's stomach.

21

On Saturday, Papa returns from town with the week-old news that a neighbor has died. Mr. Rydberg climbed his windmill to replace a bolt, got clipped by a blade, lost his balance, and fell. The fall broke his neck.

Mr. Andersen knew him from his days at the XIT. He hitches Ben to the buckboard and drives over to see what he can do to help the widow. He carries the loaf of sourdough bread we baked together. When he comes home that evening, he tells us the widow is going to move to Iowa to be with her daughter and grandchildren.

"I helped her husband build their place twenty years ago." His looks at our nearly finished house, and sighs. "She asked how I was doing here alone, so I told her about you folks. She offered me first choice of the household goods and anything else she can't take with her."

On Monday morning, Papa and Mr. Andersen hitch Sam and Ben to the Conestoga, drop Owie, Karlo, and me at school, and drive out to her farm. When we get home from school, having walked for the first time, we find the start of a herd of cattle—a bull and two cows. They are out on the unplowed acres, pawing through what's left of the snow to eat buffalo grass. There are a dozen new chickens, a second milk cow to keep Miss Lily company, a cream separator newer than the old thing Mr. Andersen uses, a butter churn with a handle that isn't broken, a No. 110 Monarch washer with rollers, and a Crawford range—a real woodburning cast iron cook stove.

Mama eyes these things, first with pleasure before turning a suspicious glance toward Papa. "Where did the money for this come from?"

We're standing by the wagon. Papa glances around, looking for Mr. Andersen.

"He's in the barn," I say.

Papa lowers his voice anyway. "Noel paid for everything. Look at the way he's been living, Glenny. I bet he's got every nickel he ever made.

She has more stuff and I thought you might like to go see for yourself. What with your furniture in the shed and what she's wanting to sell, we can furnish the entire house."

Papa smiles at me. "Nona, Noel bought you a present, too." He puts his hands on my shoulders and turns me to face the barn.

Mr. Andersen comes out leading a pinto pony.

"His name is Dan," Papa says. "He's saddle-broke and gentle as a lamb."

I've never had so much as a kitten and now I have a horse of my own. I hug Papa, Mama, and run to hug Mr. Andersen.

Dan's about half the size of Sam. To make friends, Mr. Andersen places a lump of sugar in my hand, tells me to offer it to him in a flattened palm. After that, Dan follows me all around the yard, blowing his hot breath on the back of my neck.

Mr. Andersen shows me how to saddle Dan and to adjust the stirrups. "His only flaw is he don't like the bit."

Using the rope hackamore suits me fine. I don't expect I'd take to a bit either.

That night I write Kippy to tell her I have a horse. I start to write Mamie, but all I can think of to say is how much I like it here, even though there are no girls at school my age. I'm with my family and feel too lucky to tell her all the good news *and* that I have a horse of my own.

It's the end of March and we've been here three months. The baby is due in another two weeks. Mama is uncomfortable and tired all the time. More of the work falls to me. Sam and Ben take turns plowing the garden or hitched to the buckboard for the day-long trips to town. Owie and I ride Dan to school, but I still get up at five to feed and water the horses and to milk Lily and Rose, the new cow, before we go. We get gallons more milk than we can use, so Mr. Andersen uses the separator to collect the cream. He churns it into butter, most of which Papa sells to the store in town. We keep the whole milk cold in the well house and toss the nasty tasting skim out for the chickens.

Even though the hens quit laying for the winter, Owie was happy to check under them each morning anyway for the occasional reward. Now that they've started again, he races out to check each morning and comes in with his basket loaded.

I remember our Chicago chickens quit laying in the winter, but for whatever reason, since we arrived here, we've had plenty of eggs. When I finally think to ask why, I find out it's because Mr. Andersen preserved dozens of last summer's eggs in a ceramic crock filled with water glass, which is not water or glass. It's a clear, syrupy liquid. Mr. Andersen says the eggs will keep fresh for eight months. He's going to teach me water glassing.

True to his word, Papa finishes the house a week before the baby is due. In places where the planks are a bit warped, we can see daylight through the cracks until Papa tar papers the outside. It's lovely to have windows and a door we can prop open on sunny days.

Mama makes it homey by hanging the lace curtains that belonged to her mother over the window by the kitchen sink. There's no hand pump or spigot, so we still have to haul water in from the well house. Papa puts a bucket under the sink to catch dishwater that we'll carry out to the garden.

Mama's five-drawer dresser with mirror and one of the Oriental rugs go into my parents' room, the other Papa rolls up and stores under their bed since it's too nice to put in the room I share with Owie, or in the main room where we track in mud and dirt.

Owie's and my room gets one of the parlor tables. The second one goes into the main room, the other side of which is the kitchen with the Crawford stove and a table and four chairs, also from Mrs. Rydberg. Mama puts the doilies her grandmother tatted on the parlor tables under the kerosene lamps.

Each of the two piney-smelling bedrooms has a window. Mama makes curtains for them out of the green dress she wore to that first dance with Papa. When we hang them, I watch to see if she's sad. She shrugs. "Time to let go of the past."

Coal, which Papa had delivered after the snow made finding cow patties and dry wood impossible, is in the cellar. Mr. Andersen is building shelves down there for when he teaches Mama—or more likely me—how to can what we grow in the garden.

For our first supper in the new house, Papa kills another old chicken, which Mama over-bakes to a crusty brown. We have potatoes and gravy, the corn Mr. Andersen canned last summer, and sourdough biscuits. Even the tough chicken with enough gravy, tastes as good to me as any meal Kippy's mom ever cooked back in Chicago.

Once every two weeks, Papa goes to town to bring back supplies and the mail, if there is any. He buys a Sunday edition of the *Chicago Daily Tribune*, which we read, then use sheets of it to paper the inside walls.

While in town, Papa sells our extra butter and cream and gives me half the cream money, since I do the milking and separating. He thinks I'm saving it for college when I put it in my tobacco tin with the coins I found at the dump, the nickel Mr. Fischer gave me, and my letters. I don't tell him I'm saving it for flying lessons.

Mr. Andersen says the wheat crop looks the best he's seen in years, but he's concerned there's a glut. They used to get two dollars a bushel, but last year, wheat sold for a dollar a bushel. Even so, a couple of times I catch Papa standing in the open hay doors looking out across the sprouting fields. His eyes soften like they do when he looks at one of us, and I imagine he feels relief and pride. Even though he comes in every night almost too tired to lift his fork, it's a different kind of tired from Chicago. To see him proud of his work is worth the move here.

Today, when I hear Papa in the loft, I climb the ladder. From a little behind him, I'm reminded of the *Opportunity* angel. I step forward and take his hand. "The stories about this land were all true."

Papa kneels and puts an arm around my waist. I drape mine over his shoulder. We stay like that for a few minutes, then he smiles at me, smacks a knee, and stands. "Back to work."

I stay looking out across the young wheat, close my eyes, spread my arms, and imagine lifting off, sailing out the hay doors to fly low over the fields.

It's warm enough to start the garden. We plan to plant beets, broccoli, cabbage, cucumbers, onions, green beans, tomatoes, peas, corn, asparagus, carrot, collards, cauliflower, and blueberries. It's hard to imagine ever being able to eat all that food.

Mr. Andersen and I spread horse manure over the whole plot, then he hooks Ben to a plow called a lister, to break the ground. Two weeks after we plant, it rains and the seeds sprout. I feel protective of the seedlings and walk the rows every day, weeding and picking off bugs to feed to the chickens. In addition, it's my job to carry water from the well, and mulch everything with more horse manure—except the tomatoes, which, Mr. Andersen tells me like an acid soil. And never fertilize fruit crops, he warns. It decreases fruit and increases leaves.

One day, after school, I carry the coal scuttle down to the cellar and find Mr. Andersen building shelves in preparation for our summer canning.

I'm not sure why I've waited so long to ask about the grave in the cottonwoods, but this feels like the right time. "Would you be mad if I asked you something?"

"Doubt it. Ask away." He's sawing a plank.

"Did you ever have a son?"

The question startles him. He straightens and hits his head on the shelf he's just hung.

He rubs the spot. "How'd you know about him?"

"We found a grave down by the creek."

Mr. Andersen looks so sad, I'm sorry I asked.

"It was a long time ago."

"I shouldn't have asked." I scoop coal into the scuttle.

"It weren't a secret."

"Did he die of influenza like your wife?"

"It was my first wife who died of influenza, in 1918." He sits on a keg of nails and pushes his hat back, exposing his white forehead. "My boy's name was Henry. His mother, my second wife, packed up and left after Henry died. I don't know where she is. She was too young to be saddled with an old buzzard like me anyway."

"Was it a long time ago?"

"Six years."

"He looked a bit like Owie, didn't he?"

"Some." Mr. Andersen takes out his handkerchief and wipes his eyes. "Blond, about the same height."

"You didn't see how excited Karlo was to see Owie the day we got here. It was like someone he loved had shown up after being gone a long time. I didn't start to figure it out until we saw the grave. And you had a child's wagon."

"That was his. I couldn't bring myself to give it away."

I top off the scuttle. "How old was Henry when he died?"

"Seven."

"Karlo used to go to school with him, didn't he?"

"Every day."

"Did he get sick?"

Mr. Andersen shakes his head. "Rattlesnakes. He stumbled into a nest of 'em and was bit a dozen times. Weren't nothing could be done. He died 'afore we could get a horse hitched to the wagon."

I touch his sleeve. "I'm so sorry."

He shrugs. "It don't get easier."

"May I hug you?"

"I'd be honored."

I put my arms around Mr. Andersen's neck and my head against his shoulder. I think he needs to know we love him.

Later that day, I come down the path from the outhouse to find Mr. Andersen standing outside the barn with his dirty old hat pushed back on his head. He's watching the sky, which has turned an odd yellowy-green. Odder still is the silence. No insects, no birds.

"Gonna rain?"

"Go shut the barn doors." His tone is urgent enough that, without asking why, I run to close them.

The sky darkens, and the wind kicks up. Karlo is under our porch watching Mr. Andersen zigzagging around the yard with his arm out, trying to shoo the chickens back into the coop. They run every which way.

"What's the matter?" I shout.

"Get your mother down to the cellar. Hurry."

I race to the house. Mama's sitting in her rocking chair, head back, eyes closed, her hands on her stomach. "Mr. Andersen says to get to the cellar. I don't know why, but he's trying to lock up the chickens."

Mama sighs and pulls herself out of the chair by holding onto the sides of the table. She crosses to the window over the sink, and parts the lace curtains. The sky in that direction is roiling and as black as Bubbly Creek. She rushes to the front door. "Noel," she shouts. "Where's Owen?"

"Him and the boy rode Sam off in the direction of town an hour ago." He has to shout over the growing roar of the wind. "No telling where they are." I see him look again at the sky. "It's too late. They'll have to take cover wherever they are."

"Oh my God." Mama bites her fist.

"Get to the cellar, Mrs. Williams."

"What's happening, Mama?"

Mama grabs my wrist and drags me toward the door to the cellar, but turns before closing it. "Where are you going?" she shouts to Mr. Andersen.

I have a moment to be glad she asked.

"The dugout. It's not good for all of us to be in the same place."

I follow Mama down the cellar steps.

"Bolt the door," she orders.

"What about Papa and Owie?"

"We'll have to pray."

Neither of us thought to bring a lamp down, so it's black as pitch. "I'm going to get the lantern." My ears pop as I start back up the stairs.

"Don't open that door," she screams.

I remember the stories Mama told about having to shut themselves in the cellar. "Is it a cyclone?"

"Yes." Her voice trembles.

There's a thud against the outside cellar door, then another.

"Your Papa and Owie. Thank God. Let them in."

I feel my way across the room, climb the steps and unbolt the door. There are more thuds, like someone's desperate to get in. Against the wind, I'm only able open the door a crack, but wide enough that a hailstone the size of a chicken egg whizzes by my head and explodes on the cellar floor. The door slams itself and I bolt it against what sounds like a buffalo stampede. Upstairs, a window shatters.

Mama gives a startled little cry after every thud. I find her in the dark, and put my arms around her. Each time I say, "It's okay, Mama."

The storm ends about twenty minutes later. I push open the cellar doors and we climb out into a landscape covered with balls of ice the size of lemons. I run around the side of the house to check the garden. Every sprout has been destroyed. The three chickens that escaped Mr. Andersen's attempt to get them in the coop, lay dead.

I hear Sam whinny. *Papa.* I run toward the road expecting to see Owie and Papa coming toward me, but Sam is alone. He's still saddled and has a bloody cut over his left eye. His reins are wrapped around the saddle horn. Papa must have done that and sent him home. I put him in his stall, remove his saddle, cover his back with a blanket, and empty a bucket of oats in his trough.

Mama turns from watching the road when I come in. She's holding a dustpan full of broken glass. "Any sign of them?"

I look at my feet. "No."

Her eyes get a wild look.

"I'm sure they're fine, Mama. Don't worry. Papa sent Sam home."

"How do you know?"

"He wasn't dragging his reins."

"That doesn't mean they're safe." She wrings her hands and paces the kitchen. "We'll have to move back to Chicago."

"Why?"

"If something's happened to your father, we can't stay here."

I hate when she leaps ahead with worry. "Nothing's happened to Papa."

"You don't know that."

I hear voices in the yard. "There. See?" I say to Mama and fly out the front door. Papa's talking to Mr. Andersen. Dried blood mats the back of his head and he's carrying Owie in his arms. I run to them and Papa turns. Owie is crying but doesn't look hurt. His front is covered in mud. So is Papa except where he protected my brother with his body.

Mama stands on the porch, her hands covering her mouth as if stifling a scream.

Papa hands Owie to Mr. Andersen and holds his arms out to Mama. "It's all right, Glenny." When she reaches him, he buries his face in her hair. "We're all fine," he whispers.

"Sam came back without you."

"I sent him home. Owie and I took refuge in a ditch until it passed. My back took a beating, but I'll live."

Like he said, we're all fine, but the wheat fields are laid flat by the hail. Papa guides Mama back to the house but pauses on the porch to look out at the destruction. I stand at the bottom of the steps, my arms heavy at my sides, and watch his face. Worry cracks the mud that has dried on his forehead.

Everything is ruined. The garden, the wheat. I can't stop my tears. When I look up again, Papa's watching me. "Don't, Nona. I can't stand it if this breaks your heart, too."

22

Before the cyclone and the hailstorm hit us, Mama talked about how it might make sense for her to be in town when the baby comes. She wants to take a room at the boardinghouse a friend of Mr. Andersen's owns. It's two blocks from the sanitarium where the baby will be born. After the storm, she insists.

On April 9th, a beautiful spring day a week before the baby's due, Papa helps Mama climb into the buckboard. Owie, Mr. Andersen, and I stand in the yard to wave goodbye. Karlo lies across Owie's feet, wagging his tail.

That afternoon, Papa comes back alone looking sad. In the wagon bed he has two small trees, no taller than Owie. "Chinese elms," he says when I ask what kind they are. "The fellow promised they could stand up to the constant wind and won't need much water once they're rooted. With luck, when the baby's big enough for a swing, there will be a sturdy branch to hang one from."

He unloads them and stands with his hands on his hips, surveying his options. "Where should we plant them?"

"How about we put one right outside the kitchen window so Mama can watch it grow?"

Papa looks where I'm pointing. "By golly, that's the perfect place. And it will be on the leeside of the house, so the wind won't beat it to a pulp."

Right after we moved here, Mama asked Mr. Andersen if the wind ever stopped blowing. He got a thoughtful look on his face. "It don't blow all the time, but it do blow more than it don't."

Papa carries the first tree over, places it in front of the kitchen window, and steps back to consider the location. "What about the other one?"

"By the outhouse. Mama will feel better to see another tree there."

Before Papa was forced by a second blizzard to spend eight dollars for a ton of coal, he and Mr. Andersen cut down the locust trees by the outhouse—our only trees—for firewood. The next closest being the cottonwoods a half mile away.

Papa grins. "I was thinking the same thing, and the tree will love it there."

Papa lugs the other elm to where the locust trees used to be. I watch and hope the man who sold Papa the trees told him the truth. Seems every living thing has to fight so hard to survive out here. I hope these spindly little trees are tougher than they look.

At supper the first night without Mama, Papa sits with his elbows on the table twisting his wedding ring around his finger. I put a bowl of my only stew recipe—beans, potatoes, and onions—in front of him.

He doesn't notice.

I say, "Feels strange with Mama gone, doesn't it?"

He looks at me startled, like I've appeared from thin air. "What?"

"Are you missing Mama, too?"

He nods. Steam rises off the bowl of stew. "Smells good," he says.

"Thanks." I give Owie his bowl. He's unusually quiet tonight. When I turn to fill my own bowl, I see him pick something out of the stew and stick it under the table. I lean over to look. Karlo's licking a piece of onion off his hand. "What would Mama say?"

Owie grins.

Papa glances beneath the table and sees Karlo.

"Can he stay?" Owie says.

"For now." Papa tries to look stern. "But don't tell your mother and don't feed him your sister's good cooking."

He called my cooking good. I savor making my father proud for a few minutes to the clinks of our spoons against the speckled tin bowls. When I look up, Papa's watching me. "Is your mother horribly unhappy living here?" he asks.

She is but I don't want to tell Papa. "I don't think so."

Papa's eyes drift to the lace curtains. "She doesn't seem herself."

"The work here is harder, and she hates to cook, but she'll get used to it." I sip my stew. "I like it here."

"Me, too," Owie says. He pets Karlo's head, which is now on his lap.

The garden needs replanting, but not all the wheat was ruined. After a few days of sun, the stalks that weren't beaten to a pulp lift themselves off the ground and continue to grow. The relief shows in Papa's face.

There's plenty to keep him from missing Mama too much. The barn roof needs patching. The wind banged the outhouse door so hard a few of the boards splintered. It's a good thing Mr. Andersen took shelter in the dugout. The shed's roof blew off.

With Mama gone, there is even more work for me to do. To be at school by eight, I get up at four-thirty to milk Lily and Rose. I carry the milk to the separator and pour it into the big bowl on top. There's a hand crank at the side, which pushes the milk through a series of disks and down two spouts with a pail under each. One fills with milk, the other with cream. I save enough milk for us and store it in the well house's water tank, then wash and dry the separator—a job I hate. At six-thirty, I wake Owie so he can dress, feed the chickens, and collect the eggs while I make the beds. After that, I cook breakfast, fix Papa's lunch, wash the dishes, then saddle Dan for the ride to school.

Even though I'm tired all the time, I like school and, now, so does Owie. After the first week, he was happy to sit at his own desk and I went back to the empty seat next to Joshua. I guess we can get used to anything, like the stink of cow patties burning or how bad Joshua smells.

I haven't made a friend at school. Of the nine other kids, four are in the first and second grades, one boy each in the fourth, fifth, and seventh. I'm in sixth. The only girl close to my age is in the eighth grade and she lives in Hartley. When she graduates in June, it will leave me and one of the first graders.

I already know most of what Miss Brown teaches, so I pay attention to what she's teaching the older students, one of whom is Joshua, the seventh grader. I don't think he can read. He pretends by turning the pages when we're side by side at our desk, but when he thinks I'm busy with a lesson, he reads a word at a time, touching each one. I'd help him if it wouldn't embarrass him.

I put my share of the first few cream and butter sales in my tobacco tin—eleven dollars total. This week, against Mr. Andersen's advice,

Papa opens a bank account for me and deposits six dollars. By the time I finish high school, he says I may have enough for college. *For flying lessons*, I think to myself.

Mr. Andersen is against any relationship with banks. He lived through the panic of 1893, when the banks failed, taking everyone's money. Behind his back, Papa says *pooh*. Things are different now. He calls Mr. Andersen old-fashioned. I walk a fine line between wanting to trust that Papa's right and believing Mr. Andersen that it could happen again. To be safe, I'll keep that eleven dollars in my tobacco tin with my scavenged pennies.

23

It's a girl. Glenny Grace Williams. We'll call her Gracie. She was born right on schedule, April 14th. Papa's been riding into town every couple of days to check on Mama, but he missed being there to greet Gracie by a few hours. Four days later, he brings Mama home, exhausted but glowing. The baby's as pretty as anything I've ever seen. We are blessed for sure, and Owie is smitten. It's usually impossible to get him to come in the house except to eat. Now it's hard to get rid of him.

"Our fussbudget," Mama says, when he comes stomping up the porch steps for the third time in as many hours. He goes straight to the bottom drawer of the pie safe. Mama said it was bad luck to build a cradle before the baby arrived, but has now accepted Mr. Andersen's offer to make one out of a pre-prohibition whiskey barrel.

"She's here to stay," Mama says, "and will be after you clean up for supper."

"Okay." Owie locks his dirty hands behind his back, and bends at the waist to stare at Gracie.

I'm ironing, and Mama's in her rocking chair, knitting. We smile at each other. Maybe she's settling in after all.

I come out on the porch one evening during the summer harvest and find Papa sitting on the top step. He slides over to make room for me to sit beside him. He puts his arm around me, kisses the side of my head, then cups an ear. "Listen to that music, Nona." He means the whine of the combines harvesting the wheat at the Bono's, five miles away. "Our turn is coming." He's as happy as I've ever seen him.

One afternoon, a few days later, I ride Dan out to bring Papa his lunch. He's driving the rented combine, which cuts, threshes, and winnows the wheat in one operation. A cloud of dust rises behind him giving a golden wash to the air. It's so beautiful I rein in Dan to watch. The combine circles a patch of uncut wheat in the center of the last field. With each pass, the stand grows smaller until only a thin slice is left, then it, too, is gone and the harvest finished.

In spite of losing part of the crop to the hailstorm, we harvest thirty bushels per acre and sell it for a dollar a bushel. With part of his share, Mr. Andersen buys an old tractor, so we won't have to rent from a neighbor at planting time. We'll still have to rent a combine for the harvest.

Papa puts most of our share in the bank but saves out enough to buy a used 1924 Ford Model T Touring car for a hundred and ten dollars. We all—including three-month old Gracie—ride to town in the buckboard to get it and drive it home. It's a warm day, so Papa puts the top down and tells us she'll do 45 on a paved road. Owie and I beg him to try it. At 40, Mama makes him slow down, but I still get to stand in the back, spread my arms and feel what it must be like to fly. Even over the rutted road, we still cover the twelve miles from Dalhart to home in thirty minutes. Three hours later, Mr. Andersen, with Sam pulling the buckboard, has covered the same distance.

It's not that we were unaware of the stock market crash in October of 1929. We didn't have any money in it, so it didn't affect us. If anything, Papa thinks it means wheat prices will rise. The promise of the land is coming true, he is fond of saying. I believe him. Even Mama is beginning to.

But Mr. Andersen worries. All summer and at all hours, trucks and wagons pass on the road piled high with wheat for the granaries. We were lucky to get a dollar a bushel. Soon, the price per bushel drops to seventy cents. Papa says next year we'll make up the difference by planting more acreage.

At supper that evening, Papa, without looking directly at Mr. Andersen, who now eats with us most nights, says come fall, he wants to plow up the section Mr. Andersen left to the buffalo grass.

Mr. Andersen says, "Where's the sense in planting more when there's already glut? It will only drive the price down until it costs more to plant than it's worth to sell."

I think that makes sense and turn to see Papa's response.

Papa pushes his peas around the plate, then looks at me instead of Mr. Andersen. "I heard the Catholic sisters opened a new hospital in Dalhart. That frees Doc Dawson to become a full-time farmer. And I hear Uncle Dick Coon is also buying up more land."

"With his hundred-dollar bill?" I ask.

"They are both fools," Mr. Andersen says.

"Mighty rich fools," Papa says. "Banker says the prices have bottomed out. Seventy cents is as low as they'll go."

Mr. Andersen takes his napkin out of his shirt front. "Never trust a banker. They got ulterior motives." He pushes back his chair and bows to Mama. "Good vittles, Mrs. Williams. Thank you."

Two days later, the price paid for a bushel of wheat falls to thirty cents, but Mr. Andersen is not an *I-told-you-so* kind of guy.

24

The better life doesn't last long, but I had no inkling in the spring of 1930, none of us did. I can still picture myself in the loft pitching hay down to the horses, when I looked out and saw Papa standing in the wheat holding Gracie. The sun was low and the light soft, blurring them a bit. I couldn't hear what he said to my one-year-old sister, but she was attentive and smiling.

The paper called 1930 a "wheat bonanza." At harvest time, it was shoulder high, and Papa whispered to us his resentment of Mr. Andersen for not letting him plow up the remaining 320 acres of buffalo grass. But Mr. Andersen was right again. The granaries filled and the excess rose in dunes beside the railroad tracks. Farmers couldn't give it away. A lucky few got twenty cents a bushel, less than half of what it cost to plant and harvest. We used most of ours to feed the animals.

Early on a hot July morning, I come in from milking Lily and Rose. Papa's reading the paper and eating the oatmeal I left for him on the stove. He looks up and smiles. "I guess I was wrong about lady fliers."

"What do you mean?"

He folds the paper into a square and taps the picture of Amelia Earhart, who has set the women's world flying speed record of 181 miles per hour.

I look at Papa and grin.

"Maybe she'll need a young lady co-pilot when she gets ready to fly across the Atlantic again." Papa pushes his chair back, gets up, and puts his bowl in the sink. On the way out, he kisses the top of my head.

I smile at his back as he goes down the front steps. It's sometimes hard to hold on to a dream, but it helps that Papa remembers I have one.

Papa believes 1931 is bound to be a better year. Five million people are out of work. In the big cities, thousands stand in bread lines and bread is made from wheat. He says it's beyond comprehension that the government would let people starve while our wheat decays in mountains beside the tracks. "The government will step in and buy our wheat," Papa says, "Wait and see."

At supper one night, he reads to us from the newspaper, which quoted President Hoover as saying, "Americans are nearer to the final triumph over poverty than ever before in the history of the land." Papa believes him. I want to.

Mr. Andersen shakes his head. "Politicians will tell you anything you want to hear to get your vote."

The 1931 harvest, according to the newspapers, is "the greatest agricultural accomplishment in American history." Farmers harvested two-hundred and fifty million bushels of wheat, but the prices are so low, we burn it for heat that winter. Even that doesn't stop Papa from promising that next year will be better, but his eyes have gone as dull as the bottom of a tin cup.

In December 1931, Mama tells us she's having another baby. Later that night, I hear her crying and Papa trying to comfort her. "We'll be fine," he says. "We've got plenty of food, lots of wheat, our garden, and the animals. Six can live as cheaply as five."

25

1932

On May 26, I'm in the barn brushing Dan when I hear the squeak of the buckboard's wheels and Sam nicker. Papa shouts my name. I go to the door and shade my eyes. He holds up last week's edition of the *Chicago Daily Tribune*: Woman Flying Ocean Alone. *Mrs. Putnam, Ex-Chicagoan Hops for Paris*. Blood whooshes in my ears as I take the paper from him. I grin up at Papa. "She did it."

"She did indeed."

I read that she left Newfoundland and flew almost fifteen hours before landing in a pasture in Mamie's homeland of Ireland. In the picture, Miss Earhart is wearing a jumpsuit that looks like Mama's denim Farmerette uniform. As I read, the ember of my dream to become a pilot glows brightly, then frays and fades.

I never told my parents that the money I'd saved was for flying lessons, but from now on, I will have to give up what little I earn to buy seed or fuel for the tractor. The price we get for butter and cream has dropped, and eggs sell for only seven cents a dozen. That money needs to go to buy the stuff we can't grow: sugar, coffee, rice, corn meal, beans, and tea.

I reread the story until the words get watery-looking. I'm tempted to crumple it, lift the stove lid, and burn it. Instead, I tack it on the wall above my bed next to the faded and yellowing story about her first flight across the Atlantic—the one with those two men. Then I change my mind, fold it, and put it in my tobacco tin rather than paste it on the wall for insects to nibble on. And I hate that, since she married Mr. Putnam in February, this story calls her Mrs. Putnam instead of Amelia Earhart. Mama's right, getting married erases who you are.

The Democratic convention opens in Chicago on June 27, 1932, the same day the temperature in town reaches a hundred and twelve degrees and the Dalhart bank closes, taking what's left of our savings from the 1929 harvest. All that remains is the eleven dollars left from our first two cream sales and the thirty-one cents I brought here from Chicago.

Like everyone else with an account at the First National Bank, Papa goes to town and pounds on the windows. He marches with the rest of them over to get Sheriff Foust. Foust was elected sheriff after a couple of bootleggers shot and killed Lon Anderson, our previous sheriff. The men demand that he let them into the bank to get their money. The Sheriff swears there's nothing left to get. The bank loaned it all to farmers who couldn't pay it back. The ones who bought more land during the boom lost everything. As sorry as we are for others, we all agree, it can't get much worse, and no matter what happens, we still have a place to live. Papa and Mr. Andersen own this land free and clear, so we have no debt and don't have to worry about the bank taking our property.

The convention nominates Mr. Roosevelt to run against Mr. Hoover for President. Miss Brown brings the paper to school each morning so we can read what the candidates promise to do if elected.

Mr. Andersen and Papa say they're going to give Mr. Roosevelt a chance, but Mama is vague about who she will vote for. When I ask her who she wants to see win, she shrugs and says if she rides all the way to town to vote, it will likely be for the devil we know rather than the devil we don't. In other words, Mr. Hoover.

Miss Brown says women, especially, have an obligation to inform themselves. She tells us before 1920, there were women called suffragists, who were beaten and thrown into jail fighting for our right to vote. They went on hunger strikes and were force fed with tubes down their throats.

On July 29, 1932, my baby sister is born in the new Loretto Hospital. Her name is Kathryn Noel Williams. Her middle name was Papa's idea to honor Mr. Andersen, and, I suspect, a way to apologize for not trusting his advice.

Three-year-old Gracie fusses over her like a mother hen, giving the baby the attention Mama can't muster. Mama's eyes mirror the despair in Papa's. I see her staring off at the horizon like she could wish us back to Chicago. I speak to her and she doesn't answer. It makes me want to tiptoe in the house, shush Owie and Gracie, and pray that baby Katie doesn't start crying. I find myself resenting the wind and the clackety-clack of the windmill blades. I'm afraid Mama needs more quiet than she can ever find.

On a Saturday, a few weeks before the election, Mama's got the darning egg in the heel of one of Papa's sock. She's sewing by the light of an oil lamp, holding the sock so close to her face, I'm afraid she'll stick the needle in her eye.

"How come you'd vote for Mr. Hoover when he's done nothing to help us? If I was old enough, I'd vote for Mr. Roosevelt."

Mama looks at me with that dismissive, smirky smile I hate. "What's Mr. Roosevelt going to do that Mr. Hoover couldn't do if he had a mind to?"

"Miss Brown told us Mr. Roosevelt called men like Papa, with prairie dirt under their fingernails, The Forgotten Man."

"That's easy to say, isn't it?"

"At least he knows we need help. Mr. Hoover's done nothing."

Two weeks before Election Day, Mr. Hoover says something that changes Mama's mind. She must have written to Kippy's mom with her doubts about Mr. Roosevelt because a letter comes from Mrs. Howard with an article from the *Chicago Daily Tribune*. It quoted Mr. Hoover saying, "If a man has not made a million dollars by the time he's forty, he is not worth much." Mama reads it to me, then burns it in stove.

"Why'd you do that?" I ask.

"Your father is already voting for Mr. Roosevelt. What good would it do to hear those hateful words?"

I know Mama resents Papa bringing us here. She shows it so many ways. I take a deep breath. "It's been a while since you worried about what Papa's going through."

Mama takes the lid off a pot of cabbage and potato soup and stirs. Her jaw muscles knot. "You think I should be the good wife and suffer in silence? Look at yourself—a raggedy beanpole. And me," she holds out her red, scaly hands. "I've aged twenty years."

"I'm just saying I don't think we should make it any harder on Papa than it is."

"It always about the man, isn't it?" Mama raps the spoon on the edge of the pot, and slams the lid back in place, startling Katie, who begins to cry.

My stomach roils. What's happening to us is breaking my heart, but I can't blame Papa for trying to give us a better life, or Mama, who's been miserable since we got here. I know she's right even if I can't bring myself to side with her against him. She gave up her right to choose her own way when she married Papa.

On Election Day, Mama, Papa, and Mr. Andersen all vote for the devil they don't know. So do my classmates in the mock election we hold at school. The following day, a passing farmer tells us Mr. Roosevelt won in a landslide.

26

December brings clear, windy days, but so far, no rain or snow to insulate the dormant wheat, and no moisture to give it a head start. For mid-December, it is surprisingly mild and sunny. Papa decides staring at the fields isn't helping, so he, Mr. Andersen, and Owie hitch Ben and Sam to the Conestoga and head out to collect whatever they can find to burn: cow patties, downed limbs off the cottonwoods, tumbleweeds, and broken fence posts, anything that will help conserve our dwindling coal supply.

After they leave, Mama and I do the laundry. Since we can no longer afford to buy Fels-Naptha laundry bars, we wash with the homemade soap Mr. Andersen showed us how to make by saving and straining cooking grease. When we've saved enough grease, we add lye made from wood ashes and water, and stir this mixture long and slow in a big kettle until it's a jelly-like consistency. We pour this into shallow cardboard boxes to harden, but not too hard since it has to be cut in bars.

Mama used to be so proud of her hands and never went out in summer or winter without gloves. Now hers are red and raw, as are mine. Lye soap makes them worse.

Laundry is an all-day chore. Gracie helps by dividing the clothes into piles: whites, darks, work clothes, coloreds, and rags. Thinking we'll soon have more wood to burn, I build a fire in the stove to heat a kettle of water. When it's hot, I pour it in the washer and add shavings off a cake of lye soap on top. I use the hand-agitator to wash the whites first, scrubbing the really dirty places on the washboard, then lift the dripping clothes out of the water with a broom handle, for Mama to rinse in a clean tub of water. Coloreds are next, then Mr. Andersen's, Papa's and Owie's overalls and shirts. Mama helps me carry the dirty water to the elms.

Gracie stands on a chair to turn the wringer handle after Mama gets them started, then Gracie copies the grunting sounds Mr. Andersen makes when he's working hard as she helps me carry the basket to the clothesline. I notice the pinkish color of the sky to the north, as she hands me each item to hang, but don't give it much thought.

Mama uses the rinse water to mop the kitchen floor and the front porch. After that, I'll help her carry what's left out to the garden.

We're having bean sandwiches for lunch when the wind picks up and the windows start to rattle. In a matter of minutes, it turns frightfully cold, but now we're low on anything to burn. I don't want to run out before Papa gets back with fresh fuel. I add a few chunks of coal to keep the fire from going out completely.

Mama tucks Katie into the cradle Mr. Andersen built, then she and I hang blankets over the windows to keep out the cold as best we can. I go out to round up the animals and get them safely inside the barn, and give them extra feed in case it snows and we can't get out in the morning.

The wind howls around me as I take the still damp clothes off the line and fight my way back to the house. Before slamming and bolting the door, I turn to look down the road, hoping to see the wagon.

Mama paces and wrings her hands, which I suppose helps her stay warm. I feed a little wood to the small fire in the stove. What we really need is a big fire, but we used most of our wood to do the wash.

Snow begins to fall and blow against the house. The stove pings and clicks as it cools.

"Where are they?" Mama cries suddenly, which startles me and makes Gracie cry.

I hug my sister. "They've taken shelter somewhere, Mama."

"Yes. Yes." She sits, then gets up again. The kitchen is dark except for the light from the kerosene lamp. Mama's shadow follows her as she paces the room.

We go to bed just after dark—more to get warm under the covers than to sleep. Gracie snuggles in next to me, and Mama takes Katie to bed with her. I'm reading *The Secret Garden*, one of the books Miss Brown loaned me. To keep our minds off trying to fall asleep in a freezing cold room between gritty sheets, I entertain Gracie by telling her the story of the little orphan girl and beautiful hidden garden. I tell her about Mamie, and how I hope she, too, finds a garden.

In the morning, the pot of water I left on the stove has a crisp layer of ice on it. There is nothing left to start a fire with except the newspaper on the walls and a few sticks of kindling. We decide it's not worth tearing the paper off the walls, which would let more frigid air in than a small fire could cope with. We layer on more clothes, gather around the lamp on the kitchen table, and try not to think about our numb hands and toes.

Around noon, we hear Papa's voice calling. When he opens the front door, Mama rushes into his arms and pulls Owie against her side. "I was afraid you were dead."

"Glenny, it will take more than a little blizzard to finish me off. We took refuge in an abandoned barn and had to leave the wagon there. The snow is so deep, it was hard even for the horses to get through."

Mama steps back. "You seem mighty pleased with yourself."

"It's snow, Glenny. We need the moisture."

But the snow melts and, as the months wear on without rain, the soil turns to powder and shifts with the never-ending winds.

27

I finished the eighth grade that December, but we couldn't afford the gas to drive me into Dalhart every day for high school, so Miss Brown gave me her old lessons to study until things get better.

School starts again in January but, because we've been getting frequent dust storms that come without warning, Mama won't let Owie, who'll be eight next month, ride Dan to school on his own. It falls to me to take him every day and, since I'm a girl and expected to become either a teacher, or worse, get married, Miss Brown invites me to stay and help her teach.

There's something familiar about the day that makes me edgy. It's windy, but oddly warm for February. At school, the wind whips and snaps the flag, and when the lanyard hits the metal pole, it sparks. Dan and the other horses tied to the hitching post whinny like they're nervous, too.

Miss Brown is the first to see it coming. "Oh my, children, look." She claps her hands together and laughs. "Rain."

We run to the windows to watch the rolling cloud approach from the direction of Amarillo to the south. Dusters usually come from the north or west. For a second or two, it's a praise-the-Lord moment, then I feel the air in the room change. "Miss Brown, the color's wrong for rain." I take Owie's hand.

As it tumbles toward us, the color turns from brown to black. The edges, where the sun shines through, are a watery pea soup green.

"It's coming mighty fast." Owie's voice full of alarm.

Miss Brown's eyes widen. "Get away from the windows!"

A moment later a roaring wind hits the schoolhouse with the force of a freight train. Books jump off the desks and hit the floor. The building shakes. Grit and sand blast the outside walls, and seep in through the cracks. The papers on Miss Brown's desk lift and swirl to the floor. A moment later one of the windows shatters and the room fills with a choking black cloud of dust. Outside the horses scream in terror.

"Cover your noses and mouths with whatever you can find," Miss Brown shouts over the howling wind.

I bump into desks as I feel my way to the sink and use the hand pump to wet a hankie and the bottom of my pinafore. When I turn, I don't know where my brother is. "Owen?"

"I'm here." He wraps his arms around me.

"Breathe through this." I put the wet handkerchief over his nose and mouth and cover my own with the bottom half of my pinafore.

Abigail, the only kindergartener, sobs and calls for her mother. I follow the sound of her crying until I find her. She buries her face against my hip and coughs.

"Let's pray, children. Our Father—" Miss Brown starts coughing and can't go on, but from all around the room come the muffled words of the Lord's Prayer.

The storm lasts nearly an hour. As it ends, dust settles over everything—books, our desks, the floor. Sand is piled in the window ledges and against the panes like filthy snow. The sun makes the room look full of fog. All of us are covered in black dust so thick we look like refugees from the bottom of a coal scuttle. Abigail's tears leave muddy streaks on her face. I give her my pinafore hem to blow her nose. What comes out is wet and black. Owie hacks up phlegm the same color. Where he wipes his mouth on his sleeve, he leaves a wet black smear.

Outside, the horses that didn't break loose and run are tangled together. Dan seems to be okay, but all the horses' eyes are crusted shut with sand and their nostrils caked with mud. I go back inside, take off my pinafore, soak it with water from the hand pump, and use it to wash Dan's face.

Owie and I offer to stay and help Miss Brown sweep the schoolhouse, but she says we should go home, our parents will be worried. I look back as we ride away. She's sweeping dirt out the door and crying. Seeing her, tears clearing lines through the dust on her face, reminds me that she's just five years older than me—little more than a kid herself.

There is nothing between school and home but a prairie as open as the sky. To make out the road from the buried wheat fields, we follow the fence posts, the tops of which barely show above the new dunes. Dan trudges through the deep sand, up one side of a mound of dirt and down the other. The slightest breeze lifts dust and swirls it across the road and out across the fields. I remember the morning Mama, Owie, and I arrived in Dalhart. Owie chased a dirt devil into the road and nearly got hit by a passing wagon. It now feels like that morning was only a preview of what was to come.

"Look, a car lost two of its tires." Owie points to a huge dune against the fence. Two wheels lie on top of the sand.

I get a chill. The tires are perfectly spaced, like they are still attached to the axle. I rein in Dan.

"What?" Owie says.

I get a sinking feeling in my stomach. "I think there's a car under there. What if the driver's there, too?"

We look at each other, slide off Dan's back, and sink ankle deep in the sand. Owie plunges his hand in the space between the two wheels. "You're right."

We scoop away sand until we see the running board. We dig faster until we expose the passenger-side door but there's no window. It either broke in the storm or was rolled down. Whichever happened, the car is tipped at an odd angle, as if it ran off the road and into a ditch, then the storm filled it with sand. If the window broke, there will be glass mixed in. "Move." I push Owie aside. My heart whooshes in my ears. I work my hand carefully through the sand and am past my elbow and feeling relieved— "Yikes." I jerk my arm out. "Somebody's in there." My eyes mist. "How could he just lie there and let himself be buried alive?"

Owie puts his gritty arms around my shoulders. "Maybe he got knocked out when he crashed."

Owie and I ride home to fetch Papa, who goes to town for the sheriff. It's Mr. Andersen who follows us back with the tractor, which is so slow that Papa arrives with the sheriff the same time we do. The coroner is right behind them.

Papa and Mr. Andersen wrap a chain around the back bumper, then use the tractor to pull the car out of the ditch and back onto the road. Papa says Owie and I should go on home. Has he forgotten I saw the dead boy in Chicago when I was not much older than Owie is now? I pretend I don't hear him over the noise of the tractor engine.

The coroner opens the driver's door, and the sand pours out exposing a dead man, still in a seated position, arms bent at the elbows, fingers frozen into claws around the steering wheel. The left side of his head is caked with blood.

The coroner pats my shoulder. "He died hours ago, and I doubt he suffered."

"How can you tell?" Owie and I ask at the same time.

"Rigor mortis takes a couple of hours to set in, and—," He points to the blood on the side of his head. "Probably knocked him out cold."

Almost every night, for a week or so, the sound of his fingers breaking as they remove his claw-hands from the steering wheel, wakes me.

28

I think Owie is going to be tall like Papa, but is as skinny as a stream of pump water, with knobby knees and feet too big for his body. I'm afraid I take after Mama. At fourteen and a half, I'm exactly her height—five feet, three inches. I think a woman pilot should be tall. In pictures, Miss Earhart—still Miss Earhart to me—looks tall.

Owie may be big for his age, but he still has his little boy love of collecting cow patties. When the last Sunday in March dawns clear and crisp, giving every indication it will be a beautiful day, Owie, Gracie, and I beg to stay home from church with the excuse that we will spend the time collecting fuel. Though they've never said one way or the other, I'm pretty sure Mama and Papa only go to church to be neighborly, and for Mama's sake, since church is her only social life. Mr. Andersen swears that if he showed up at church on a Sunday, it would endanger the entire congregation, although it would surely save many of the damned, because hell would have frozen over.

Papa says he doesn't think it will hurt us to miss one Sunday. Mama agrees after I promise not to let Gracie, who'll be four in next month, out of my sight.

When we got the bull and two cows from Mrs. Rydberg, Mr. Andersen and Papa put a gate in the fence that separates the wheat fields from the acreage where the cattle graze on buffalo grass. Lily and Rose like it there too, but the bull is mean, so we can no longer cross the pasture on foot.

After our parents and Katie leave for church in the Model T, Mr. Andersen helps me hitch Sam to the buckboard. I lay in a pile of grain sacks too old and worn to be used as clothing or dishcloths, and call Owie and Gracie from feeding the chickens.

Karlo is deaf and blind and no longer able to follow us. Mr. Andersen says that may be true but he can still tell time. Every day, at three-thirty, he gets up from wherever he's been sleeping and walks out to the road to wait for us to return, as if every day is a school day. Today, when we leave to hunt fire wood, he's asleep and dreaming on the porch.

Owie holds the gate open for me to drive through. I watch for the bull while keeping Sam on a slow, straight track toward the creek and cottonwoods. Gracie's job is to hand Owie an empty grain sack while Owie follows the wagon, running from side to side, poking the patties with a stick to make sure they are dry enough to burn. When the sack is full, he catches up with us and makes an exchange with Gracie.

Tumbleweeds are easy to find. The wind rolls and bounces them across the prairie like balloons until they lodge against a fence or the side of a building. The hard part is stomping them down into small enough pieces to put in a sack. They have sharp little spikes that stick to our socks. We decide to save tumbleweed collecting for last in case we find enough wood and patties.

Not surprisingly, the creek bed is bone dry. While Gracie and Owie collect downed limbs, I walk the white sand bottom to Henry's grave. If it weren't for the cross I repaired, I'm not sure I would have found it, buried under this winter's crumbly, brown leaves. I clear them away, straighten the cross, and whisper to Henry that his dad and Karlo still miss him.

We've got a nice load of cow patties, twigs, and limbs when I turn the wagon for home. Owie and Gracie sit at the back, feet swinging off the edge. In the distance, next to the gate to the pasture, I see Papa, already home from church, waving both his hands over his head. I wave back and he jabs a finger at the sky behind us.

"Look, Nona, it's gonna rain," Owie says.

I turn to see what Papa's pointing at. A towering cloud rolls toward us from the west. My heart thrills. *Rain!* But the cloud is a strange brownish yellow color, and it's moving faster than any storm I've ever seen. Fast as a freight train.

"Get up here behind me," I shout to Owie and Gracie.

"How come?" Owie whines.

"Do what I say. Hurry."

The look on my face scares them. Owie grabs Gracie around the waist and climbs over the limbs and branches and onto the bulging sacks of cow patties.

"Hang on." I click to Sam, who's plodding toward home. I've never slapped his reins, but I do now, and see his eyes roll to show the whites.

He lurches forward against the weight of the wagon. An instant later, the cloud rolls over us, pelting us with sand carried by a frigid, howling wind.

"Cover your faces," I shout.

Sam screams in fear and races across the field toward home, steam blasting from his nostrils. I hear Gracie wailing. I glance back to make sure they're okay and get a face full of blasted sand and a glimpse of branches and bags of patties disappearing off the back of the wagon as if being pulled into nothingness. The earth looks like it's crumbling away behind us faster than Sam can run. I face forward, but can't see where we're headed. I hope Sam finds the gate.

He doesn't. He crashes straight through the barbed wire fence, stumbles, and goes down shrieking in pain. The wagon stays upright only because the wheels get snared by the fence, too. We must be in the yard, but I can't see the house or the barn. I hear Papa calling over the roar of the wind.

"We're here." I turn to check on Owie and Grace. Their hands clutch the wagon seat and both are crying. Behind us the air is clearing and sunlight filters through the last of the blowing sand, turning the sky to the west a hazy shade of red.

Papa appears beside the wagon, lifts me off the seat, then Gracie. Owie leaps over the side and throws his arms around Papa's chest. The four of us cling to each other for the time it takes the wind to die, and the sun to come out.

Sam whinnies and tries to get up.

Papa removes our web of arms. He walks over to where Sam lies in the dust. Both front legs are tangled in barbed wire, but his left front leg bleeds from where a splintered bone pierces the skin. Papa closes his eyes. "Owen, go to the house and get my rifle."

Gracie takes Papa's hand. "Help Sam, Papa."

"I can't, sweetheart. His leg is broken."

"Why do you need your rifle?" Gracie's voice quivers.

Papa kneels in front of Gracie. "You don't want him to suffer, do you?"

"No."

I am crying too hard to speak. I walk over and kneel by Sam's head. I stroke his face until his terrified eyes soften with trust. "You saved us, Sam." His eyelashes are crusted with sand, and his nostrils are caked with mud.

"We have to put him out of his misery," Papa tells Gracie.

"You're going to shoot Sam?"

"I have to, honey."

Owie comes back and hands Papa the rifle.

I kiss Sam's face and struggle to my feet.

"Papa, please don't," Gracie pleads. "I love Sam."

"Take her in the house, Nona."

"Papa, please don't kill him." Gracie sobs. "I'm begging you with my whole mouth."

"Go in the house children."

I pick Gracie up and carry her sobbing against my shoulder to where Mama stands calmly on the porch. Too calmly. She's staring into space and swaying from side to side with Katie on one hip. With her other hand she's plucking out one strand of her hair at a time. She looks at each one, then opens her fingers, and lets it float away as if she's setting something free.

"Come on, Mama." I take her hand and open the screen door.

Papa is watching, waiting for us to go inside. After I shut the door behind us, there's an earsplitting crack, followed by the cackle of startled chickens, then silence.

Inside the house, everything, every surface—floor, chairs, plates, all Mama's tables, and her lace window curtains—is covered in a layer of sand. We cross the room and dust rises and eddies in the sunlight coming through the west window.

Tears cling to Gracie's lashes in muddy beads. When I put her down, she runs and throws her arms around Mama's legs. "Papa shot my horse," she wails.

Katie, who's still straddling Mama's hip, crinkles her brow, and begins to cry.

Owie sits at the table. Tears swim in his eyes. He lifts the tablecloth, causing the layer of sand to shift toward the center, and looks under the table. "Where's Karlo?"

29

Owie goes to the door. "Karlo?" He calls and whistles.

"He can't hear you." I remind him. "He's probably under the porch."

Owie bursts out the door and jumps to the ground. He gets on his hands and knees, and crawls behind the steps.

Mama's nursing Katie, holding her loosely, staring at my grandmother's lace curtains sagging under the weight of yellow dust.

"I'll wash them for you, Mama."

Her eyes flick toward the sound of my voice and back to the curtains. She doesn't answer. The way she's staring, so quiet and detached, scares me. "Are you okay?"

She looks at me. "What do you think?"

It's been four years since we were packing to leave Chicago, and she held up the green satin dress she'd worn to a dance with Papa, and admired herself in the mirror. I remember thinking how beautiful she was. Now, I see what living here is stealing from her, and I realize I don't know how old she is. I study her face and the brittle gray hairs escaping her scraggly bun. She was born in 1900. She'll be thirty-three in a couple weeks. Last month she lost a tooth and sucked cloves for the pain, until Papa finally pulled it with a pair of pliers. It's three back from her front teeth, but now, when she smiles, which isn't often, she puts her hand up to cover the hole. I wish I could think of something to say to her, a word or two to let her know that I, too, believed in Papa's dream, and am sorry.

Papa has unhooked the buckboard and is clearing the barbed wire away from Sam's front legs. Mr. Andersen's brought the tractor from the barn, and is looping a rope around Sam's hind legs.

I step out onto the porch as Owie reappears. "He's not under there." He brushes the dirt off his hands, then stops to watch Papa tie the other end of the rope to the tractor seat. Owie looks up at me. A single tear rolls down his cheek. He wipes it off on his shoulder, turns, and touches Mr. Andersen's sleeve. "Mr. Noel, have you seen Karlo?"

Mr. Andersen straightens, puts a hand on the small of his back, and squints in pain. "No, Son. He was on the porch when you kids left. Did you check the barn?"

"Karlo?" Owie trudges across the yard, sinking ankle-deep in sand with every step.

Sam's eyes, filled with trust and love a few minutes ago, are now dull. It surprises me to realize the light in living eyes comes from within. "Where are you going to bury him?" I ask Papa.

"The ground's too hard to dig a hole," Papa says. "We're going to drag him out to the pasture."

"And let the buzzards eat him?"

Papa looks at me. "It's them or us."

"You'd eat him?"

"Ate plenty of horsemeat during the war, Nona. Only reason not to butcher him is he was family."

"That's disgusting." My lip curls, but I'm immediately sorry. I know it broke his heart to shoot Sam. His history with Sam goes a lot deeper than mine.

His disappointment in me shows in his eyes and I imagine he wants to say, "Grow up," but he knows I loved Sam. He may even know I'm blaming myself. It was my idea to skip church. If we hadn't stayed behind, Sam would have been safe in the barn when the storm hit. Papa takes a deep breath. "I feel as bad as you do, but before this drought is over, we may be forced to do a lot of difficult things."

"I'm sorry, Papa."

He nods. "Why don't you go back inside and help your mother clean up." He looks past me, and I turn. Mama's standing on a chair taking down the filthy curtains.

The sandstorm changed the landscape of our yard. Papa left the car in front of the house, and sand piled to the top of the running board. Where tumbleweeds mounded against fences, the sand covered them and created dunes. Walking anywhere outside takes effort.

None of us have ever seen a storm like this, but Mr. Andersen says at supper—where everything we eat has grit in it—that sandstorms are common enough in March and April if the winter has been dry. I think he means this to be reassuring. It's not.

Mr. Andersen admits it was bigger than any he can recall during the drouth of 1890s. Mr. Andersen says "drouth" and Papa says "drought," but they mean the same thing—tough times if we don't get rain or a slow melting snow to put moisture into the soil.

Karlo doesn't show up for his supper Sunday night. Monday morning, after milking Lily and Rose, I saddle Dan for the ride to school and call Owie. He comes out on the porch, crosses his arms over his skinny chest, and says, "I'm not going."

"Why?"

"I'm staying until I find Karlo."

"He'll come home. The storm probably scared him and he's taken cover somewhere. Remember how he always hides when it thunders?"

"He's blind and deaf. 'Sides we didn't have any thunder."

Papa comes to the door, a napkin still jammed into his shirt collar. "Noel and I will find him, son. You go on to school."

Owie makes prayer hands. "Please, Papa."

"You heard me."

I maneuver Dan parallel to the porch. Owie drops his arms and scowls at Papa before climbing on behind me.

At the gate, when I turn to wave goodbye, Dan lowers his head to a pile of sand by the road and snorts, then paws the ground. My stomach roils. "Papa," I scream.

"What?" Owie says.

Papa runs toward us.

I should have noticed this odd pile of sand. Dunes only form against something that blocks the sand from blowing. I swing my leg over Dan's head, slide to the ground, and tear into the mound with my gloved hands.

Owie lands beside me. We look at each other, then both dig until our fingers hit Karlo's cold, stiff body. He's where we should have looked in the first place. Of course, he would have gone out to wait for us by the gate. He couldn't have known yesterday was Sunday, and we went off—not to school—but in the opposite direction.

Owie throws an arm across his eyes. Tears stream down his face.

I put my arms around his shoulders, my head against the side of his. Dan's head is down there with us, his warm breath blows little circles in the dust.

Papa reaches us. "Damn it," he whispers.

30

When we uncover Karlo, he's facing the road, waiting as he always did for us to come home. His head rests on outstretched paws like he'd fallen asleep.

Papa doesn't make Owie go to school. He and Mr. Andersen put Karlo's body in the buckboard. We're taking him to the cottonwoods to bury him next to Henry. On the ride to the ravine, my eyes follow the broad furrow made when Mr. Andersen dragged Sam's body across the pasture. There are buzzards on the ground and more circling. I look away.

Mr. Andersen and Papa take turns digging a hole next to Henry's grave; Owie sits on the ground and strokes Karlo's gray muzzle. I watch the blue veins in Mr. Andersen's hands, crooked as worms, moving under his loose skin as he digs. I've seen this kind of pain on his face only once before—the day he told me about Henry. He's now lost every being he loved.

Karlo belonged to Mr. Andersen, then Henry, then Owie, to us all really, but none of us can manage any words of goodbye. We cover the grave with rocks, and leave Mr. Andersen there with his son and his dog.

On the ride home, seated next to Papa, with Ben pulling the buckboard, I can't help but wonder, if we knew in advance how terrible each loss would feel, would we risk loving anything ever again.

All spring long, rain clouds tease us. They look promising from a distance, black and towering. Sometimes, I can hear thunder and imagine I feel the coolness on my face and smell the rain, but it never reaches us. The wheat doesn't sprout, and the garden and the elm trees have to be hand-watered every day.

More and more often, fat men in dark suits drive by in big, open cars. They wave and smile. We don't wave back. They are bankers, who everyone considers no better than thieves, on their way to a foreclosure. We're sad for the folks they're after and relieved it's not us.

Soon they will be riding out to Mr. Loonan's, our neighbor, who did what Papa wanted to do, and mortgaged his farm to buy more land and equipment. Now he can't make the payments or pay his taxes. The bank is taking his farm and auctioning off everything the family owns.

Last week Mr. Loonan drove his old Model T truck through the gate. He said he was moving his family to California, where he hoped to find work. He asked if Papa would be kind enough to "store" the car for him until after the auction. It was loaded with mattresses, their kitchen table, four chairs, with pots and pans tied to the sides, clanging and banging. Papa and Mr. Andersen talked it over, then Papa clapped Mr. Loonan on the back, and let him drive it into the barn. To keep it from being seen, should someone stop by, Mr. Andersen, Papa and Mr. Loonan stack hay bales in front of the car with Lily, Rose, Dan and Ben watching closely. Mr. Loonan must have thought Papa would say yes, because he'd tied his horse to the rear bumper for the ride home.

In May, Mr. Andersen receives a letter from the widow Rydberg. In it, she tells him she couldn't find a buyer for her farm, so she leased her place to a tenant farmer when she moved to her daughter's in Iowa. He went broke, packed up, and left for California. With no rent, no crops, and no other income, she hasn't been able to pay the taxes. Now the bank is foreclosing. In the letter, she asked Mr. Andersen if he would be kind enough to meet her train on Friday. She and her daughter want to look the bankers in the eye when they auction off everything she and her husband worked so hard for.

We hear about these auctions, but I've never been to one. Owie asks to go, so do I, then so does Gracie.

"Not me." Mama shakes her head. "I can't bear to kill a chicken. I sure don't want to see this kind of beheading. Katie and I will stay here."

Papa says yes to Owie, but I can tell by the way he hooks his thumbs around his suspenders, that he's going to say it's no place for girls. The farmers are mad, and this is a chance to confront the only people they can get their hands on to blame. I put my hands on my hips and look him right in the eye.

He raises both hand in defeat, and says to Owie. "When the cussing starts, put your fingers in Nona's ears. And—" he says to me. "You put yours in Gracie's."

I work as hard as anyone else and hate when he treats me like I'm softer. "Who does that leave to plug Owie's?"

Papa smiles and nods. "You got me."

Mrs. Rydberg's farm is a few miles east of us. From the front porch, Gracie and I see a line of wagons and old cars parked out on the road. Papa is talking to a group of farmers. There's something about the way they're bunched together that reminds me of boys at school when they're about to get in trouble.

When Mr. Andersen comes back from the train with Mrs. Rydberg and her daughter, Gracie and I climb in the wagon with them for the drive to her farm. Papa and Owie ride with one of the other farmers.

At her house, the sheriff and one of his deputies stand on either side of the steps leading to her front porch. The once fine house is a wreck. The windows have been broken out by vandals or squatters, and the front door leans against an outside wall. Tumbleweeds have piled up against the west wall, and the accumulated sand forms a dune high enough to seep into the house through one of the broken windows. The fields, which once waved with golden wheat, have been blown bare, right down to the hardpan.

I glance at Mrs. Rydberg. She's a tall woman. I hear her gasp at the condition her house is in, before taking her daughter's hand, straightening her back, and lifting her chin.

Two bankers, wearing dark suits, are on the porch with the auctioneer. The bankers smile down at the promising number of men who have shown up for the sale. One shouts for the auctioneer to get the bidding started.

The auctioneer smiles. "Well, alrighty, here we go." He snaps his suspenders and steps forward. "What ya gonna give me for the lot—."

Referring to the furnishings the tenant farmer left behind. "Do I hear ten dollar, ten dollar, bid it now."

There is silence.

"Do I hear five dollar? Who'll bid a fiver?"

Nobody answers.

The fatter of the two bankers laughs. "Guess we could afford to give this stuff away. Might make good kindling."

The chairs and table he thinks might make good fire starter look as good as what most of us live with. The men stare at him. No one smiles.

The banker clears his throat and nods toward the rusty tools, milk cans, a lister, an old harness, and a wagon wheel piled against the sagging barn.

The auctioneer says, "Do I have an opening bid?"

A farmer from Hartley glances at the men standing with my father, but says nothing.

"Come on folks," one of the bankers says. "These tools are worth something."

The farmer standing next to me spits a wad of tobacco juice into the dust.

The two bankers shift uneasily, then one says, "Tell you what folks. We'll move on to the land and house and throw the contents and tools in for nothing. What do I hear as an opening bid for this fine piece of land and the house?"

Mrs. Rydberg sits dry-eyed and ramrod straight in our buckboard. Her daughter's face glistens with tears.

The men look at Papa, who nods. All together they pull their empty overall pockets inside out. Before Mr. Roosevelt was elected, empty pocket linings were called Hoover-flags. One man holds up a nickel. "This here's all I got left after the bank closed."

There's a murmur in the crowd and a few muffled laughs. The farmer from Hartley says, "I'll bid a—" but before he can name a sum Papa claps him on the back, friendly like, and whispers something to him. The farmer nods, walks to his wagon, and climbs up next to his wife.

The banker stares at my father. "What's going on here?"

"I heard rumor of an auction," Papa shouts. "Get on with it."

My heart leaps with joy. I haven't seen my father stand this straight and proud since he finished building our house, and harvested that first fine crop of wheat four years ago.

The other men, weighed down by the massive unfairness of what we've all come to, shuffle closer, tightening the circle, staring coldly at the bankers.

"We have a nickel," the auctioneer says. There's a hint of a smile on his face. "Do I hear—"

"I'll see your nickel and raise you five cents." A farmer holds up a dime.

"We have ten cents, do I hear a quarter," says the auctioneer. His eyes sparkle with amusement.

"Looks like that's it," Papa says. "Take it or leave it."

The fat banker in charge wipes sweat from his forehead and looks at Sheriff Foust. "Do something."

"What would you like me to do? Hold a gun on 'em 'til it rains?"

"A dime going once," says the auctioneer. "A dime going twice."

"Stop," the banker shouts.

"Sold," says the auctioneer.

The banker's face goes scarlet.

The farmer who bid a dime makes his way through the crowd of men, who reach to pat his back. He hands the dime to the banker. "You'll take this and be happy to have it."

"Let's get out of here," one of the bankers says.

"Not without my deed, you don't," says the new owner of Mrs. Rydberg's farm.

The banker scrawls his signature and hands a piece of paper to the farmer. Cheers erupt and the men shake hands with each other. Though I don't think Gracie knows what happened, she hops up and down the bed of the buckboard, clapping her hands. I look over at Papa. He's being congratulated and he's beaming, but when our eyes meet, he drops his gaze as if he's ashamed to feel any joy for this little victory. I hop over the side, walk over, put my arms around his waist, my cheek against his chest.

The farmer who got the house and land for a dime ambles over to Mrs. Rydberg and hands her the deed. The men crowd around. She looks at it, then at their grinning faces. "You mean—" Her hands tremble. Tears spill down her face.

The men nod.

"Thank you," her daughter says, and hugs her mother.

The men wait, battered hats in hand. When she composes herself, she says, "Please, gentlemen, take whatever you need. Tools, furniture, anything you think you can use, something for your wives. There's nothing left here I need or want, except this piece of land for my grandchildren."

"Next year, when it rains," Papa says, "the land will recover and all our farms will grow wheat again."

Nothing in his tone makes me think he believes those words.

The men aren't too proud to take Mrs. Rydberg up on her offer. They sort through the tools and their wives go into the house. Gracie jumps down, follows them, and comes out carrying a radio.

"Can I have this?" She holds it up to Mrs. Rydberg.

"Of course, you can," Mrs. Rydberg says.

"It should belong to someone who has electricity, Gracie. Put it back." I reach to take it from her.

She wraps her arms around it. "No!" Her bottom lip juts. "I can listen to it when the dust comes."

"We don't have electricity, Gracie."

"We do when the dust comes."

"No, we—" I laugh, and look at Mrs. Rydberg. "She means static electricity." I squat down. "It's not the same thing, sweetheart."

"Let her keep it, Nona," Mrs. Rydberg says. "It's a farm radio. You crank it by hand, and it charges itself."

Mr. Andersen picks up the mail when he takes Mrs. Rydberg to catch the train back to Iowa. Along with another half dozen notices of upcoming foreclosures is a letter for Mama from Mrs. Howard. Mama is ironing when I hand it to her. She folds the envelope and puts it in her apron pocket. "Bring me the other iron, will you?"

"Aren't you going to read it?"

"I want to finish this." She smiles. "Then I can take my time reading it."

Ironing is the only household chore Mama has ever liked. Back in Chicago, she always seemed content when she was ironing. Out here, I think it settles her mind to stand over an ironing board, forcing wrinkled things to become crisp and smooth.

I fetch the iron heating on the stove, put it on the ironing board, and take the cold one back to the stove to reheat.

"Thanks." She dips her fingers in the bowl of water on the table, flicks water on the pillowcase, and applies the hot iron. The damp cloth hisses and steam rises.

Later that afternoon, when I come back from milking Rose and Lily, Mama's sitting at the table reading her letter. She looks up. "I've gone through it three times now and feel luckier after each reading."

"How come?"

"Celia says she only has one boarder left—"

"Mr. Fischer?"

When she doesn't answer, I turn. She shakes her head. "Not Mr. Fischer, Nona."

I know what she's going to tell me. "Did he die?" I blink back tears. She nods.

"From what?"

"Old age, I guess. She says he was skin and bones near the end, but still insisted on giving the better share of his food to Kippy." She hands me the letter. I read to the part Mama hasn't told me.

We're down to oatmeal and a loaf of bread a week. Any meat we manage to get from the butcher is rotten and has to be washed to get rid of the maggots.

I know you're having a time of it, too, but you can't imagine how terrible it is here in Chicago with so many out of work, the air still thick with ash, smoke and stink. You did the right thing leaving, but I miss you so.

I found out Kippy and two of her friends have been foraging at the dump. Now we're no better off than the poorest of the poor. I've sunk so low that I didn't tell her to stop going.

Please tell Winona how sorry I am to be the bearer of sad news. I know she adored Mr. Fischer. He was just as kind to Kippy. She cried her eyes out when he passed.

Your friend always, Celia

That night, I get on my knees beside my bed, with the Indian head nickel Mr. Fischer gave me clutched in my fist, and tell him goodbye.

31

After Mr. Roosevelt is sworn in as President in March 1933, he begins talking to the nation every week over the radio. They're called fireside chats. Papa cranks Gracie's farm radio and we gather 'round to listen.

Roosevelt creates a new cabinet post called the Department of the Interior, appoints a Mr. Bennett, the former Secretary of Agriculture, to head it. First thing Mr. Bennett says is the prairie was only meant for grazing: cattle and buffalo, not for planting wheat. That's totally opposite of what the government told the farmers before. They said the soil was the one "resource that cannot be exhausted."

In a story in the *Dalhart Texan*, Mr. Bennett said Americans were "changing the face of the earth more than the combined activities of volcanoes, earthquakes, tidal waves, tornadoes, and all the excavations of mankind since the beginning of time."

At school, Miss Brown says the way humans are mistreating the earth, maybe we don't deserve to inherit it. That same night, after listening to another fireside chat, Papa says we should have known better than to vote for a Democrat. I'm not so sure. I remember that cowboy outside the pool hall on the day we arrived in Dalhart, the one who sneered and called us sodbusters. Maybe that's the right word for what we've done to the land. I don't risk telling Papa what Miss Brown said.

About the time Mama and Papa start being sorry for their vote, Mr. Roosevelt says from now on the government will insure all money deposited in banks up to ten thousand dollars. It's safe to put our money into a bank account again. Of course, we don't have a bank left in town to put money in, or any money to deposit. I'm keeping my eleven dollars and thirty-one cents right where it is—in Mr Andersen's old tobacco tin on a shelf in our bedroom.

The government starts buying up surplus corn, beans, and flour to give to the needy. We qualify to receive those goods, but Papa is too proud to take a handout.

On April first, like a sign from heaven that things are looking up, it rains. With Mr. Andersen watching and clapping, Gracie and I hold hands and dance. At first, raindrops pock our dusty arms then the dirt runs in rivulets down our faces. Mama joins us, holding a giggly Katie on her hip. We dance with our heads back, mouths open to catch rain on our tongues. We dance until the ground turns muddy. I grab a fistful and throw it at Owie.

"Stop that," Mama shouts before the mudball Papa throws hits her in the shoulder. We children freeze, eyes wide with shock.

Mama looks at her shoulder, then at Papa, puts Katie down, scoops up as much mud as two hands can carry and gives chase as Papa dodges and weaves to escape her. We shriek with laughter and blast away at each other.

Within days, the bare, brown fields bloom with mats of purple verbena and evening primrose in pink, white, and lemon yellow. Papa and Mama drag the table out onto the porch so we can have supper in the sweet-smelling air.

Mama wears her hair in a bun, but wisps escape. On these warm evenings on the porch, with the air barely stirring, the loose curls dance like butterflies, but her face looks tired even when she smiles.

Out in the unplowed pasture, a few patches of Buffalo grass appear, and there are rose-colored blossoms on the cactus. Trumpet vine sprouts and wraps tendrils around the fences. Hawks teeter on the wing. Nighthawks peent and boom in dives. I'm full of envy.

After the rain, the cottonwood trees bud. As spring wears on, the air fills with their cottony seeds and their green leaves are a relief from the drying fields and Papa's disappointment. On warm days, when my chores are done, I take a book and ride Dan out to the cottonwoods mostly just to be alone.

This Saturday, as I head out, my eyes are drawn to the white cage of Sam's skeleton. One of our beef cows stands near it, mooing. The way she's standing makes me look again.

She's giving birth. I check the pasture for the bull and spot him lying near the fence. He's watching me, but not aggressively.

The calf's head and front legs dangle a foot above the ground. I edge Dan closer and turn him so I can keep an eye on the bull and the birth—the first I've ever seen. The calf's head has broken through the birth sac, and its eyes are open. It shakes its head like cows and horses do when flies bother them. I hold my breath.

The cow's sides heave twice and the calf drops to the ground, followed by a gush of blood from the mother. Our little herd of beef cattle—if you can call three head a herd—has grown to four. The cow turns and begins to lick the calf and eat the placenta. I'm covered in goosebumps as I watch until the little black calf struggles to its feet and begins to suckle. I ride on toward the cottonwoods, ignoring the feelings of affection that well up in me for the wobbly little calf. I don't want to love any other animals. It hurts too much when they die, or when we kill them to eat.

At the top of the ravine, I rein Dan in to listen and watch for a minute. I think my favorite thing about living here is the sound of the cottonwood leaves rustling, watching them flash and sparkle in the wind. Out here, life feels more normal. I lean back, gaze up at the clear blue sky, and breathe deeply.

I'm smiling as turn my head to watch the new calf nursing. A dirty red cloud, stretching east to west as far as I can see along the horizon. It's barreling toward us. I whip Dan's head around and spur him toward the mother and calf. We skid to a stop. The startled cow runs, leaving the calf behind. I leap to the ground. Up close, the calf looks like it must weigh seventy or eighty pounds. I don't know if I can lift her high enough to get her across Dan's withers. I look again at the rolling dark red cloud and feel the first sting of sand. I squat, grab the calf around the middle, take a deep breath, and throw her across Dan's back like a sack of oats. The little calf cries for her mother. The red cloud rolls over us as I scramble back into the saddle. "Go." Dan's charges for home.

32

Mr. Andersen sits in a chair tilted back against the side of the barn. His eyes are closed, his face lifted to the sun. When he hears me shout, he opens his eyes and sees what's coming. "Sweet Jesus!" He lets the chair land on all four legs, jumps up, and tries to chase the chickens into their coop.

Gracie comes to the screen door of the house.

"Get inside and close the door," I scream as I gallop past on Dan. I ride him straight into the barn, lift myself out of the saddle and slide backwards off his rump to the ground. I pull the calf off and guide her into the stall with Lily, who turns to look at her, then resumes chewing her cud. I slam the barn doors, but dust pours in through the hay doors. I climb the ladder to the loft, but I'm not strong enough close the doors. It's all I can do to keep from being pulled out of loft. Grit and sand blind me and I struggle to breathe.

Down below, I see dirt swirl up as Mr. Andersen forces his way into the barn, then hear the wind slam the door behind him.

"I'm up here," I shout.

A moment later, he's beside me. He leans out and, with me holding onto his overall straps, pulls the hay doors closed.

The barn walls block the wind, but dust seeps through every gap, knot hole, and around the doors, filling the air. Mr. Andersen begins to cough and can't stop. He wets his handkerchief in a water trough, but hands it to me to cover my nose and mouth. He sits beside me on a hay bale and covers his own face with his shirttail.

The calf cries for its mother.

"What's that?" Mr. Andersen croaks between spasms of coughing.

"A new calf. I watched her being born this morning. When I saw the storm coming, I took her from her mother. I was afraid she would die like—"

"Karlo?"

"Uh huh."

"Quick thinking."

Ben sneezes, then Dan. Lily and Rose moo. Their breathing sounds like they all have head colds. I get up and lead the calf back to where Mr. Andersen and I sit on a hay bale, and give her my thumb to suck. Her nostrils are muddy where the dust sticks to her wet nose.

"Do you think we could make masks for the animals," I say.

"I'll make some tomorrow."

I smile to myself, imagining Mr. Andersen's working with a needle and thread, then think, why not? Maybe he likes to sew. "How'd you learn to sew?"

"I went to Alaska during the gold rush. I had to learn to cook—" a spasm of coughing grips him "—and sew."

I pound his back with the palm of my hand. "Did you find gold?" I pull one of my boots off, then a sock, and wipe the calf's nose.

"A little." He starts coughing again. When he catches his breath, he says, "There was more money to be made buying claims and reselling them to the next fool."

The barn and hay doors rattle and the air is dense with grit. For a moment, I stop to marvel at how we're adjusting to these storms enough to sit and chat as if this is a normal way to live.

"How'd you end up here?"

"I came to Texas the first time when I was seventeen. After the freezes killed most of the cattle, I went to seek my fortune in Alaska. When the gold rush petered out in 1899, I had enough money saved to come back to here. After the XIT ranch bellied up, I bought this place. The difference between me and other prospectors is, I didn't gamble or drink. Saving your money is the only way to get what you want."

"You were right about banks. I had fifty-eight dollars saved for flying lessons. All I have left is eleven dollars and thirty-one cents in the tobacco tin you gave me."

He pats my leg. "Don't give up. This drouth will end, things will get better, and you can start saving again."

I rub the calf's soft little ear. "Do you think the mother cow will take her calf back?"

"Pretty sure she will, and be grateful to you for saving her."

After the storm ends, I check on Mama, Gracie, and the baby, then ride out with the calf slung across Dan's back. It takes me a while to spot her mother. She's lying down. Sand has mounded against her back and her head is tucked into the curve of her body. I'm afraid she's dead, until her calf bawls. She turns her head toward the sound. Her eyes are caked shut, but that doesn't stop her from struggling to her feet. She shakes off the sand, and stumbles toward us. I dismount, slid the calf off Dan's back, and put her on the ground. The calf wobbles to meet her, finds a teat, and begins to nurse. I take my canteen, which is hanging off the saddle horn, and walk slowly toward his mother. Air whooshes in and out through the mud caking her nostrils. I'm not sure what she'll do when I touch her, so I uncap my canteen, and step to one side in case she bolts. I pour water over the eye nearest to me. She blinks it open and turns her head, as if asking me to rinse her other eye. Next, I pour water over her nose and use my free hand to loosen the mud clogging her nostrils. She turns to sniff her nursing calf, then nudges me. With the last of the water, I rinse her eyes again. There's still a lot of sand in her eyelashes but now she can see. I brush sand from the sides of her face, and giggle when she stretches her neck and licks my chin.

33

The winter and spring of 1933 were dry and not cold enough to kill the next generation of insects. By the summer, we're overrun with centipedes and spiders. Bull snakes get into the hen house and eat our eggs. Mr. Andersen put chalk eggs on Papa's shopping list. Owie puts one in each nest after he empties them in the mornings. The hens know the difference, but the snakes don't. Swallowing a chalk egg kills the snake. I feel bad about that until Owie drags me out and shows me a bull snake coiled around a fence post with three eggs in its stomach. We watch it squeeze the post to break the shells.

This morning, I open my eyes when the rooster crows and turn to see if Gracie is awake. The sun's not up, but there's enough light to make out her black-haired rag doll at the foot of her bed. Gracie's sitting up, her back pressed hard against the wall. She turns her head to look at me; her cheeks glisten with tears.

"What's wrong, honey?" Out of the corner of my eye I see what I think is her rag doll lift two long, hairy, black legs and wave them in the air.

"Nona."

"Don't move, Gracie."

There was a story in last week's newspaper about a Hartley boy who was bitten by a black widow spider hiding in the wood he carried into the house. The paper said he died, screaming in pain, before his parents could get him to the new hospital in Dalhart. Thankfully, this isn't a black widow spider. It's a tarantula. Not poisonous, but its bite can really hurt.

I slip out of bed and creep toward the foot of Gracie's bed. The tarantula swings around, rears up, and exposes its fangs. I stop. If I try to jerk the bedspread off, it might run right at Gracie.

"Hurry," Gracie whispers.

"Hush." I walk the other direction. The spider scuttles farther along the foot of her bed.

Gracie has the bedspread pulled to her chin and she's holding the edge so tightly, her knuckles are white

"Let go of the spread, Gracie."

She lifts her fingers. I take a corner, ready to rip the spread off, but the spider dashes across and disappears over the far edge of her bed.

Gracie scrambles away and runs screaming into the kitchen. I hear Mama's startled cry, "What? What is it?"

"Giant spider," Gracie wails.

The tarantula is now on the floor on the side of her bed next to the wall. I'll never be able to sleep in here again if I don't find it.

Mama appears in the doorway. "Where is it?"

"I don't know. Over there somewhere. Where's Papa?"

"He and Noel and a bunch of other fools are at the newspaper office letting the editor, John McCarty, talk them into signing a pledge not to give up and leave this godforsaken place."

"We just need rain, Mama. Would you rather be back in Chicago?"

"Maybe. In spite of what Celia says, it can't be as bad as here." She turns.

"Where are you going?"

"To get the broom and kill that spider."

"I'll do it."

I strip Gracie's bed to make sure it hasn't gotten between the blanket and sheet, then crawl on my hands and knees looking for the tarantula. It has scrunched itself into the corner. When Mama hands me the broom, I poke it with the handle. It tries to back up but it's trapped. It flails the air with its two front legs. I feel sorry for it, even though I'm sure the tarantula's raised legs are in defense, not defeat.

I read a poem in school called the *Rime of the Ancient Mariner* about a sailor who killed an albatross. After he kills it, the ship ends up stranded in the doldrums, which Miss Brown told us means no wind. I envied them until we finished the story. The crew blames him and makes him wear the dead albatross around his neck. Eventually, the entire crew dies for lack of water and only the ancient mariner is rescued but is doomed to wander the earth telling the story. Facing the tarantula, I'm reminded of the last two lines from that long poem: *For the dear God who loveth us / He made and loveth all.*

"Don't be afraid," I whisper to the spider. "I'm not going to hurt you."

"What are you doing?" Mama, with Gracie cowering behind her, is at the door.

"I'm going to catch it and put it outside."

"Don't be silly. Just kill it, Nona. If you put it out, it may come back in again."

I straighten and look at her, but don't know what to say. I can't tell her I'm not killing it because of a poem, or that maybe, by not killing it, we won't lose everything like other farmers have. Maybe that's the problem. We've nearly killed the land, and now, like the mariner, we're marooned, but in an ocean of dust.

Mama goes to pick up Katie, who's crying, but Gracie squats down so she can watch.

"Go get the dustpan," I say.

"I'm gonna tell."

"Tell what?"

"You're supposed to kill it."

"Get the dustpan or I'll put it back in your bed."

I open the window and pull her bed away from the wall. Gracie puts the dust pan on the mattress, and runs back to the doorway.

The thought of trying to pick up the tarantula with the dustpan nearly makes me change my mind. I walk between the bed and wall and put the dustpan in front of it. I hold the broom so I can pin it against the wall if it tries to rush me and sink its fangs into my hand. I inch the pan forward. The tarantula's front legs wave. It's too dark to see if its fangs are out. I glance at the open window, which is between our beds. If I convince the spider to climb in the pan, I'll have to carry it around the foot of Gracie's bed to get to the window.

I slide the pan forward until it's under its second pair of legs, then it's third, then the fourth. My heart pounds as I place the head of the broom perpendicular to the handle of the dustpan, lift, and back out of the corner.

"She's got it," Gracie shouts. "Mama, she's got it."

I can't see under the broom, but I can feel the weight of the tarantula in the pan. Every nerve in my body tingles as I back around the end of the bed toward the open window. Out of the corner of my eye, I see Mama in the doorway holding Katie, who is still wailing. I reach the window, lift the broom, and flip the tarantula out, then lean over in time to see it scuttle under the house.

Mama turns away. "I don't know why you didn't kill it."

She can't know that I just saved us, and myself, from having to roam the earth telling the story of what went wrong here.

34

1934

We thought 1934 would be a better year. We were wrong. Again. The first duster barreled down from the north in late January.

Everything in our house, no matter how hard we work, is always coated with dust. We stack the plates upside down on the shelves and they still have to be rinsed before each meal. Every bite of food feels gritty. Dust floats on top of the milk. Sand sinks to the bottom. We sweep and it blows back in. Laundry is a daily chore, but no sooner is the wash done than another duster comes and everything needs to be washed again. Mama's oriental rugs have been rolled up and stored under our beds for over a year, and all the carved scrolling on her furniture is gray in spite of her constant polishing.

The chickens begin to die. The first was an old hen, so we assumed age took her, but when we cut her open, her crop and gizzard were filled with sand. It's the same with others that follow. Nearly every day, we're breathing dirt, eating dirt, drinking dirt.

Papa got turned around during a storm a couple of days ago. It was just luck he found his way to the dugout. Afterwards, he tied a rope from the barn to the porch so we can find the house during a duster.

In March, snow falls in dark flakes the *Texan* calls a "snuster." Later that same month, dust storms blot out the sun for six days in a row.

We hang washcloths over the doorknobs to keep from getting knocked off our feet by a jolt of static electricity. Cars drag rattling chains to ground them, and still the static causes the engines to die. We go out of our way not to touch each other. Two-year old Katie been shocked so many times, she's terrified of being picked up.

The tar-papered walls of our house are little protection against the windblown sand and dirt. Grit finds cracks in the boards and around the windows and swirls in. The air in the entire house is hazy. To protect

Katie, Mama puts her in her cradle, covers her with a sheet, and opens an umbrella over her. We hang damp sheets over the windows and stuff every exposed crack with wet rags. Nothing keeps the dust out. Katie and Owie develop the same hacking cough Gracie and Mr. Andersen have. Mr. Andersen tells Mama the best thing for a cough is a teaspoon of sugar and a few drops of kerosene. It doesn't help. Gracie cries because her little throat is raw and she complains her stomach muscles ache from coughing. Soon, Papa and I develop coughs. Between the rising heat and the chorus of coughing, we're awake most of every night.

Spring 1934 is marked by an invasion of insects: centipedes, blister beetles, and cutworms. Tent caterpillars in the cottonwoods are followed by swarms of grasshoppers. They stream across the fields, consuming anything that sprouts, including the bark off fence posts as they march in noisy waves toward our garden.

Mr. Andersen makes a poison of bran, lemon, molasses, and arsenic—a disgusting mess—and spreads it around the perimeter of the garden every night. In the mornings, hundreds of grasshoppers are dead.

Owie and I are raking up the bodies to burn when Gracie goes to gather eggs. Though I shout a warning, she lets the chickens out. A few rush over to eat the bodies we're raking before we can scare them away. By morning, those chickens are also dead. We burn them, too.

Dirty winds rage all through April, but die to a breeze too weak to turn the windmill for much of May. We're drawing barely enough water for the livestock. The garden dries up, and in the fields, the wheat sprouts are buried under loose and shifting sand. For weeks, the sky is painfully blue, and the daily weather report is the same: dry with dusters.

Mrs. Howard writes to Mama in May and says dust from the Great Plains has blown in and blanketed Chicago. "How can you stand it?" she asks.

That night, Mama reads the letter to Papa, then pushes it across the table for him to read for himself. He does, then looks at her. "Do you really want us to pack up and move back to Chicago?"

I'm setting the table; Mama's wiping out the bowls we'll use for supper. "I'd rather risk starvation in Chicago, than worry about the very air we breathe."

"If we leave, we'll never have another home of our own," Papa says.

"Do you hear the children coughing all night? This place is killing them."

An ache spreads in my chest as Papa puts his head in his hands. "You want to go back there and have me shuffle along in a bread line for a meal? At least here we have our own land. We have a roof over our heads and food to eat."

"None of this is *ours* yet," Mama says.

She means as long as Mr. Andersen is alive. When I look at her, shocked, she says, "Well, it isn't."

The summer is brutally hot—days and days of 110-degree weather and no rain. Nearly all the Turkey Red wheat Papa and Mr. Andersen planted last fall withers and dies in the fields. Even the garden struggles, in spite of being watered every evening when the air cools. While I water, Gracie helps by plucking bugs and putting them in a jar to feed to the chickens.

The only food we have left is what we've grown and canned from the garden. We have plenty of eggs from the chickens, and milk from the cows. As worried and scared as we sometimes feel, we're so much better off than people living in cities, and luckier than some of our neighbors. Many went into debt to buy more land, tractors, and wheat seed. Now, if it doesn't rain, or if it does and the prices don't go up, the farmers around us will lose everything like Mr. Loonan did.

Mama cherishes the Chinese elms Papa planted five years ago when Gracie was born. I think she cares more about those two trees than the entire garden. On the rare windless days when the windmill can't pump well water, Mama still sees to it the elm trees get water before a drop goes to the garden. I worry her fate is tied to theirs. It scares me to think what might happen to her if these trees don't survive. It pleases Papa that she loves them, but I don't think he sees how important their survival is to her.

In June, we have a hailstorm that kills a dozen baby chicks. The hail also ruins what's left of the garden and pounds the wheat that's still struggling to survive to a pulp. A screen over the tomatoes saves them, but everything else is lost.

By July, we've had a half dozen sand and dust storms, and the ground looks like brittle tiles, curling at the edges.

I've learned to tell the difference. Sandstorms, depending on which direction they come from, are beige, red, yellow, or brown, and blow through quickly, and for days afterwards, everything we eat is full of grit. Dust storms are black, can last for hours, and are so full of static electricity that touching something metal like a car door can knock a grown man off his feet. Sometimes it's so bad, the spark jumps out to meet you.

July also brings heat and the constant wind. Everything thing that's left, withers. We harvest potatoes as small and hard as marbles. The wind howls most nights. When it stops, my ears ache for other sounds: coyotes calling, mice scampering, insects in the walls—anything but the wind.

The temperatures have been well over a hundred for days on end, barely cooling off enough to sleep until midnight. To escape, I sometimes take a lamp to the cellar and read. I envy Mr. Andersen in the dugout, which stays cooler than the house.

Mama's so afraid we'll run out of food, she's been fixing saltine-cracker pancakes for breakfast. It's a recipe Mrs. Howard sent her, and we love it. She uses old, stale saltines, an egg, a little vanilla, shapes them into pancakes, and fries them in lard. Covered with molasses, they are the best thing she knows how to cook.

In August, days of hundred-degree weather and searing wind finally kill the Chinese elm by the house. The one Papa planted by the outhouse hangs on, shielded, depending on the direction of the wind by the knoll, the barn, or the outhouse.

For all Mama's efforts to keep that tree alive, she takes its death without a word. When Papa suggests he should cut it down, since we'll need dry wood come winter, she only shrugs.

"When the rains come, we'll plant another," he says.

Mama's eyes narrow, then she turns and goes back in the house.

Papa's outside the kitchen window, sawing up the elm, when I bring water in from the well. Mama's at the table shelling peas the size of BBs. I lean and kiss her cheek.

She's not an affectionate person and looks up, startled. "What was that for?"

"I feel bad that your elm died."

"It was just a tree."

"But you loved it."

"I suppose I did."

Later, when I come out of the barn from the afternoon milking, she's standing next to the pile of cut up branches—an entire tree, spindly as it was, now reduced to a few small logs and kindling. I put the bucket of milk down. I should go and be with her—put my arms around her and let her cry if she needs to. I worry about how much more of this place Mama can take. How long before her strength gives out? Instead, I step back into the barn, out of the sunlight, and watch her select one of the forked branches. She holds it like a candelabrum, and stares across the rippling sand dunes. Maybe she's chosen this piece to put in a jar of water—a keepsake to tide her over until the rain returns and Papa plants another for her.

Even at this distance, I see her jaw muscles knot. She starts snapping off the smaller branches, tearing loose the ones that resist. When there's nothing left but one naked limb, she breaks it over her knee, and throws the two halves on the pile with the others.

I stay concealed in the shadows. Even when she puts an arm across her eyes and her body is wracked by sobs, I watch. Not until she lifts her apron hem and dabs her eyes do I pick up the pails of milk and come out into the sunlight. She sees me, leans down, gathers an armful of twigs, turns, and goes into the house. Only then do I realize that caring for Mama is exhausting, and comforting her too often feels like a betrayal of Papa. We're suffering—the whole world is suffering—and I feel forced to take sides.

35

With no rain and nothing left for them to eat, rabbits descend on us. The first few are a welcome source of meat. Papa long ago butchered and smoked the hog we got from Mrs. Rydberg. Since then, aside from the occasional tough old chicken, supper usually consists of beans and rice. The appearance of the rabbits has temporally stopped Papa from eyeing the calf I rescued during the sandstorm.

A few rabbits soon turn into hundreds. At a distance, they hop like fleas on a mangy dog. Nothing survives as they rampage across the fields. Mr. Andersen and Papa put a fence around our garden, but it has to be checked and repaired daily. The rabbits dig under it.

Papa goes into town for a meeting of his Last Man Club and brings home a flyer: *Big Rabbit Hunt Sunday, Air strip—Bring Clubs.* The air strip a little north of town is the home of a useless crop duster.

"Why clubs and not guns?" Owie says.

"There will be hundreds of men and thousands of rabbits. We'd be too likely shoot each other.

"Are you going?" Mama asks him at supper that night.

Papa glances at me. "Yes." He's expecting me to want to go with him like I did to the auction, but he's wrong. I don't want to watch rabbits get killed. Gracie calls them her bunnies and will only eat rabbit if she's told it's chicken.

"Can I go?" Owie says.

"No," Mama says at the same time Papa says, "Maybe."

"What hunt?" Gracie says.

"Never mind," Mama says.

He told Owie "maybe," and I'm six years older than he is. I'll decide if I want to go to the hunt, and if I don't, I won't. It's not up to Papa to say if I can or can't. That would be discrimination, a word Miss Brown taught me when I said I wanted to be a pilot.

"We shouldn't treat girls differently than boys, or expect less from them," she said. "With the example Miss Earhart is setting, by the time an opportunity for you to take lessons comes, lots of girls will be pilots."

The day of the rabbit hunt dawns clear and sunny. Papa and Owie leave in the Model T while I'm in the barn milking Lily and Rose. I feel like they've rushed away while my back was turned.

I'm putting the cow's milk through the separator when I hear Mr. Andersen coughing. He comes into the barn.

"How come you didn't go to the hunt?" I ask.

He takes a spool of wire off a peg by the door. "I don't need to watch grown men take out their frustration on helpless critters."

"Is that what you think they're doing?"

"I don't think it's what they are planning to do, but it's what it will turn into."

"But we're overrun with rabbits."

"Yep, we are, but we'll never win against a force of nature greater than we are. Bashing in the heads of a few hundred rabbits won't solve the rabbit problem or the drouth, and it will leave every man ashamed of himself."

If Mr. Andersen's right, I don't want Owie and Papa doing it.

After putting the milk in the wellhouse, I hear Mama kneading dough long before I reach the porch. She's slamming it down on the table, kneading it, then slamming it down again. I was going to tell her what Mr. Andersen said and that I'm going to get Owie and bring him home, but think better of it. She's already upset about something.

"Do you need me for anything?"

"Why?" She lifts her arm and runs it across her sweaty brow.

To avoid looking at her, I smile at Katie, gurgling and happy on a blanket in the corner of the kitchen. "It's a pretty day. I thought I'd take a book to the cottonwoods."

"Go ahead." She opens a cupboard drawer, puts the dough in to rise, covers it with a towel, and closes the drawer in the useless attempt to hide it from the dust in the air. Everything we eat is flavored with dirt from some other state.

"Are you sure?" I feel guilty for lying.

"I'm sure," she says.

I saddle Dan and ride him west toward the cottonwoods. Whenever I come this way, I try not to look at Sam's bones picked clean, but I always do. His ribcage has trapped tumbleweeds, which have let the sand pile up. He finally has the burial he deserved.

When I'm out of sight of the house, I turn northwest toward Dalhart and urge Dan into a trot. It will take an hour or more to cross the eight or so miles of sand-covered fields. In front of us, startled rabbits hop in all directions.

Long before I get there, I see a huge cloud of dust stirred up, not by the wind, but what looks like thousands of people who've arrived in cars, wagons, and on horseback for the hunt. The men have built a large triangular-shaped enclosure of chicken-wire. Other farmers on horseback and on foot have been joined by young boys beating on tin cans, including, I suspect, Owie, though I don't see him. They have fanned out over the prairie in a huge semi-circle and are herding rabbits toward the enclosure. There's so much dust I can't actually see the rabbits, but the closer I get, the clearer the numbers become. Hundreds leap and tumble over each other, trying to get away. Any that succeed in breaking through the line are clubbed by a second line of men on foot. The circle shrinks until hundreds of rabbits are throwing themselves against the chicken-wire. Men on either side of the wide open end of the triangle lift a long wire gate into place, blocking any escape. Dozens of men, including Papa, enter the pen and begin clubbing the screaming, flailing, frantic rabbits. Blood spurts in streams from crushed skulls, but it's the rabbits' child-like shrieks rising above the shouts of the men that sickens me.

The mass of dying rabbits writhe beneath clubs swung with such fury I feel as if I might throw up. I close my eyes, and when I open them again, Papa, covered in blood, walks toward the gate of the pen. Men clap him on the back as he steps out through a gap someone opens for him.

I'm alone and quite a distance from the slaughter, but he spots me. Mr. Andersen was right. These men, including Papa, took their misery out on the rabbits, and I can see it in his face. He's ashamed. I turn Dan for home.

36

When I ride into the yard from the hunt, the car is already back. Papa and Owie must have left soon after I did. In the barn, I find Papa's shirt and overalls soaking in a wash tub. The water is red. I unsaddle Dan, brush him, put him in his stall, give him oats and hay, and feed Ben.

The cows' udders are again full. I get the stool and pail and start with Lily. When she turns to look at me with her sad, understanding, brown eyes. I put my forehead against her side and cry.

Papa's sitting in the kitchen with his forearms on his thighs, fingers laced, head down, when I come in with the milk. He straightens and looks at me. He's wearing a clean shirt and has washed the blood off his face, hands and arms, but his tanned neck is still streaked.

Mama turns from the stove. "I thought you were going to the creek bed to read."

He's told her I was at the hunt.

I don't answer.

Owie bangs through the front door, the odor from the outhouse wafting in with him. His eyes are red-rimmed. I'm not sure whether it's from the dust or if he's been crying. He crosses the kitchen and puts his arms around me. "It was sad, Nona. I'm glad you didn't see it."

I look at Papa over Owie's shoulder.

"We can't let the rabbits eat the food we need." Papa's tone is defensive.

"I didn't say we should, but the fencing keeps them out of our garden."

Papa sees the tears swimming in my eyes, gets up, and holds his arms out.

"Don't." I put a hand up.

I'm not grieving for the rabbits, left as food for the vultures, flies, and ants. The tears spilling down my cheeks are for the man, always so tall in my mind, now looking thin, weathered and old, wearing his sorrow and regret in the hunch of his shoulders.

Papa looks socked in the stomach. I may never get the memory of this day out of my head, but I can't bear hurting him. I step forward and put my arms around his waist, my head against the beat of his good heart.

The rabbit hunts go on until the weather gets too hot to swing a bat, but Papa doesn't go again. The others must feel some shame, too, for killing more than they could ever eat, because the town votes to send the meat up north to feed the hungry. That ends when the first and only shipment, which was expensive to send, rots before it arrives. The rabbit hunts are finally over when the Chamber of Commerce hires someone to poison them. It doesn't take long before we begin to see sick and dying coyotes and vultures as the poison moves up the food chain.

Late in summer, the government passes a relief bill that will pay farmers not to plant their land.

Papa says not planting is an outrage. We're farmers. Planting crops is what we do. But as fall approaches, with no improvement in the chances of rain—or in the market for wheat, Mr. Andersen argues we should leave the land fallow. He says turning the soil and exposing more of it to the wind is stupid. Let whatever will grow wild, grow. It may hold the soil in place. Papa says if we don't plant and it rains, we'll be out in the cold.

In the end, the government offers $498 to each farmer not to plant. It's more money than Papa can afford to refuse. With it, he pays our overdue taxes and buys coal for winter. Our share of the $9600 from the 1930 harvest seems a lifetime ago.

37

The dust and blowing sand have chafed Lily's and Rose's udders so badly they bawl when I milk them. Mr. Andersen treats them with a little axle grease, which helps, but doesn't improve how the milk tastes.

Papa couldn't bring himself to kill our pastured cattle—a bull and three cows—including the young heifer I rescued during the sandstorm. He probably should have. Their skin hangs on their ribs and bony rumps. Any remaining buffalo grass is under the dunes. By August, there's nothing to feed them except tumbleweed. Along with collecting cowpies, gathering those becomes Owie's job, using the buckboard with Ben pulling it. When he returns, Gracie and I break tumbleweeds up with our feet, leaving our shoes filled with splinters. As hungry as the cattle are, they won't eat the tumbleweeds until Mr. Andersen suggests we salt them. That works.

For Lily, Rose, and the horses, Owie adds collecting prickly-pear cactus, which is more nourishing. Mr. Andersen shows us how to stick the pads into a fire to burn the spines off before chopping them up for the animals. Come fall, we'll save the red cactus pears for Mr. Andersen, who promises to make "Indian fig" jelly from them.

One of the pasture cows gives birth but rejects her calf. While we're at school, Papa shoots him and we again have meat. When the second cow gives birth, she, too, butts it away when it tries to nurse. Gracie begs Papa not to kill this little heifer. "Lily will give her some of her milk." She takes his hand.

"You children need the milk," Papa says.

"I don't like milk," Gracie says. "She can have mine."

"Owie and I will drink less," I say.

"We need to sell the cream," Papa says.

"You should let us try," I say. "If our other cattle die, she can be the start of our herd when the rains come again."

Before the rabbit roundup, I don't think Papa would have given in. Now he shrugs. "Go ahead. But you'll just get attached, and it will make whatever happens harder."

Lily rejects the calf, and so does Rose. We're trying to figure out what to do, before we have to tell Papa, when we hear Mr. Andersen's hacking cough. He's crossing the yard from the dugout. Gracie runs to the barn door, clasps her hands behind her back, elbows locked, and swings her body side to side. "Hi, Mr. Noel."

"Hey there, Missy. Whatcha up to?"

"Nona and I have a hungry calf and the cows won't let her milk. Miss Lily tried to kick her and so did Rose."

"I'm not surprised, them cows is pretty miserable." He comes in to take a look at the bawling calf. "Why she's a real honey, she is." He strokes her head and sticks his thumb in the calf's mouth. She sucks on it. "Did the mother feed her at all?" he asks me.

"No, sir. She ate the after birth and walked away."

"That means this little heifer never got any colostrum."

"What's that?"

"The important first milk. It's full of vitamins and other stuff to protect newborn mammals. We'll have to make a substitute. I've still got the XIT recipe in my old head." He taps his temple. "Nona, you milk Lily. Gracie, go in the house and bring me the castor oil and some sugar. And bring along a measuring cup, a spoon, and fetch me an egg. Can you remember all that?"

Gracie counts to herself and holds up a hand with her fingers spread. "Five things."

"Good girl."

Gracie darts out of the barn.

"And one of your sister's old baby bottles." Mr. Andersen shouts as he crosses to the dugout.

As gently as I can, I begin to milk Lily.

Gracie comes back with everything Mr. Andersen asked for clasped to her chest. Mr. Andersen's right behind her with the pitcher from his washstand and a long, wooden spoon. With us watching, he measures in two and a half cups of warm milk, a cup and a third of water, a half teaspoon of castor oil, a tablespoon of sugar, cracks and adds the egg and beats the mixture. He pours in as much as the baby bottle will hold. "If you're serious about keeping this calf you'll have to feed her three times a day for the next three days, then we can switch her to regular milk. Got it?"

We nod.

He hands the bottle to Gracie.

"After that, we'll give her milk twice a day for the next month. Then you can add dry feed until she's weaned."

Gracie sits on the milk stool, lifts the calf's head, and tilts the bottle. The calf slurps the milk, pushing against the bottle so hard, she tips Gracie and the stool over. Mr. Andersen and I laugh, then he pats my shoulder. "We've been missing that sound for too long." To Gracie, he says, "Have you named her?"

"I like what you called her." Gracie looks up at him. "Honey."

"I love that name," I say.

"Honey she is," Mr. Andersen says.

Later that afternoon, I go to the barn to call Gracie in for supper. Honey is curled up in a bed of hay with her head in Gracie's lap. Gracie's asleep, too. Her cheek rests against Honey's side. My book, *Heidi,* lies open on the ground beside them. Gracie can't read yet, but I've read that book to her so many times in the last four and a half years, she knows the story by heart. My eyes brim. She's been reading to Honey.

Not a day goes by that we don't hear a car or a truck passing, look up and see an entire family with their belongings tied to the roof, fenders, and truck beds, headed toward the main road to Dalhart. People are pulling up stakes and leaving for California, where it's rumored there are jobs. We also get a lot of hobos stopping by asking if we can spare a bite to eat. Mama tells them no, she has four kids to feed, but if Mr. Andersen's around, he scrambles them an egg and shares his hardtack.

Mama complains to Papa that if the word gets out we're a place to find food, we'll never see the end of hungry people. Papa says an egg or two once in a while isn't going to kill us.

Papa takes a job shooting cattle for two dollars a day. The government sent men down to round up any cattle left with meat on their bones, and those men hire a few locals—including Papa—to shoot them. They're shot and butchered and sent to market up north. It's an effort to lower the prices people have to pay for beef. Papa tells us they need to kill eight million to get beef prices stabilized. Farmers are paid sixteen dollars for each cow and four dollars for a calf. Papa doesn't say so, but I imagine he must feel terrible to be back killing animals like in Chicago.

Starving cattle, too far gone to be butchered, are rounded up, shot and burned, or left for people to scavenge bits of meat until the carcass is buried by the next sandstorm. When the wind is right, the air fills with ash and the same burning-flesh smell Chicago had, now mixed with dust.

Papa tells us wherever he goes there are abandoned homesteads with doors missing, windows broken out, and collapsed roofs. The houses have filled with sand. Trees planted by some hopeful housewife, are buried in dunes with only bare, black branches poking skyward.

On a Sunday, a couple weeks after Papa takes the job shooting livestock, he tells us a little girl about four was left sitting on a bench in front of Doc Dawson's sanitarium. "She had this note pinned to her flour sack dress." He unfolds it, hands it to Mama. She reads it and hands it to me.

Our boy, he can work, the girl is just a mouth to feed.

"How come you have this?"

"I'm the one who found her."

"What happened to her?"

"I took her to the nuns at the hospital."

I haven't thought of Mamie in a while. The last two times I wrote her, the letters came back marked "Undeliverable. No forwarding address." This little girl's story reminds me of her. "You mean her family left her behind?"

Papa nods. "I took her hand and she walked with me to the hospital. Didn't say a word. Didn't cry. When I tried to let go of her hand, she tightened her grip and looked up at me with eyes like black marbles. It was the saddest thing I've ever seen. That's why I took the note. I hope she won't remember what her parents did."

On Monday, after school, Gracie comes running in from the barn with Honey loping along behind her. They run up the porch stairs together and burst into the kitchen.

"Someone stole Rose."

"Get that calf out of the kitchen," Mama says.

"Rose is gone!" Gracie stomps her foot.

"No one stole her, Gracie," Papa says. "Her milk was full of dust. We couldn't afford to keep her."

"Where is she?"

"She's . . . in a better place."

Gracie stares at Papa, sees him lower his eyes and shouts, "You shot Rose?"

Oh, Papa. My second thought is thank heavens it wasn't Lily. But then, she isn't ours to kill. She's Mr. Andersen's cow.

Gracie whirls and runs from the house. Honey scrambles after her, breaking through the screen on the bottom half of the door.

"We can barely feed ourselves," Papa says. "We can't keep animals as pets." He sighs, grips the side of the table with both hands, and pulls himself to his feet with a grunt. "I need to fix that screen."

The look on Mama's face as she watches Papa cross the kitchen chills me. Eyes narrow, lip curled. *Disgust.* Maybe even—I take a breath—hatred. She sees me looking and turns back to stirring the beans.

I continue setting the table for supper then leave to use the outhouse. My hand is on the outhouse door when I hear a sound like a water pipe sucking air. It's coming from inside where there is no plumbing. I put my ear to the wood. It's Papa sobbing.

"Supper," Mama shouts from the porch and rings the triangle hanging from hook in the ceiling.

I hear Papa blow his nose.

I back away so when the door opens, it looks like I'm on my way to the outhouse and not like I've been standing there listening to him. I wonder if he'll see in my eyes how my heart breaks for him.

"Where's Gracie?" Mama says. She, Owie, Noel, Papa, and Katie are seated when I come in. Papa eyes are still red-rimmed with deep creases in his forehead.

I wash my hands in the basin. "I don't know."

"Well, call her again. Her soup's getting cold." Mama sounds mad at me, too.

I go out on the porch and shout her name. There's no answer. "I'll check the barn."

She's not there. And neither is Honey.

38

I come to the screen door and tell them Gracie's missing. Chairs scrape away from the table.

"The outhouse?" Mama says.

I shake my head.

She grabs Papa's arm. "If there's a duster—" Her voice turns shrill.

"We'll find her, Glenny. She can't have gone far." He reaches to pat Mama's hand. She jerks it away.

Papa closes his eyes for a moment, then says, "I'll take the car and head toward town. Mr. Andersen, you take Ben the other way. Owie, check the cellar."

Mama begins to pace, probing where her tooth is missing with her tongue.

"Sit, Glenny." Papa guides her back to her chair. "Things will be all right." He pulls the napkin from his shirt collar and throws it on the table.

"Papa," I say.

"What?" he snaps.

"There's no place to hide except the creek bed," I say. "I'll go there."

"Hurry." Mama's biting her knuckle. "It'll be dark soon."

In case I'm wrong about where Gracie's gone, Papa and Mr. Andersen head down the road in opposite directions, but not before I hear Papa tell Owie—back from checking the cellar—to stay with Mama.

I lead Dan from the barn and ride bareback across the dunes toward the creek. Dust rises in puffs behind us. For something that is choking the life out of us and the land, I can't help notice how it turns a lovely reddish gold in the setting sun.

As I approach the edge of the ravine, I hear Gracie coughing and Honey bawling. I slide off Dan's back and walk to the edge. They are side by side, nestled between Henry's and Karlo's graves.

GINNY RORBY 169

"Did you bring Honey's supper with you?"

Gracie twists and looks up at me. "I forgot." She sniffles.

Honey scrambles to her feet and bawls at me.

"Come on. I'll give you a ride home."

"Is Papa going to shoot her?"

"No, Gracie. Lily belongs to Mr. Andersen, Honey is yours. He can't kill her without your permission."

"Are you sure?" she demands.

"I'm positive."

Last week, while I was helping Miss Brown clean up the schoolhouse, she mentioned that she has a contract with the county to teach. She also told me, it's for a hundred dollars a year, and that they haven't had enough money to pay her for the last two years.

"When we get home, we'll draw up a contract for Papa to sign, making Honey yours all legal and binding."

"Okay." Gracie brushes the leaves off her bottom and climbs up to me. Honey follows.

I wipe her tears with my thumbs and put her on Dan's back. Honey rushes over to Dan and butts his belly trying to find a teat. Dan dances away from her and trots toward home with Gracie alone on his back.

I whistle. Bless him, he returns and holds still while I climb on, too.

Honey scampers along behind us.

Our food supply is down to a couple dozen jars of tomatoes, plus six or seven each of green beans, peas, and carrots. We've eaten all but two cans of corn and one jar of cooked rabbit meat. We're so low on flour, rice, and potatoes that we eat the only two things we have plenty of—beans and eggs—for nearly every meal.

Lily's milk has to be strained and left sitting overnight in the well-house to let the rest of the grit settle to the bottom. It, and the butter we churn, taste of axle grease and dirt no matter how long we wait.

Mr. Andersen says the Indians used to eat tumbleweed sprouts. They are green when young. Owie, Gracie, and I scout the landscape breaking off the tips. It takes a lot of them to make a meal, but brined and steamed, or cooked with rice, they don't taste bad.

Mr. Andersen also remembers Indians eating the fruit of the flowering yucca with its tough, sword-shaped leaves. He says cowboys call them 'ghosts in the graveyard' because they seem to prefer growing in cemeteries, and at night the stalk of pale flowers looks like a spirit hovering.

Harvesting the flowers is a painful job since it's hard to avoid getting stabbed by the leaves' sharp points. The flowers are okay raw, but they make my throat itch. Cooked, they taste a little like green beans. None of this keeps our stomachs from rumbling between meals.

I find a letter Mama started to Mrs. Howard.

We've been reduced to eating weeds, and Owen still won't consider joining the migration west. I don't know how much. . .

That's all I manage to read before I hear her coming up from the cellar. I dart into my room. *How much what? More she can take?*

By fall, we run out of, of all things, wheat for flour, and Mr. Andersen suggests we try grinding tumbleweeds, the only thing we have in abundance. "If cattle can eat Russian thistle," he says, "so can we." It tastes exactly the way I expected: dry, flavorless, and prickly.

We all need shoes. Bare feet in the summer are fine, but winter is coming. When Papa goes to town for the monthly Last Man Club meeting, he comes home with news that Doc Dawson has opened a soup kitchen in the old sanitarium building to help families trying to ride out the drought. He calls it the Dalhart Haven. And Uncle Dick Coon has started a shoe-swap.

"Does he still have his hundred-dollar bill?" I ask.

"Didn't ask him," Papa says. "But he's hired a cobbler to repair the shoes people bring in, no matter the condition, and will let us swap ours for repaired shoes other people leave."

The following week, we gather all the shoes we've outgrown, or with holes worn right through to bare ground in spite of the cardboard patches everyone still calls Hoover leather. Papa won't let us have a meal at the soup kitchen because people without a homestead need it more, but we all come home with shoes that fit.

⁓

A large piece of cardboard blew into the yard during today's dust storm. When the storm ends, I get a ladder from the barn and call Gracie and Owie. Owie comes out of the house, and Gracie comes up the steps from the cellar, where she took cover from the duster. She glances at the front door, then at me, puts a finger to her lips, turns, and pats her thigh. Honey bounds up the steps, then twirls and leaps around the yard.

Owie smiles at me. "Honey'd sleep in Gracie's bed at night if Mama would let her. What's the ladder for?"

"I'll show you. Bring the cardboard."

I lean the ladder against the back of the knoll, climb up, and take the sheet of cardboard from Owie. "Do you remember the hill near our house in Chicago after a snowstorm?"

He shakes his head.

"Well, watch this." I lay the cardboard at the top of the dune, which has buried the roof of the dugout, lie on it, launch myself, and fly, screaming, out into the yard.

I hear Gracie, shout, "Me, next," then "Not you, Honey."

I turn and see Gracie on the ladder, pushing against Honey's forehead with her foot to keep the calf from following her onto the roof.

39

When Mr. Andersen took sick, I offered to bring him his meals every day. Now I've got whatever he has. Breathing is hard enough with all the dust in the air, but I have a fever, itchy eyes, and a dry, hacking cough that makes my throat burn.

On Sunday, the family goes to church and leaves me home to rest. I'm in bed when I hear voices. At first, I think I've been asleep and the family is already back, but these are male voices, and they're whispering. Every nerve in my body tingles.

My bedsprings squeak as I get up and creep to the window to listen. Nothing.

I decide it's my imagination and I'm jumpy because the number of hobos stopping by has grown. I'm about to crawl back into bed when I hear the outside door to the cellar open.

On tiptoe, I run to the kitchen, and put my ear to the inside cellar door. I hear the stairs creak and the raspy whispers of two men. There's no lock on this door. If they've a mind to, they can come right up into the house.

"Ain't much here," one says.

"Beggars can't be choosey." The other laughs.

I begin to tremble. I can't let them steal the last of our food.

Mr. Andersen's in the dugout, but if his door is closed, he won't hear me shout. Even if it's open, he's gotten deaf as a fence post. I'm afraid to move. If those men hear me walking across the floor over their heads, they may grab as much as they can carry and make a run for it. We can't afford to lose a single jar.

Nowadays, Papa keeps his 30-30 rifle by the front door. The shells are an arm's length away in a drawer in the cupboard. I know how to load and fire it. Papa taught Owie, and I insisted on learning, too.

I hear the clink of glass jars below. If I'm going to move, it has to be while they're making noise enough to cover the sound of me crossing the room. I slide the drawer open, slip my hand inside, and get two shells from the box. When I hear the rattle of jars again, I tiptoe across the room, pick up the rifle, and open the front door. The hinge whines.

"Shh," one voice says.

I freeze.

There's only silence, though I swear my heart sounds like a herd of buffalo in my ears. Somewhere outside a chicken squawks and a barnyard squabble erupts.

"It's them chickens," the other says.

"Quit pickin' and choosin'. Take 'em all."

I load the rifle and keep out of sight behind the screen door. The cellar door is lying open. I wait. I don't want them to see me before they're out of the cellar. If I startle them, they might drop and break the jars.

The first man's head appears. My heart ricochets in my chest. He looks around but can't see me behind the screen. He signals all clear and steps out into the sunlight. He's got a duffel bag slung over his shoulder.

I wait for his partner.

"Let's go," says the one with the duffel bag.

The second is a younger man. He's carrying our last bag of rice. "Wait." He closes the cellar door, and grins. "Don't want 'em figuring out they've been robbed too quick."

I'm shaking, as much in anger as fear. I shove open the screen door and step onto the porch. "Put our food down."

They freeze then turn to look at me. The young one smiles. "Ain't you just a speck of a girl."

"Down!" I motion toward the ground with the rifle barrel.

"She ain't gonna shoot us," the older one sneers. He adjusts his grip on the duffle bag.

I remember how, when I first shot the rifle, the kick knocked me off my feet and left a big, black bruise. I point the rifle at the ground near their feet, and pull the trigger.

Boom.

My ears ring and the recoil punches me hard in the shoulder, but I stay on my feet. In the barn, Dan whinnies. The bags are on the ground and both men have their hands up. I take aim again.

"We're hungry," the young one whines.

"We're all hungry, but we're not lowdown enough to steal food from others."

"Let us have a jar or two." The old one leans to pick up his bag.

"Take another step and it'll be into the arms of your maker." Mr. Andersen, with his white hair wild from sleep, stands in the doorway of the dugout, with his shotgun aimed at their backs.

They whirl around, see him, turn tail, and run toward the road. They reach the gate just as the buckboard carrying Papa and the family comes up the rise. The two men change direction and run down the road toward Hartley.

Mr. Andersen fires the shotgun over their heads. We look at each other and laugh, which sends us both into coughing fits.

40

On Monday morning, August 20, the day after my sixteenth birthday, I'm in the barn milking Lily. Blue, the skin-and-bones cat that showed up recently, rubs against my leg waiting for his share of the gritty warm milk.

"Nona," Mama screams from the porch. "Hurry."

I jump up, knocking over the milking stool, and run to the barn door. A black duster is rolling in from the northwest. They're always the worst—heavier than the red ones from Oklahoma, or the yellow-brown ones from east Texas. They come at us like a rolling mountain of dirt and dust.

I grab Ben's and Dan's masks off the nails by each stall, then Lily's and Honey's. The masks aren't much protection, but they're better than nothing. I'm latching the barn doors when the blast hits, knocking me to the ground. I drag myself to my feet and swing my arm wildly, trying to find the rope Papa tied to the door handle. My hand hits it and I grab hold.

With my head down and my eyes squeezed shut, I follow the rope, hand over hand, across the yard. Sand blisters my bare legs and arms. It's only about twenty yards to the house, but the wind is so strong it's hard to put one foot in front of the other.

I bump into the porch and let go of the rope. My left hand hits one of the steps. I crawl up and across until my head bangs into the screen door. When I pull the door open, the wind catches it and rips it off its hinges. I hear it hit one of the spindly porch-posts before disappearing into the curtain of blowing dirt.

Mama opens the kitchen door, grabs my arm, pulls me inside, and slams the door behind me.

My hair is caked with sand, but it's my eyes I need to wash out. I feel my way to the stove and rinse the grit off my face in the pail of water we keep covered with a lid. When it's safe to open my eyes, I hurry to help Mama and Gracie stuff wet rags into every place we see dust blowing in like black flour. I put towels along the windowsills and under the front door, then cover our beds with sheets.

No matter how we prepare, the dust seeps in, fills the crawl space between the roof and the ceiling, and sifts down on us. The steady stream of sand pouring from the ceiling forms a pyramid on the kitchen table. The damp sheets Mama hung over the windows turn muddy and sag under the weight.

Katie is in her cradle under the table. Mama has covered her with the newspaper Papa read to us this morning before he and Owie left for town. Mama, Gracie, and I sit at the table with damp tea towels made from flour sacks over our heads, listening to the windows rattle and the wind whistle through every crack and chink. The room grows darker and darker. I get matches from the tin wall holder by the woodstove and light the lamps.

Mama stares up at the stream of sand, and then at me. "I've written my sister in Carthage. Things aren't as bad up there. Maybe we can go spend some time with her. What do you think?"

"Papa, too?"

Mama shakes her head. "He will never agree to leave this godforsaken place."

Katie wakes coughing and begins to cry.

I rock the cradle with my foot. "Where would we get the money to go?"

"You've got a little saved."

A jolt goes through me like I've touched metal. She's found my cream money. When Papa opened the bank account for me, where my saving disappeared along with everyone else's, I remembered Mr. Andersen's warning and never deposited the eleven dollars left from the first couple of sales, or the thirty-one cents I brought from Chicago. It's all still in the tobacco tin with my letters from Kippy, Mamie, and my Amelia Earhart crossing the Atlantic story.

"That money's for—" I don't finish and feel ashamed I've kept it a secret when there are so many things we need. I'm never going to be able to take flying lessons. Even school has become a luxury we can't afford.

Come winter, Owie and Gracie will have to quit because we don't have money for warm clothes. Learning to fly is out of the question.

She glances at Gracie, who's drawing the outline of a house in the sand on the table. "With what you have," she says, "and what we could get for L-I-L-Y and H-O-N-E-Y, we'd have enough."

Gracie looks at me and smiles. "Honey," she says and prints H-O-N-E-Y in the sand. The N and E are backward.

"You're a smart cookie," Mama says, "and it's time for your nap." To me: "Think about it. I don't know how much longer I can stand this." She puts both hands on the table and pushes herself to her feet.

"I'm hungry," Gracie whines.

"You won't feel hungry if you take a nap. I'll wake you for supper after this duster blows through."

Katie's asleep again. When Mama comes back from tucking Gracie in, I remind her Lily isn't ours to sell, and Honey belongs to Gracie.

"Ownership of the livestock doesn't concern me. Getting you children out of here alive does. People are dying, Nona. Think of your sisters."

"What about Papa?"

"If he's that stubborn, we go anyway."

"You'd leave him behind?"

She levels her gaze at me and doesn't answer.

"If he stays, so do I." I stare at her. "And so will Owie."

"It's not up to you."

I'm sixteen. She can't make me go, but I don't say that.

We sit in icy silence after the storm ends, she knitting, me darning socks. I'm not sure how long we go without speaking before Papa bursts into the kitchen with Owie right behind him. They cough clouds of dust.

"Where were you?" Mama says. "I've been frantic."

She hasn't given his whereabouts a single thought. Papa looks at me; I roll my eyes.

"I saw an ad in the paper. We went to town for this." He looks sheepish when he holds up a 500-foot roll of house-sealing tape.

"How much did that cost you?" Always Mama's first question.

"Thirty-five cents."

"That's seven dozen eggs! I hope it will be worth it." Mama stands up and points at Owie. "Go fetch Noel for supper."

I feel Mama watching me as I rinse our plates and slice the loaf of bread we are having with gravy. I avoid looking at her when I go to call Gracie for supper.

When Mama tucked Gracie in for a nap, she covered her with a sheet. When I carry a lamp into our room, the weight of the dirt has outlined Gracie's small body. She looks dead and buried. My heart leaps to my throat. "Gracie?" I tear the sheet away.

She opens her eyes and puts a finger to her lips. "Don't let Mama sell Honey. Promise?" she whispers.

"I promise."

"If she goes to Missouri, we'll stay here and take care of Papa, okay?"

I nod, and marvel that, once again, we children throw our support behind Papa in spite of Mama's suffering. I often wonder why, but have only managed to think it's because, even more than Mama, Papa blames himself. Someone has to be on his side.

41

1935

The second week in January, Miss Earhart flies 2408 miles solo from Hawaii to Oakland, which is somewhere in California. She's the first person, man or woman, to do this. Even though it's now clear flying will never happen for me, I cut out the story and add it to the wall above my bed.

Early the next Sunday, Papa looks up from reading the paper. "There's going to be another war with Germany."

Mama's at the sink, staring out the window, lost in her own thoughts. She sighs. "The world can't be that stupid a second time."

"It doesn't have to be stupid. It only has to be silent. Hindenburg is dead and the German people have let that madman Hitler declare himself supreme ruler." He passes the paper to me and taps the story about Hitler re-arming Germany and introducing a military draft. "Mark my words." Papa says. "It's only a matter of time."

"Umm," Mama says.

I'm more worried about the silent war brewing right here in this house. Mama hasn't mentioned going to her sister's again, but I know that's what she's thinking about when she seems a million miles from us.

Papa's worried, too. He waits for Mama to say something more or turn from the window before he finally gives me a weak smile and gets up. He squeezes my shoulder, takes his hat from the nail by the door, and leaves for the comfort of his ruined land.

In early March, we have twelve straight days of heavy, gritty, black blizzards. According to the newspaper, one came with forty-mile-an-hour winds that blew for a hundred hours. During that one, our house vibrated so hard the tin plates slid off the shelf and clattered to the floor. Papa reached up and pressed his hands against the ceiling beam. I watched, gnawing a callus in my palm, as his arms jackknifed up and down.

Another trapped the children in a Hartley school where they spent the night cold and hungry until their parents dug them out the next day. After that, the schools close.

We kids try to keep up with the cleaning. Mr. Andersen, sick as he is, helps care for the animals. Papa, wearing his disappointment in hump-shoulders and downcast eyes, does the constant patching. Mama holds Katie and rocks. A stranger might see her as the calm eye of the storm, but to us, it feels more like we are dead to her.

In late March, the schools reopen, but Mama refuses to let Gracie go back. She tries to stop Owie, too, but he wants to catch up with me so when the rains return, we can go to high school together. He thinks it's funny that we might start ninth grade at the same time. I don't tell him that Miss Brown says, if I keep up with my studies at home, I can probably test up a grade level or more.

Miss Brown has loaned me some of her old schoolbooks so I can teach Gracie to read and do arithmetic. I'm studying algebra and history on my own—especially the war Papa fought in Germany. The Treaty of Versailles disarmed Germany and now Mr. Hitler is breaking it.

Spring arrives gray as a stillborn calf. It gives us no hope that this year the drought might end. Even the cottonwoods fail to leaf-out, and whatever manages to come up in the garden, in spite of constant watering, survives only to be buried by dust during the next storm. By April first, we've had only nine dust-free days this year.

Mr. Andersen's health worries me. I recovered from my cold, but his has hung on for two months. He says his chest hurts and he can't keep solid food down. He's got a raspy cough and fever but refuses to go to the doctor.

"Quacks, the lot of them."

We've all got one symptom or another—sore throats and coughs so bad it's hard to sleep at night. We either wake ourselves coughing, or wake because someone else coughs. The paper says people all over the Great Plains are coming down with dust pneumonia, and that people up in Boise City, Oklahoma, just fifty miles north of Dalhart, have died from it.

After every storm, Papa, or Owie, shovels the path to the outhouse and clears the dugout doorway so I can bring Mr. Andersen his meals and empty his slop bucket. All he can keep down is broth.

When I come in this morning, his fever is up, and each breath comes out as a whistle followed by a crackling sound like balling paper to start a fire. I wet a rag for his forehead. The dugout reeks of onion. He's been trying to cure himself with onion poultices applied to a foot. I take his left sock off and remove last night's poultice, apply a fresh one, and put his sock back on. He's also smeared a salve of kerosene and lard on his chest and throat. I don't know which smells worse—the mushy onions or the salve.

"I got something for you," he whispers between efforts to breathe.

His blanket has slipped off onto the floor. I cover him with it, and tuck in the sides.

"You still want to learn to fly?"

"That's never going to happen. I need an education first and money for lessons."

"The drouth's bound to end soon." He breathes in shallow, short gasps. "Then you'll go back to school."

I help him sit up and spoon broth into his mouth.

He presses a handkerchief to his lips and swallows, then doubles over and begins to cough. Horrible, deep, chest-crushing coughs. His face turns scarlet with the effort and he jabs a finger at the bucket beside his bed. I hold it near his head so he can spit out phlegm the color of mud.

He falls back and wipes his mouth. "Look over there." His handkerchief has black blood on it. "In that trunk."

I'm staring at the blood.

"Never mind that. Do what I tell you."

I cross the room and open the trunk. Inside are old maps of Alaska, a little book that looks like a record book, a pair of spurs, an old pistol, and two tobacco tins like the one he gave me when I started school. "What am I looking for?"

He doesn't answer. I turn. His eyes are closed. "Mr. Andersen?"

"The tobacco tins," he whispers.

I carry them to his bedside.

"Open 'em."

I put one on the floor by my foot and open the other. There are a few old coins, a small canvas bag with a drawstring, a smaller tobacco pouch, a few arrowheads, his wedding ring, and a well-worn picture of Karlo and Henry. They are standing on top of the dugout. Henry's holding a home-made bow and arrow. A turkey feather sticks out of the headband that has slipped a little and rests on one ear. No wonder Mr. Andersen and Karlo took to Owie. Henry looks enough like him to be his brother. There's another picture, this one of Mr. Andersen, with a full head of black hair and droopy mustache, standing with his hand on a woman's shoulder. She's seated. The top edge of the picture is burned as if he lit a match, then changed his mind. Half the woman's face is gone, too much of it to tell what she looked like. On top of all this is a folded piece of the same pink writing paper he gave me six years ago.

"That." He taps it.

It's one sheet with a few sentences written in a shaky hand: *I leave the contents of these tobacco tins to Winona Williams for her flying lessons. I am of sound mind. Noel Andersen.*

I put my head down and blink back tears. "I don't want—"

"Hush."

"But—"

"The coins date from the Civil War and may be worth something someday." He tries to take a deep breath and winces. "There are gold nuggets in the larger bag and a few twenty-dollar gold pieces." He closes his eyes.

After a bit, I think he's drifted off to sleep, and I start to get up. The side of the bed creaks and he opens his eyes. "What's left of my savings is in the other box. You keep it all. Don't go wasting any of it on seeds or some other trumped-up necessity." He shifts a little and moans.

"Mr. Andersen, I can't keep all of this for myself."

"Yes, you can. Owie will take over the farm and . . ." he pauses to catch his breath. "By the time Gracie and Katie are old enough . . . to know what they want to do with their lives, you'll be able to help them."

"I'm grateful, Mr. Andersen, but—."

He lifts his hand to stop me. "I ain't got nobody but you kids, and you're the strongest of the lot." He tries to take a deep breath but winces. "You're the family rock. Ever since you was a little thing, you've been the one they lean on. When life gets us down, you're the first to bounce back, tough as buffalo grass." He starts to cough. When it eases up, there's more black blood on his kerchief. He lies quiet for a while, eyes closed.

I get so used to the silence with only the whistle of wind blowing across stovepipe and the rattle in his chest that I jump when he starts talking again.

"I'm entrusting what I have left to the person who can take care of the others. If your mother had it, she'd cut and run like my wife did. If I gave it to your father, he'd sink it back into this place to dry up and blow away."

I know he's right. I take his bony hand and press it to my cheek. "Okay."

He smiles at me, bare gummed. His teeth are on the table. "That's my girl."

I layer everything back in the tobacco tin. He hasn't mentioned the tobacco pouch. It feels like there are small stones in the bottom.

"I ain't got long now, so you need to find a place to hide them tins so your folks don't find 'em. I never thought I'd say this, but I rented one of them new safe deposit boxes at the bank, then never got back to town to put this stuff inside. It's in your name and mine. Until I can . . . or if I can't, you do it."

I nod. Tears roll unchecked down my cheeks.

If Mr. Andersen notices, he ignores them. "Take 'em now. Hide 'em in the shed. Nobody'd think to look in there for nothing."

I'm not convinced this is right, but I carry the tobacco tins to the shed. It's dark inside, made more so by the thin streaks of light coming through the many cracks in the walls. What I can see looks pretty much as it did when we lived in the dugout and Mr. Andersen slept here. All of Mama's furniture, except for two lamps, is in our house. We had electricity in Chicago and she's saving these for when we get it here. I see Mr. Andersen's old rope bed, a woodstove, the lister, and some rusting tools all with the handles broken off: rakes, hoes, and shovels. A tall, narrow crate stands in a dim corner. I don't remember seeing it before. I move around in the tight space trying to decide where to hide the tobacco tins. It's not until I'm standing in front of the crate that I realize it's a coffin, though the lid is not attached. It's the only thing in the shed not covered with layers of dust, which is ankle deep on the floor. This is what the sawing and hammering was about before Mr. Andersen got too sick to leave his bed.

I wonder how much Papa knows about Mr. Andersen's preparations. I stand in the middle of the shed, sniffling, and decide there's no good hiding place for the tobacco tins except inside the woodstove. I open the door and start to put them inside, but my curiosity about the tobacco pouch gets the best of me. I take it out, untie the drawstring, and empty Mr. Andersen's teeth into my hand. Each one has a gold filling.

What should make me cringe, instead breaks my heart.

I come in from hiding the tobacco tins in the shed to find Owie and Papa greasing their boots. "How's he doing?" Papa says.

I shake my head. "Not good. Maybe you could get Doc Dawson to come out. Mr. Andersen at least likes him."

"Maybe." Papa glances at Mama.

They've been arguing. I can tell by the set of my mother's jaw.

I unwrap the old onion poultice, add it to the bucket we keep for vegetable scraps to compost, and carry the cloth it was wrapped in to the washbasin.

"How much did you give?" Mama says.

"To what?" I say.

Papa doesn't get a chance to answer.

"Those Last Man Club fools have hired a rainmaker," Mama says.

I swallow my urge to laugh by turning to scrub away the onion smell. "Really?" I try to sound neutral.

"So, how much?"

"A dollar or two." Papa slaps more grease on the boot he's holding. "His name is Tex Thornton and he's had good success up in Kansas."

"Who says so? Him?" Mama doesn't wait for Papa to answer. "How much are they paying him?"

"Three hundred, initially, but he needed a little more to buy enough TNT and solidified nitroglycerin to reach the clouds."

She puts her hands on her hips. "How much more?"

"Another two hundred, I think."

"Five hundred dollars! Jesus, Mary, and Joseph. You're all crazy."

"I can't expect to reap the benefit without contributing."

"You bought yourself a two-dollar share of a pipe dream."

I'm sure Mama is right, but it doesn't do any good to scold Papa. She's a pessimist and he's a dreamer. She should know that by now.

"How's it supposed to work?" I ask.

"A rainmaker seeds clouds by blasting them with silver iodide crystals. That changes the cloud's structure to produce rain."

"We're gonna learn about the Silver War when I go back to school," Gracie says.

I burst out laughing, so does Owie, then Papa. Mama at least smiles.

Later that evening, when I take Mr. Andersen his supper, I tell him about the rainmaker. "Fools," he says.

"You don't think it will work?"

"Hell, no. We ain't had a rain cloud pass over in four years. Can't just fire away at any old cloud."

Two days later, Mr. Andersen thinks he broke a rib coughing and is in enough pain that he finally agrees to see a doctor.

The main road to Dalhart is kept passable by dragging tractor tires up and down it to flatten the dunes. Our road is a different story. While Papa digs the car out of the sand, Owie saddles Ben and ties two long ropes to the saddle horn. The other ends are tied around the railroad tie he and Ben will drag down our road to smooth and even the dunes.

In case there's a duster while they are gone, Papa hooks the chain to the rear bumper of the car. This will keep the static electricity inside the storm from shorting out the engine.

While they are getting ready, I go to see if Mr. Andersen needs help dressing.

He shoos me.

But he can't manage. In the end, he goes in his long johns, a work shirt, which I button for him, and a buffalo hide robe. He leans on me as we walk to the car. Before I help him into the front seat, he grips the roof of the car and looks around at the farm, now buried by drifting sand.

"I never thought the place would end like this. Or me either."

"You'll be home in no time." I say.

He pats my cheek and smiles. "You have greatness in you, Nona. Don't forget that. And don't let anybody talk you out of your dream."

I hug him—carefully.

"Bye Mr. Noel," Gracie calls from the porch. Her bottom lip is quivering.

He presses his bandana to his eyes, and then, holding onto the car door, lowers himself onto the front seat. I lift in each thin leg and kiss his cheek. Mama, Katie, Gracie, and I stand on the porch to watch them drive out the gate. Mr. Andersen turns to look at us and raises a hand. Tears stream down my face. I don't think he's coming back.

42

It's after dark when we see Papa's headlights coming along the road. We run out to meet him. He's alone.

"Well?" Mama says as he comes up the steps.

"It's dust pneumonia all right, and he has three broken ribs."

We follow him into the house.

"But he's going to be okay," Owie says like a statement of fact.

I watch Papa's face. He never makes eye contact when he fibs. He walks to the sink and takes a glass from the drain board. "Sure he will." He stares out the window for a moment and puts the glass back.

The next day starts out depressingly sunny. A little before noon, I'm in the kitchen fixing bean sandwiches for our lunches. I hear a plopping sound on the roof and glance out the window. It takes me a minute to realize those little explosive puffs of dust are caused by big raindrops hitting the ground. I shout for everyone to come look and run outside.

The rain doesn't last long, but it renews our hopes that the drought may be over soon. At lunch, Gracie says, "Did the rainmaker do it?"

"Who knows." Papa pats her cheek.

"Humph." Mama stares across the table at Papa.

I wish, just once in a while, she would let Papa be.

When Papa took Mr. Andersen to the hospital yesterday, he saw a notice about a meeting at the Dalhart Courthouse this afternoon. Some of the farmers want to ask Mr. Bennett, the Secretary of the Interior, to come to Dalhart to talk about ideas he has to stop the soil from becoming airborne. According to the paper, Mr. Bennett thinks contour planting is the answer. We don't know what that means, but I talk Papa into taking me along. I want to see Mr. Andersen and go to the bank.

Papa drops me off in front of the hospital, where I wait just inside the door until he drives away, then cross the street to the bank. I want to be able to tell Mr. Andersen that I did what he asked.

I have to wait on a bench for the manager to take me to the vault. When he comes, it's Mr. Ferguson, the man our teacher, Miss Brown, is sweet on.

We shake hands. "I've been expecting you. How's Noel feeling?"

"He's got dust pneumonia. I'm on my way to see him, but figured I'd come here first so I can tell him."

"Good. I need you to fill out a signature card, so we have that on record, then I'll take you to the vault."

He leads me to a desk where he opens a cabinet drawer and thumbs through a row of cards until he finds the one Mr. Andersen signed. It has my name on it, too. I sign it, feeling grown up and sad at the same time.

After I sign, he gives me the key to box number 514 and takes me to the vault. It takes his key and mine to open the door in a wall of little numbered doors. Inside is a rectangular metal box. I have the contents of the tobacco tins in a small duffel bag along with a clean shirt and pants for Mr. Andersen.

Mr. Ferguson carries the metal box to a shelf in the vault and leaves me alone while I empty the bag. I don't know how many gold nuggets there are, and I don't bother to open the bag and count them. There are thirteen gold-filled teeth in the pouch. I counted them before. There's a hundred and seventy-four dollars in paper money, five twenty-dollar gold coins, and a bunch of old coins from last century. One is not American. I pick it out. It's an 1875 2 Kroner coin from Denmark. That's the year Mr. Andersen told me he left Denmark to try to find a cousin in America. He was twelve and an orphan. He never did find the cousin and ended up a cowboy in Texas. I slip the coin in my pocket, put everything else in the box with his will on top, and close the lid.

At the hospital, I ask for directions to what Papa said they are calling the dust ward. I find it on the second floor and I ask the first nurse I see where to find Noel Andersen. She goes to a desk and looks through charts until she finds his. She reads it, then looks at me. "Are you a relative?"

"Not exactly."

"What does that mean?"

"We're not blood kin, but he's a part of our family. We're all he's got."

She puts a hand on my shoulder. "I'm sorry, but Mr. Andersen passed away."

"He's—" I can't get the word 'dead' out.

She pats my shoulder. "Will your family claim his body and see to his burial?"

"When?"

"Soon."

"No, when did he. . . die?"

"An hour ago."

I was at the bank. He died alone while I was across the street. Images of him flood my mind: coming down the path from the outhouse that first day, giving Owie Henry's wagon, showing us how to make wallpaper paste out of flour and water, showing Gracie how to bottle-feed Honey, and yesterday, only yesterday, waving goodbye. I put my face in my hands and sob.

The nurse puts her arms around me. "Wasn't he lucky to be so loved."

My crying ends with a case of hiccups. She gives me a glass of water and asks again if we'll see to his burial.

I nod. "Papa's at the meeting at the courthouse. I'll go get him."

I feel gutted as walk up Denrock to the courthouse and climb the steps. Inside, I hear raised voices coming from one of the meeting rooms. Eyes raw from crying, I sit on the bench in the hallway, listen to the clock tick, and wait for Papa.

He's with a group of men who exit the meeting room, still arguing. I stand. "Papa."

He glances at me and he knows. He pulls me into his arms and whispers, "I'm sorry," which brings more tears.

Mama sews a shroud from an old sheet while we wait for the undertaker to bring Mr. Andersen's body to the farm. Papa insists we wait inside while he and the undertaker lay him in his coffin and hammer down the lid. I stand at the screen to watch them load the coffin in our wagon. I hear the undertaker ask where we'll bury him, since the ground is either exposed right down to the solid-as concrete hardpan or covered with sand dunes that will be picked up and blown somewhere else with the next storm.

I don't need to hear Papa's answer. I know.

We bury him between Karlo and Henry under the cottonwoods, where the trees will give his grave some protection against dust storms. Papa makes a nice cross for his grave and a new one for Henry's.

We're quiet that night at supper. Out of habit, Gracie puts a plate on the table for Mr. Andersen. We don't take it away. After we eat, Papa goes out onto the porch and stands looking across the rolling dunes. I watch him through the screen as I wash dishes and Gracie dries. It's hard to believe. Five years ago, Papa stood waist deep in golden wheat, holding baby Gracie in the crook of his arm. His free arm swept the horizon, and he smiled down at her. He was sharing his dream come true with our newest addition. I remember her eyes fixed on his face, hearing her giggly laugh, and wishing with all my heart that it would be all he hoped for and more.

When we finish the dishes, I carry the water to the garden. Papa's in the rocking chair, his head back, eyes closed. "All this is ours now." His voice is flat and he speaks without opening his eyes.

I put my hand on his shoulder. "It will be okay, Papa."

He nods, but when I come back from pouring the dish water on the garden, he has his head in his hands.

"Are you asleep?" Gracie says from her bed.

It's dark and for a change there's no wind. "No."

"Is Mr. Noel in heaven yet?"

"I'm sure he is."

"Miss Brown told us that when someone dies, they go to heaven as a shooting star."

"I like that."

"Could we go outside and watch Mr. Noel go?"

"It's pretty late, Gracie. He might have already gone."

"Can we just go see?"

"I guess but be real quiet so we don't wake anyone."

Outside, off in the distance, I hear coyotes yipping and remember our first night here, listening to Mr. Andersen yip back at them.

The windmill stands gaunt and dark against the sky. Gracie takes my hand and leads me toward the barn. The horses nicker when we come in. Honey scrambles to her feet and bawls at Gracie.

We climb the ladder to the hayloft and open the doors. It's a lovely night. I pull a haybale over and we settle side by side with our backs against it to watch the sky. I always find myself wishing the same thing when I'm in the loft—to spread my arms, drift out the doors, soar across the devastated fields, and over the tops of the cottonwoods headed in any direction away from here.

My eyelids are heavy and I must have dozed off, because I start awake when Gracie speaks. "There he goes, Nona. There he goes. Did you see him?"

I take my sister's hand. "I sure did, sweetheart."

Of the lies we've told ourselves and each other for all these years, this is the sweetest.

43

It's hard to remember a day since we moved here that sun-up hasn't arrived through a fog of dust. But, today, April 14, Gracie's sixth birthday, dawns clear as glass and windless—the prettiest day any of us can remember. The ruined landscape may look like the pictures I've seen of the Great War battlefields, but the air is clean and sweet. None of us can stop grinning.

I pull the sheets from the windows and off the beds and add them to the pile of linens on the porch to be laundered. While Mama washes the grime off the dishes, Grace sweeps, and I do the wash. Gracie likes working the wringer, so I stand by to keep the sheets from folding over on themselves onto the porch floor. I carry them, the pillowcases, and dishtowels, to the clothesline to dry in the lovely warm breeze.

What we want more than anything is to scrub ourselves as clean as this morning's air. Since we no longer waste wood to heat bath water, Papa puts the tin tub behind the wagon for some privacy and covers it with a sheet of black tar paper to let the sun warm the water. It's deliciously hot when Katie and Gracie—the least grimy of us—go first. It's still comfortably warm when I follow. Out of habit and hope, Owie helps me carry the water to the garden full of plants killed by static electricity, then we pump and carry clean water for Mama's, Papa's, and Owie's turns.

With most of the chores done, and all of us as clean as possible, we gather around the table to watch Gracie open her presents. Papa gives her a dime for candy next trip to town, and a new pair of used shoes.

For years now, Mama has made our clothes—including Papa's work shirts—out of old flour sacks that she washed and boiled until the company's name faded away, but when Gracie opens her present from Mama, I recognize it as one of my old Chicago school dresses, made over to fit my little sister. Long ago, the kitchen window curtains, ruined by Mama's constant attempts to keep them clean, disintegrated. But she must have salvaged pieces of them because the dress has a lace-curtain collar. I've never been interested in clothes, but even I see the effort that went into remaking that old dress so it looks store-bought.

I grin at Owie when our turn comes. He pulls a package wrapped in newspaper from behind his back. When Gracie opens it, a hand-woven rope halter for Honey slides out and drops on the floor. I wove one of my old pink hair ribbons into the noseband. Gracie hugs me then her brother, which makes him blush.

Later in the day, Mama, Papa and Katie are driving out to the cemetery for the funeral of a neighbor who also died of dust pneumonia. Gracie gets to stay home because she shouldn't have to see someone buried on her birthday. I don't have to go because she can't stay alone. We haven't left the farm unattended since those men tried to steal our food. Owie's going to a rabbit roundup because we need the meat.

Gracie and I stand on the porch and wave. The chain dragging from the bumper kicks up a rooster-tail of dust that we can see rising above the road long after we lose sight of the car.

Honey, wearing her new halter, romps in the yard. She's playing with a tumbleweed. She either butts or kicks it to make it roll, then jumps in front of it and leaps side to side like a game of tag. When it quits rolling, she tosses it with her nose, and starts the game all over again.

Gracie's beside me on the porch steps, watching Honey and laughing. We both look up when a small flock of screeching birds flies over, headed south. It's spring, they should be headed north. I cup my hands around my mouth and shout, "You're going in the wrong direction."

Gracie giggles.

Another flock, larger and noisier, races by. Chill bumps spread up my arms. Our house faces south. I walk to the side of the porch and look north. The sky is clear and blue for as far as I can see.

I glance at her and smile. "Let's get to work."

We leave Honey trying to entice a chicken to play and go inside to gather the clothes that need washing. I scrape lye into water, wash and rinse, then feed the clothes into the wringer before letting Gracie turn the handle.

"Bunnies." Gracie giggles.

I look where she's pointing. Dozens of rabbits race across the yard. So many they frighten Honey. She runs up the porch steps and would have bolted right through the screen door if it hadn't still been propped open when I carried in water for the wash tub.

We laugh, but I walk to the side of the porch and look north again. Still lovely.

I pile the damp clothes in the basket and carry it out to a line that stretches from the east side of outhouse to the shed. The sheets are dry. I bury my nose in one and breath in the sunshine smell. I take them down, fold them, and call Gracie to carry them into the house. Birds and swarms of insects flow overhead. More rabbits race in the same direction. Something's wrong. I feel it in the pit of my stomach.

"Nona." Gracie's voice is so small, I think it's a trick of my mind.

I turn. She's standing in the yard looking up at the windmill. Its blades glow with an eerie blue light and beyond it, along the single row of barbed wire fencing still showing above the dunes, every spike glows.

I run to the side of house and look north. A black duster, wider and higher than any I've ever seen, spans the horizon. The cloud rises thousands of feet and rolls like a tornado on its side.

Gracie is trying to drag Honey into the shed.

"Get to dugout," I scream.

Chickens race for cover. I watch in horror as the rooster flies up and lands on the metal tractor seat. There's a zap and a spark of electricity. He falls dead.

The clean shirts flutter in the breeze and the afternoon sun bathes Gracie in a golden light. I scream. "Let her go. Get to the dugout." Seconds later, the temperature plummets, the duster swallows the light, and bowls me over.

"Nona," Gracie screams.

44

It's as if I've gone blind. A moment earlier there was the glow of the afternoon sun with Gracie trying to drag Honey through the door to the shed, then total darkness. Each panicky breath I take is full of dirt and dust. I swing an arm above my head, searching for the clothesline, snatch a shirt loose, and hold it over my nose.

The wind roars like a freight train. "Gracie," I shriek.

"Help me, Nona." Her voice is to my left.

"Get on the ground," I shout.

"I am," she wails.

I try to orient myself. She and Honey were only feet away. I follow the clothesline to the side of the shed and feel my way to the door.

"Where are you?"

"Here." She chokes.

"Keep talking." I wave my free hand from side to side until I find her.

"I can't breathe."

I give her the shirt. "Cover your face." I find her shoulder, follow her arm to her hand, and pull her to her feet.

"Honey ran off."

"We'll find her when this is over." Even though she's right beside me, we have to shout to be heard over the freezing wind.

With my free hand I find the wall of the shed, then feel along it for the door handle. I pull as hard as I can but can't get it open against the wind. From the barn, I hear Dan's screams and his hooves pounding the wall of his stall. Lily bawls, too. The barn doors were wide open and they face north. There's nothing I can do for them. I can only try to save myself and Gracie.

"Get on my back and hold on." I turn, bend my knees, and help boost her. "Keep your face against my shoulder and breathe only when you have to."

The distance between the shed and the east side of the knoll is only about five feet. I run straight across. The door to the dugout faces north, too, and will already be blocked by sand. I turn left instead. The wind pushes me along until it slams us into the outhouse. I turn right. On the leeside of the hill, sand and dust blow over the knoll and down on our heads. I keep going.

The dugout's only window is on the west side of the hill. I know we've come out from behind the knoll when the wind hits us broadside, nearly toppling me. "Hold your breath and hang on." I make the turn. The blast of black wind stops me in my tracks. It takes all my strength to move us forward. I swing my right hand above my head searching for the edge of the roof. I find it and feel beneath the eave for the window.

Every time I take a breath, I am racked with coughs. When I reach the end of the roof without finding the window, terror nearly overwhelms me. I'm trying to take in air in short little gasps, and I feel dizzy. If I don't find the window, or pass out before I do, we'll be buried alive.

"We're almost there," I croak.

I start back along the roof line. This time my hand finds the glass window. I tug on it, but there's too much sand built up along the bottom. It doesn't budge. I gulp the gritty air and dig like a dog to find the handle. If it's been latched on the inside, we're dead. I yank as hard as I can. The window creaks open.

Six years ago, I was a skinny girl of eleven when Papa shoved me through this window after a snowstorm. Not anymore. I take Gracie's hands and fit them over the windowsill and slip out from under her. "Pull yourself through, Gracie. Hurry." She's crying, but does it until she's dangling down the wall on the inside with me holding her ankles. I work my head and arms in and lower her until her hands touch the ground. She flops onto the floor.

With the window open, dust swirls into the already black interior. I work one shoulder in, then the other until I'm wedged like a cork in a bottle. My hands flail in the darkness trying to find something to grab to pull the rest of me through.

Gracie is coughing and crying somewhere in the pitch-black room.

"Gracie. I need you to help me."

"I can't see you." She sneezes.

"I'm going to keep talking until you find me, then I want you to take my hands and pull as hard as you can. I'm stuck in the window. Find the wall and swing your arms above your head."

"Which wall?"

"Follow the sound of my voice."

Her foot hits something metal, probably the woodstove, and she cries out.

"Keep coming. I'm right here."

Her hand hits my wrist. "That's it. Grab hold. Here's my other hand. Now hold tight and pull."

I don't budge at first, and I can feel the wooden frame scraping my chest. A coughing spell makes Gracie lose her grip on my wrists. I press my hands to the wall under the window and push as hard as I can. I ignore the burning pain as I leave a layer of skin on the sill, and I keep pushing until I'm dangling by my waist inside the room. I swing my arms wildly until my hand hits the stove. I grab the edge, pull, and hit the floor. I jump up, feel for the window, close, and latch it.

"Gracie?"

"Here I am."

"We're okay now."

"I can't breathe, Nona."

"Where's the shirt?"

"I don't know."

"Breathe through the hem of your dress. I'll try to find matches and light the lamp."

"Okay." She sniffles.

Not an ounce of light gets in. I feel my way across the room, bump the table, and find the kerosene lamp. I run my hands over the wooden top, hoping Mr. Andersen left matches nearby. There's nothing here except the lamp. I turn and feel for the woodstove. There used to be matches in a holder attached to the wall to the right of the stove pipe. I find the window again and move down the wall and to the left until I hit the metal container. It still has matches. I take one and strike it on the stove top. It flares and casts a yellow-gray circle of light. I shield it and carry it to the lamp, remove the chimney, and light the wick.

"There, that's better."

Gracie runs at me from a corner of the room, grabs me around the waist, and sobs against my stomach.

"It's okay, honey. We'll be fine in here until the storm ends. Then Papa will come for us." I hold her at arm's length. Her face is black except where her tears cut muddy tracks. She coughs and dust puffs out of her mouth like cigar smoke.

"You're bleeding." She touches my chest.

I look down. The front of my dress is shredded. My camisole is bloody and sticks to a raw layer of exposed skin.

"Does it hurt?"

"A little." It hurts like the devil.

Outside the wind howls. For a while it batters the door. When the door stops rattling, I know we're sealed inside.

45

We fall asleep on Mr. Andersen's old bed. When I wake, the lamp's gone out. I get up and feel my way to the table, turn the dial to raise the wick, and relight the lamp. There is no way to know how many hours have passed.

"My eyes hurt." Gracie's sitting up with her fists pressed to her eye sockets.

"Don't rub them." I go to the water pitcher and lift the cloth covering it. There's still water in it even though Papa "cleaned up" in here after Mr. Andersen died. In reality, he went through things searching for Mr. Andersen's bankroll. I remember Mama looking up expectantly when he came in from the dugout.

Papa shook his head. "Poor bugger, didn't have a dime left."

Mama closed her eyes and sighed before turning back to the stove.

It took all my will not to tell them the truth, or at least remind them that he left us this farm, but I kept my eyes on the sock I was darning.

Since there's water in the pitcher, Papa must not have done too much cleaning. I pour a little in the basin and carry it to the bed. "Wash your eyes out with this."

"When's Papa coming home?"

"Soon." I try not to think about what's happened to our parents and Owie.

"How soon?"

I shake my head. "I don't know."

"I'm hungry."

"I am, too."

"I'm cold."

"I'll build us a fire. How would that be?" I get up.

The air has cleared in the room, but as I walk to the stove every step raises a small plume of dust. I press my ear to the stove pipe, but don't hear the wind or anything else. Dust seeps in where the stove's chimney pipe punctures the dugout's ceiling. I wonder if the sand's coming in over the top of the pipe or just around the sides. I don't want to light a fire and have the dugout fill with smoke. I tap it and hear the dull thud of a chimney full of sand.

The lamp flame starts to flicker. I shake it. There's no slosh. Cleaning out the stove will have to wait. We need light. I carry the lamp to the shelves to search for a can of kerosene. I find it on the floor behind the stove. There isn't much left, but hopefully it will last until Papa can find us and dig us out. I don't let my mind consider they might be dead, or the consequences for Gracie and me if they are.

After pouring what's left of the kerosene into the base of the lamp, I carry it to the woodstove and carefully lift one of the burners. The stove is filled to the brim with sand.

"I'm still cold, Nona."

"I know, honey, but I have to clean the stove out first. Get under the blanket."

"I am under the blanket."

"Curl into a ball. That will help."

I carry the ash can to the stove and use the little scoop to shovel out sand the consistency of black flour. I lower a shovelful at a time into the ash pail, moving slowly so the dust won't bloom into the air. I keep scooping with a wet hankie over my nose and mouth, but for every scoop I take out, sand from the stove pipe fills the gap and puffs up into my face. If a dune is covering the top of the pipe, I may be letting all the sand into the dugout.

Gracie's asleep by the time I fill the second bucket. I look for another place to empty it. I dumped the first one in the corner and it puffed dust into the air. I decide under the bed is safest. The blood that soaked my camisole has dried. The strain of lifting and shifting the bed tears the fabric loose from my chest like ripping off a scab. Gingerly, I pour the contents of the second bucket on the floor, grit my teeth against the pain, and shift the bed back without waking Gracie.

Digging out the dirt is like dating a tree by its rings. There's dust, then sand, then a foot of dust, then more sand, some yellow, some reddish-brown, some black. I have no way of knowing if the stove pipe is refilling from the top as I dig from the bottom. After the fifth bucket,

I began to believe that's exactly what's happening. I quit digging, sit cross-legged on the floor and rest with my cheek against the edge of the stove. Something tickles my forehead. I think spider and swat at it before realizing it's air moving wisps of my hair. I reach into the stove and feel cool air on my hand. A moment later I hear the creak of the windmill blades turning.

I scramble to my feet looking for something to burn, a rag, anything. There are plenty of cow chips and a small bit of kindling, but no paper to start a fire—except what's on the walls. I pull off a few sheets, wad them up, add kindling, and strike a match. The smoke is sucked up the chimney and the little fire blazes. I add cow patties. At least Papa, when he gets home, will know where we are. I blow out the lamp to save kerosene, crawl into bed and spoon myself around Gracie.

46

I bolt upright, heart pounding. Did I hear Papa calling for us, or was I dreaming? "Gracie?"

"I'm here."

Enough light comes through the filthy window to let me see Gracie wave from the corner where she's using the chamber pot. The fact it's light outside means at least a full day has passed.

"Did you hear Papa?"

She shakes her head, and I see her bottom lip start to quiver.

"Don't cry."

"I need to."

"Then I guess you'd better go ahead."

She covers her eyes with an arm, but I see her smile.

I try to get out of bed but every muscle in my body aches like I've gone ten rounds with Joe Louis, Papa's favorite boxer. My skinned chest hurts worse than it did yesterday. I lie back and close my eyes.

Gracie touches my shoulder. "I'm hungry, Nona. When's Papa coming?"

"Soon."

"That's what you said last time."

I take her hand. "Help me up."

The fire in the stove has died to embers. Another indication that hours have passed. Once again, I try not to think about what's happened to the rest of our family. I tear more sheets of newsprint from the walls, re-kindle the fire, and add cow patties.

"How long have we been in here?"

"I don't know. Not too long."

"Seems long. Do you think Papa's looking for us?"

"When he gets home," I say, "the smoke from the chimney will let him know where we are."

I cross the room to inspect the shelves and open a drawer in the cupboard. Inside is a can with the label missing. Its sides are caked with crusty, hard chunks of something the color of Texas dust. I pick at it. Dough. Mr. Andersen must have used this to roll out his sourdough. The can's not swollen, so I search the other drawer for an opener and take a pot from a nail in the beam.

Nothing but a hard rain could smell better than those beans heating on the woodstove.

The bit of light from the window glows red. The sun is setting. I add cow patties to the fire, and crawl back into bed next to Gracie. We both fall asleep. I'm not sure what wakes me, but when I open my eyes, Papa is standing over us. He sinks to his knees beside the bed and wraps us in sweaty, sand-covered arms.

"Is everyone okay?" I ask.

"Your mom and Katie are safe."

"And Owie?"

"I don't know." He shakes his head. "I—" He takes a deep breath. "I don't know where he is."

"He'll be okay, Papa. I'm sure of it."

"Me, too." He lifts Gracie, who's still asleep, puts his other arm around me, and we walk out of the dugout into the bright, noonday light.

Papa sees the dried blood on my camisole. "What happened?"

I smile. "The dugout window is the same size it was when I was eleven."

Gracie opens her eyes. "Hi Papa." She yawns, then her eyes widen. She clamps his face in her hands. "Have you seen Honey?"

He kisses her cheek. "No. It's you I was looking for. We'll find her after we eat."

"What day is it?" I ask.

"April sixteenth."

The storm was two days ago.

The door to the dugout was buried to the roof. Sand, in mounds taller than I am, rise on either side of the entrance. Outside, the entire landscape has changed again. The back of the house is buried to the roof and the dune wraps down both sides like a muffler. At the front, on the side away from the storm, the cellar door and the porch steps are still visible. The barn doors must have blown shut because a dune blocks the entrance. I hope this means Dan and Lily survived. I shush any thoughts of Honey.

"When did you get home?"

"About three hours ago. Seeing that smoke coming from the chimney was the happiest moment of my life. I've been digging ever since." He tightens his arm around my shoulders.

"Honey ran away." Gracie's got Papa's neck in choke hold, her legs knotted around his waist, and her head on his shoulder.

"We'll find her." He pats her back.

We're making our way through the black dirt toward the house. "Where were you when the duster hit?"

"A couple miles south of town. After the funeral, we went in to buy more kerosene. When the news came that a big one was coming, we left to try to get back before it hit. The static electricity shorted out the engine. Your mother, Katie, and I were trapped in the car the entire time."

I think of the dead man Owie and I found. "How'd you get out?"

"After it ended, I rolled down a rear window and tunneled out through the sand."

"Where are they?"

"Your mother's at the hospital with the baby. Katie was having trouble breathing, so we walked back to town."

"And then you walked the whole twelve miles home?"

"Guess I did." We climb the porch steps.

"Is Katie okay?"

"I hope so."

We reach the screen door, stop and stare. The weather on Gracie's birthday started out so perfect, we'd opened all the windows. The scene in the kitchen is chilling.

Papa puts Gracie down and opens the door. The center portion of the ceiling has collapsed and dumped its load of sand onto the kitchen table, forming a peaked dune chest-high on Papa. The perimeter of the room is mostly ankle deep. Papa goes around, past the door to the cellar, and tries to open the door to Gracie's and my room. It opens enough to see the dirt in there is also ankle deep. He continues to his and Mama's room, which faces north, the direction the duster came from. He puts his shoulder against it, but it doesn't budge. The dirt inside is that deep.

Papa looks at me over his shoulder. "This will finish your mother."

I was thinking the same thing. "Maybe she and Katie should go to Carthage for a while. Until we get this cleaned up."

Papa's lips compress, before nodding in agreement.

Gracie's at the screen. "I'm going to look for Honey."

"No, you're not." Papa manages to get to the door, kicks it open, and catches her around the waist before she gets past the bottom step. "I'll look for Honey. You help Nona find something to eat and take it to the dugout. We're going to get some food in our bellies before we start cleaning. Got it?"

"Yes, Papa." Gracie says.

Papa goes down to the cellar from the kitchen. A few minutes later, he pushes up on the outside cellar door and comes up carrying the ladder. He crosses the yard, and places it against the side of the barn. From the behind the screen, Gracie and I watch him climb up and go in through the hay doors. He disappears and reappears quickly. "I think they're alive. Dan may be in the shed. The wall of his stall is broken out."

The path to the shed is blocked, and only the outhouse roof shows above the sand.

"And Lily?" I ask.

"Honey?" Gracie says.

"I don't see either of them." He climbs down and crosses to the dugout for the shovel he left by the door. Each step creates an explosive puff of dust. "Okay, you two." He waves for us to help. "There's another shovel in the cellar."

When I come up with the second shovel, Gracie is on the porch calling for Honey.

She turns to look at me, her little face streaked with tears. "She's dead, isn't she?"

"I don't know, sweetheart." I hug her.

"Do you think she is?"

I take a breath, trying to decide whether to lie and say no, or tell her the truth. I'm not even sure our brother is alive. "Probably. There was no place for her to hide."

She nods and wipes her nose on her shoulder. "Do animals go to heaven?"

"Sure, they do. What kind of place would it be without the animals we love there, too?"

We're so worried about the animals, that we forget about eating and start digging. It takes Papa an hour to clear a path to the outhouse while I work on reaching the shed door. As we dig, we find the bodies of chickens, beaks open, mouths full of sand. If any did survive, they're probably still tumbling through the air toward Amarillo. I carry their bodies to the wellhouse. We'll clean them later and try to salvage some meat to can.

When I'm finally able to pry open the door to the shed, both Lily and Dan are inside. And they're not alone.

I walk outside. "Gracie."

She's sitting on the top porch step, arms wrapped around her knees.

"Come here." I'm smiling.

She kicks up a dust storm of her own running across the yard. She flies past me and into the shed. Honey's standing on the mound of dirt that covers the woodstove. Lily and Dan are buried to their bellies in sand, but they're alive. They struggle to breathe through the mud caking their nostrils, and their eyes are sealed shut with grit.

"How do you suppose she got in here?" Papa says.

"Gracie was holding the shed door open when the duster hit. Honey must have bolted in and the wind blew the door shut after her. We tried to hide in there, too, but I couldn't pull the door open against the wind."

Papa leads Honey out, and hands her rope to Gracie, who smothers her with kisses.

I pump two pails of water—one for Gracie to clean Honey's face, the other I lug to the shed to wash Dan's and Lily's while Papa digs them out.

I'm at the pump refilling a bucket, when, over the clacking of the windmill blades, and the jet rod rising and falling, I think I hear someone call my name. When I hear it again, my heart flipflops. I turn and see a figure who looks rolled in talc walking a beaten down gray horse over the dune that's drifted to cover the gate.

Chill bumps spread up my arms. It's Owie leading Ben. I plow toward them through the sand, elbows pumping for momentum. When I reach my brother, I throw my arms around his neck. Not everything that could have gone wrong did. Our family survived.

I lift my head off my brother's shoulder when Gracie grabs us both around the waist. Honey presses her clean, wet nose against Ben's.

Owie lifts Gracie in the air and kisses her, leaving dusty lip prints on her cheek.

"Where were you? You look awful."

"You don't look all that great yourself." He pats my hair. It's still full of sand and grit.

"So?"

"I was in the White's barn."

Bam White and his family live a few miles east of Dalhart. We live twelve miles south. Owie and Bam's son, Melton, are friends.

"Must have been a hundred of us at the round-up when we saw it coming." We're walking side by side, leading poor Ben to the water trough. His saddle is still covered in dust, which means Owie walked him all the way home.

"I don't know what happened to the families who arrived in cars. Those of us on horseback tried to outrun it in a dozen different directions. Melt and I were inches ahead of that black cloud when Bam saw us coming and flung open the barn door. We rode in and he slammed it behind us. He'd been headed in to join his family in their cellar. Instead, the three of us rode it out in the barn. Wasn't 'til it ended that his wife knew Bam and Melt were alive." Owie looks at the mountain of sand blocking our barn doors. "Their barn faces north, too. Melt's brothers dug us out."

Papa comes out of the shed, leading Lily and Dan. He sees Owie, bows his head, then bends at the waist and puts his hands on his knees. I take Ben's reins from Owie, who crosses the yard and wraps his arms around Papa. They are the same height. My baby brother is a man.

Back in our ruined kitchen, I pour the sand out of the skillet, put six of the eggs we collected before the storm into it, get some lard from the can by the stove, and carry everything to the dugout. The woodstove is still warm. I add cow patties to get it hot enough to cook the eggs. I send

Gracie to the house for more forks since the two Mr. Andersen had are caked with dried beans. She comes back with forks and her birthday cake from the pie-safe. It's as black as if it's been frosted with coal dust. I put it on the table next to the pan of eggs and hand out the forks. After we eat, Papa slices off the top and the sides of the cake. We sing Happy Birthday to Gracie, then the four of us eat the sand-free center.

47

Gracie's cough is worse. Rather than have her in the house while we start to clean, I give her the task of plucking the dead chickens, which she can do outside in the sunshine.

I start shoveling the sand out of our bedroom while Papa and Owie patch the ceiling in the kitchen. We want it looking as back to normal as possible before we bring Mama and Katie home.

Once the room Gracie and I share is clean, I put her to bed and rub a little lard and kerosene on her chest. When I go in to check on her later, I find Honey asleep on the floor beside her bed.

It takes another full day to clear the house of sand. On the third day after the storm, we take the buckboard out to find the car. Owie and Papa spend hours digging it out and getting the engine clean enough to start. By that time, Gracie's cough is a little better, but Papa and I agree she should see the doctor when we go in to fetch Mama and Katie. Owie leaves us and takes the buckboard home. This time, he'll stay to guard the farm.

There's a room full of coughing people waiting to see Doc Dawson. When we do get in, the news is good. Gracie doesn't have dust pneumonia—not yet—but she mustn't be exposed to another storm without protection. The doctor gives Papa one of the Red Cross gas masks from the box on the floor beside his desk. Papa stares at it for a moment before turning to Gracie, who shakes her head. "No." She covers her face with her hands.

The masks they gave us at school were cloth with straps to tie around your head. This one has leather goggles and an air-purifier.

"Let me." I take it from him and put it on.

Seeing me, Papa closes his eyes.

The doctor puts his hand on Papa's shoulder. "I was there, too."

I know he means the War. The mask looks like the one Papa wore when the Germans lobbed poison gas canisters at our army.

Gracie uncovers her eyes and laughs. "Let me try it." She holds her arms up, and dances impatiently.

I take it off and let Doc Dawson fit it over her little head. She looks like a giant fly, with big glass eyes and a tin-can-sized air filter for a nose. She sees her reflection in one of the organ-display cases, giggles, hunches her shoulders, makes claw-hands, and tiptoes toward me. "Grrr."

It's such a beautiful day, we decide to walk the nine blocks to the four-story hospital. Our moods match the clear blue sky, littered with puffy white clouds. Papa and I laugh at Gracie, who's wearing her gas mask and trying to outrun a cloud-shadow. She skips ahead of it, dodges left, runs around its edge, then pretends to chase it down the sidewalk.

We're directed to a ward with two long rows of beds, each occupied by a hacking, coughing dust pneumonia patient. It takes a while to spot Mama sitting in a rocking chair on the far side of the crowded room. I can't make out her face because of the light coming through the window behind her. One hand rests on Katie's back, who's sleeping peacefully. Papa waves. I think she sees us, but she doesn't wave back. The fingers of her free hand twirl a lock of her gray hair, which cascades like strands of tarnished silver.

I glance at Papa and smile, but the look in his eyes makes my stomach lurch. He drops Gracie's hand, rushes across the room, and kneels in front of Mama.

I follow, dragging Gracie, still happily wearing her gas mask and slapping the foot of each bed we pass. When Gracie sees Mama, she pulls free, runs, and throws her arms around her neck. Mama blinks, but otherwise has no reaction. I take Katie's little hand. It's stone cold. I swallow the scream that fills my throat. Agony etches Papa's face. He puts his big, crusty, brown hand over the top of Mama's, and turns his face to the ceiling, tears streaming. "Sweet Jesus, not our baby."

"What's wrong?" Gracie's voice is muffled by the gas mask. She starts to cry, fogging the glass lens. I pull her off Mama, remove the mask, and hug her tightly.

"What's wrong with everybody?" Gracie's voice is almost inaudible against my shoulder.

Mama suddenly throws her head back and screams. She does it over and over, like a siren. When Papa reaches to hug her, she clutches Katie to her chest, leaps up, knocking over her chair, and runs past us toward the exit.

A nurse tries to catch her arm as she passes. Mama dodges her, but is stopped by a doctor before she gets to the door.

"She's sleeping," Mama pleads. "Don't wake her."

The doctor lifts Katie from Mama's arms as we reach her. "Glenny—" Papa cups the back of her head, and tries to pull her to him.

Mama jerks free. "Don't you touch me!" She hits him in the chest with her fists. "You wouldn't leave. I begged you." She collapses to the floor, sobbing.

I think of Mr. Andersen and his confidence in me as the strong one in the family. I don't think I have it in me to lift us up from this.

At the cemetery two days later, the preacher who presides over Katie's funeral is from a church in Hartley. Our minister packed up and left Dalhart months ago. This man doesn't know us and the words meant to comfort, like God needed our baby more than we did, only make me angrier. He keeps calling her Little Kathryn. Katie hasn't been Kathryn since the day she came home from the hospital.

Gracie tugs my sleeve and whispers, "Who's Kathryn?"

"That was Katie's real name," I whisper back.

Mama stands on one side of the open grave, the rest of us on the other. There is no forgiveness in her eyes. She stares at Papa across the lid of the little casket Papa made from the last of the furniture crates.

The preacher drones on until it's time to bow our heads and pray. My prayer is that they bury her too deep for the wind to find. After that, we each take a fistful of sand and drop it onto the casket. He says, "Dust to dust, ashes to ashes."

I look around as we're leaving this treeless, wind-ravaged place. There are three open holes waiting. Before we get to the car, the gravedigger begins to shovel dirt into Katie's grave. I hear dirt thumping against the box. The thud-thud-thud follows us all the way to the road.

After Katie's funeral, our instinct—Gracie's, Owie's, and mine—is to protect Papa. Even though Mama experienced the loss every mother fears most, it's him we keep watch over. His guilt is eating him up. He's gone from reed thin to skeletal with dark circles under his sad eyes.

Mama never wanted to leave Chicago in the first place. Now her grief over Katie's death has been replaced by undisguised hatred of Papa. She moves through the days silently. She responds if one of us asks her something, but if Papa speaks to her, she doesn't answer. If he tries to touch her, she flinches. I watch him wilt inside his clothes.

On top of everything, a letter comes from Mamie.

Dear Nona, I hope you still live in Dalhart and that your family hasn't been forced to move on like so many others. I was luckier than many of the other orphans I've heard from. The Johnsons treated me kindly from the beginning, but the drought and dusters have taken their toll. Sadly, a few months ago, the bank finally took the farm that had been in Mr. Johnson's family for three generations. It was more than he could stand. The day after the auction, he went out to the barn and hanged himself. Ma Johnson and I are now on our own without money or a place to live. This Friday, we will join her brother and his family when they leave for California. Some say there is work there; others say the state is overrun with people like us. All we know is we can't stay in Texhoma. I'll try to write again when we get settled. In the meantime, pray for us.

Your friend always, Mamie

48

The papers are calling April 14, Black Sunday. The worst of the worst. It even reached the Gulf of Mexico.

The day after Katie's funeral, Owie and I ride out to look for our bull and the last surviving cow and the little heifer I rescued last spring. We find the bull lying by the fence, blinded by sand, nostrils caked with mud. He's been eating the boards and dies before Papa gets back with his rifle. Papa butchers him, smokes enough meat for us, and sells the rest in town for four cents a pound. With that money, he buys a couple layers and four baby chicks we hope won't turn out to be roosters.

We find the cow and her calf in the ravine, both dead too long to make the meat safe to eat.

We start another garden and I keep it watered even knowing it will be buried by the next dust storm. How we keep going when everything feels pointless, is beyond me.

I never came into the kitchen in the days after Katie's funeral, that my eyes weren't drawn to the cradle. I don't know why, but it comforted me, as if it was only empty because one of us was holding her until her coughing quieted and she was asleep again. Today, I come up the steps with an armload of scavenged kindling and see that Mama has hacked up the cradle and stacked the pieces next to the stove to be burned.

"Why did you do that?" It's almost like Katie died all over again.

Mama turns back to the sink. "We need the wood."

At supper that night, she announces that she's going to Carthage, Missouri, to visit her sister. Gracie shrinks in her chair and sneaks a peek at me. No one speaks. I think we all expect her to say she's taking Gracie with her, but she doesn't say anything more.

I glance at Papa. He's looking at her ring finger. I do, too. Her wedding ring is gone. Even in the hot kitchen, chill bumps spread up my arms. "How long are you going to stay?" I hope my voice doesn't sound suspicious, like I really believe it's just for a visit.

She shrugs.

A week later, at the train station, she hugs each of us, gives Papa a quick kiss near his mouth, and boards without looking back. We stand on the platform in the blazing sun and watch Mama walk the aisle past open seats. When she doesn't take a seat on the platform side of the tracks, Owie turns and walks away. The rest of us stand there anyway, and wave when the train pulls out. Papa watches it the longest.

As if trying to make Mama's departure seem ordinary—like a long-awaited trip to visit relatives—Papa offers us ice cream. When we come around the corner, Uncle Dick Coon is standing on the sidewalk in front of his drugstore. His Desoto Hotel has been boarded up for a couple of years now, and they say he's as broke as the rest of us, except for that famous hundred-dollar bill.

A young family's Model T has run out of gas smack dab in the middle of the street. Like nearly every car that passes through town, it's piled high with their belongings. Their children—four of them—are bare-foot and dirty. The father asks Papa if there's work to be had, anything he can do to get enough money to buy gas and a spare tire. Of course, there isn't. There's nothing to harvest and no more livestock to shoot. Papa's been earning a little money helping to keep the roads passable, and after Katie died, he swallowed his pride and began accepting the government's handout of beans and flour.

The young father turns helplessly to his wife after Papa shakes his head.

"Son." Mr. Coon reaches into the breast pocket of his shirt. "Take this."

People stop in their tracks to watch Uncle Dick hand the young man the hundred-dollar bill.

"Sir?" The man looks at it, then at Mr. Coon. "You can't mean all of it."

"It's yours. Take care of that fine family."

The man shows his wife. She touches the paper bill in awe and bursts into tears. Mr. Coon tips his hat, then holds open the door to his drugstore, and follows us in.

When we settle at the counter, Papa orders us each two scoops of strawberry ice cream. We turn on our stools and raise them in a toast to Uncle Dick, who's at his table in the back dealing cards to his friends.

He looks as happy as I've ever seen him when he smiles back at us. Or maybe he just feels lighter, the way you do when there's nothing left to lose.

The dust storms continue—blowing from the north one day and the south the next. The last week in May, one blows in from New Mexico, where the soil is red. After it's over, Gracie and I —with Honey loping after her like a dog—go out to collect tumbleweeds for kindling. The fence that once separated plowed land from the last of the buffalo grass is buried. We can cross anywhere, but we always walk through the gate. On the ground, where we've crossed a hundred times before, I find an arrowhead. Gooseflesh covers my hot, bare arms. I turn it over in my hand. It's black and sharp. I try to imagine how it came to be here, how many decades since it felled a buffalo. I wonder if it was left for us to find by the ghost of an Indian who's seen what we've done to the prairie. Maybe as reminder that the land will someday be rid of us, and we, too, will be ghosts like the ghost buffalo grazing on ghost grass.

Letters from Mama arrive every week. In them she never asks after Papa. She says she misses us and I write back saying we miss her, too, which is true. I used to ask when she was coming home, but she never answers that question, so I stop asking.

After a couple months go by, we get used to her being gone. I do everything I've been doing—the cooking and most of the cleaning. Our food—rice, beans, flour, and sugar—comes from the government, which still hurts Papa to accept. Nothing else changes. In between sand and dust storms, Papa clears roads for a few dollars a week. He says more and more farms are abandoned, swallowed to the height of their stove pipes by the sea of sand. Some days I wish we'd never come here. We'd still be a family and Katie would be alive. It's easy to forget how awful things were in Chicago when our day-to-day lives here continue to be a struggle.

Until this summer, I thought nothing could be worse than the hot, stifling, filthy, smelly air of Chicago's Back of the Yards. Maybe my memory is faulty, but this is the hottest I can remember, here or there. The temperature has been over a 110 degrees every day. When there's a breeze, we can't open the windows because the air is full of dust. If we open them at night, we wake in the morning with sand rippling on the kitchen floor. Papa's taken to spraying the dust with kerosene to keep it down, which makes it easier to sweep, but it smells terrible and means taking extra care when lighting the stove or the lamps.

My thoughts of Chicago must have caused Kippy to think about me. In September, I receive the first letter I've had from her since I wrote to tell her Mama left.

29 August 1935

Dear Nona,

Just because I haven't written in a while doesn't mean I don't think of you often and wonder how life is for you. Your mother wrote mine about your sister's death. I didn't know her, of course, but I'm sorry all the same, and should have written then. Your mother also said she was staying with her sister for the time being and has found a job. That upset my mother. She says once a woman gets a taste of independence, she's never satisfied with being just a wife and mother again. I wouldn't worry if I were you. Your mother will come home when she's ready.

Life has gotten a little easier here. The government programs supply basic food and the slaughterhouses have been hiring. We've got new tenants in Mr. Fischer's attic. They come from Germany, where I guess things aren't so good for Jewish people since Mr. Hitler took power. None of them speaks English, so I don't really know much about them.

I met a nice boy in January and—I hope you're sitting down—we tied the knot in May. I'm Mrs. Charles Butler. He works at the Armour plant and is handy with tools, so he's making needed repairs around the boarding house. We'll be living here with mother, probably forever, since this place will be mine someday. I know you and I swore we'd never marry, and I sure didn't want to live in the Back of the Yards all my life, but we never know God's plans for us, do we? So far marriage is pretty good and we're looking forward to the arrival of our first child in February.

I hope you are well and will write back. The miles and the years have separated us, but I still consider you my best friend. Happy Belated Birthday!

Yours forever, Kippy

I'm surprised when a tear hits the paper, blurring her signature. I fold the letter and put it back in the envelope. In the fifteen weeks Mama's been gone, she never mentioned she had a job. I wonder if Papa's realized she isn't coming back. He does, I suppose. He never talks about her anymore. None of us do. When she first left, he would say, When your mama comes home, we'll do such and such. He stopped that weeks ago.

If I'm honest, the news my best friend in the world is married and having a baby is what's really upsetting. I just turned eighteen; Kippy's a year younger. I'll never forget Mama telling me about marrying Papa when she was seventeen and how her dreams of being a dress designer ended. Kippy and I haven't kept in touch enough for me to know what her dreams were—except to escape the Back of the Yards, or at least to never marry a man who worked in a slaughterhouse.

I suppose I should be happy for her, but I'm not. I'm heartbroken and frightened. She's locked into the very life we swore to escape unless someday she deserts her family like my mother and Mr. Andersen's wife did. Even if I give up my dream to be a pilot, I swear I'll never marry a farmer.

49

1936

In April, men from Mr. Roosevelt's Civilian Conservation Corp come to talk to the farmers about contour planting so the wind will ripple across plowed fields instead of lifting and blowing the soil. They bring African grass seed to stabilize the soil, claiming it will grow better in this desert we're blamed for creating.

Many of the farmers blame the government for luring us here in the first place and refuse to listen. Papa listens. He says if enough of us try it their way, and it works, the others will follow. If they don't, there's nothing to keep their soil from blowing over and covering a neighbor's success.

To encourage the holdouts, the government offers to pay farmers who contour plow a dollar for every acre they own. No one can turn down that offer.

Our turn comes in May. Papa and Owie go out with the CCC men to survey our fields before plowing. I drive the car into Dalhart to sell our eggs, buy a few supplies, and the Sunday *Chicago Daily Tribune*. I don't admit this, even to myself, but I read it for news of Miss Earhart. This week's paper has a small, hard-to-find mention that she is planning a round-the-world flight. Others have done it, the article says, but her attempt will be the longest, 29,000 miles, because it will roughly follow the equatorial route.

When I get home, Papa's at the cutting board butchering a rabbit. "I invited one of the CCC boys to supper." He smiles at me over his shoulder.

My mouth waters at the thought of meat with our usual potatoes, onions, and beans. "Want some help?"

"I'll do the cooking. You get cleaned up."

I hold my arms out and turn slowly. "Think I need to?" I'm wearing Owie's hand-me-down overalls, one of Papa's flannel shirts, and a pair of secondhand boots from Uncle Coon's shoe-swap.

Papa laughs. My heart leaps when I realize how long it's been since I've heard that sound. "If you start now, you may be presentable by supper," he says.

I grin at him. "Tonight's or tomorrow's?"

"Owie's still out in the field so you're free to bathe in the dugout. I lit the stove and there's water heating."

"It's only Tuesday." I'm suddenly suspicious. "Papa?"

"Huh?" He severs the rabbit's last leg and adds it to the bowl of baking soda and water to tenderize the meat.

"How old is this boy?"

Papa keeps his back to me and shrugs. "'Bout your age, I'd guess. Seems like a nice boy, too. Wants to own a farm one day."

I don't know whether to be angry or amused. There are no young men left around here. Only burnt-out men clinging to their ruined land and watching the blue sky for rain clouds. I don't care what Papa's got up his sleeve, I'm keeping the solemn oath Kippy and I made, even if she didn't.

In spite of that, I carry my church dress to the dugout.

In the front yard, Gracie's got a vulture feather stuck in her hair and is whooping as she circles Honey, whose role as a buffalo is not very convincing. Gracie reins in her broomstick pony. "Where you going?"

"We have a guest coming for supper. You need a bath, too. I'll save the water for you."

"Who's coming?"

"I don't know. Some boy," I say, and realize I'm a little nervous.

"A boy's coming to see Nona," she tells Honey.

Even Gracie figures out what Papa's up to. "He's not coming to see me." I turn and march to the dugout.

Papa has Gracie set the table with the pieces of Mama's good china that have the fewest chips. Meanwhile, I'm getting more and more nervous. I don't know how to talk to a boy. My stomach knots when I hear a car drive in.

"He's here." Gracie yells like a banshee and bangs out the door. I busy myself filling jelly glasses with water and refolding the flour sack napkins. Owie's laughing at something and I'm surprised; at eleven, his laugh sounds just like Papa's.

I take a deep breath when the boy and Owie clomp up the front steps and stomp the dust off their boots on the porch. Gracie holds the door open, looks at me, and giggles.

Owie introduces Zack to Papa and Gracie. He's as tall as Papa, brown as a berry from working in the sun, and movie star handsome. His hair is blue-black, but his eyes are winter sky blue. He smiles and his teeth are straight and white. It's like having Errol Flynn to supper.

"Sit here." Gracie pulls out the chair that used to be Mama's opposite Papa's.

"Next to you, I hope," Zack says.

"I usually sit here." Gracie speaks in a most grown-up voice, then plops herself in my chair, which *is* next to Zack's.

"And this is my sister, Winona." Owie blushes.

Geez, I think. He and Papa are in this together.

Zack turns his smile on me, puts out his hand, notices how dirty it is, and pulls it back. "Pleased to meet you, ma'am."

"Ma'am?" Gracie hoots. "She's no ma'am. She's Nona."

"You boys wash up." Papa puts the platter of rabbit on the table.

Zack's a talker, for which I'm grateful. He's from Iowa, where he says his family had over a thousand acres of corn, which dried up and blew away like everyone else's. Last he heard, his father, mother, and seven brothers and sisters are now somewhere in the central valley of California.

"Do you have a wife?" Gracie asks.

"Not yet, but I'm leaning toward asking your Papa for your hand."

Gracie laughs. "I'm too young to get married."

"Well, I'm willing to wait."

"She comes with a full growed cow," Owie says.

Zack laughs. "What a package."

Gracie giggles, then asks, "How old are you?"

"Seventeen."

"I'm seven." Fingers fan out as she tallies the age difference. She smiles at Zack. "You'll have to wait ten years."

"To get you and a cow in the bargain, I'd wait eleven."

I find myself smiling at this likable guy.

After supper, Papa says it's a beautiful night for a walk.

Gracie jumps up.

"Not you," Papa says. "You clear the table."

"He's my financy."

We all laugh.

Owie stands and reaches for his jacket.

"He can be your *financy* after—" Papa points at Owie. "the pair of you do the dishes."

It's a starry night. I turn toward the cottonwoods. If I worried about what we'd talk about, I shouldn't have. Zack picks up his life story pretty much where he left off at supper. He tells me his family acquired most of their land when his grandfather, a banker, foreclosed on failed farms. That knowledge would take some of the shine off him in Papa's eyes.

"My grandfather got crushed when his tractor rolled over on him. Dad inherited the whole kit and kaboodle and lost it all to foreclosure. What goes around, comes around." His laugh has a bitter edge.

"Papa told me you want to be farmer."

"Maybe one day, after the war."

"What war?"

"With Germany, of course."

"You and Papa." I shake my head.

"He thinks so, too?"

"Yes."

"I'm saving for flying lessons," he says. "I'm going to be a fighter pilot."

I stop mid-stride and turn. "So was I—once."

"So were you what?"

"Saving for flying lessons. I want. . .wanted to be a pilot, too."

All his straight, white teeth shine in his suntanned face. His head goes back and he laughs, a deep belly laugh that rings out across the dunes.

I do an about face and march for home.

"Wait." Zack catches up and grabs my arm.

"You have no right to laugh." I jerk my arm free.

"Girls can't fly."

"Amelia Earhart is a girl."

"Who's she?"

For years, I've thought Papa was wrong sticking to his dream and continuing to hope for a better future. Now, standing amid the barren dunes, with Zack still looking amused, I realize that, in spite of all the disasters we've lived through, Papa succeeded. He has what he wanted: a farm of his own. If he can hang on to his dream, I can hang on to mine. I hike my church skirt and take off running for home.

50

In late May, we get a couple of nice rains. Our corn sprouts and the wheat Papa and Owie planted gives a green blush to our contoured fields. The cottonwoods leaf out and shimmer in the breeze. Late one day, after the chores are done and before I start supper, I ride Dan out to the creek bed for the pleasure of listening to the wind in the cottonwoods and sitting in their shade. On the way home, I feel renewed. I cross the dunes, climbing to glimpse the line of lush green leaves, then dip and lose sight of them. Knowing they are there is enough.

A couple of mornings later, after finishing the breakfast dishes, I sit down at the kitchen table to write Mama. I want to her know we're doing fine, and that if she ever considers coming home, she needn't be afraid, we all love and miss her. I tell her about the rain and the cottonwoods and the corn and wheat sprouting, and still have half a page to fill, so I ask if she's excited about Miss Earhart's plan to fly around the world. It will be days before I get to town to mail it, so I don't seal the envelope, in case I think of something else, or Gracie, Owie, or Papa want to add anything.

I'm carrying the dish water to the garden when I hear an odd buzzing sound and turn to see a strange cloud approaching from the north, thick and dark, and moving erratically, not like a dust storm. Sunlight flickers through it the way it does through dense leaves in a wind. The buzz becomes a whir of white wings and, a moment later, like a wave crashing. Every surface, including me, is covered with locusts. I scream and try to brush them off, but there are thousands, crawling, chirping, chewing. Their claws scratch my face and get tangled in my hair.

I hear the screen door bang. "Nona?"

"Get in the house. Shut the windows."

Between me and the house is an undulating sea of hoppers. They pop under my feet as I run toward the porch.

Gracie's frozen in place as the hoppers swarm up the porch steps. When they start up her legs, she shrieks and stomps her feet. I slip on their slimy insides as I run up the steps, and nearly fall. I grab Gracie's hand, drag her into the house, and slam the door.

I use a dish towel to beat them off her. Some fly to escape the towel, bashing themselves against the windows. Others fly toward the screen door, which is soon covered inside and out. The racket of their chirps is almost deafening.

Gracie's crying, but she helps kill them, smashing as many as she can with a rolled-up newspaper. The stove still has embers from breakfast. I get the broom and the dustpan, corral as many as I can, run, and dump them into the stove. They sizzle and pop.

Outside the sound of chirping ebbs. I dump another dustpan full into the stove and go to the window. In less than fifteen minutes, they've eaten our garden down to the ground and are leaving. I open the door and use the broom to brush off the ones on the inside of the screen. They, too, take flight, and for one cursed moment, their white, transparent wings remind me of that damn *Opportunity* angel that ignited Papa's dream all those years ago. Tears stream down my face as I cross to our ruined garden, where they have even eaten the rake handle.

Back in the house, I lift a stove lid and add the letter I wrote Mama to the crisp remains of locusts.

On the radio the following week, the farm report estimates we had fourteen million locusts per square mile. Our farm is two square miles. After that promising rain, the wheat Papa planted is gone. They ate all the cottonwood leaves and their weight broke off most of the branches.

Without a garden, we have to go back on relief, taking the government's handout of rice, flour, and beans.

~

A week later, I come in from feeding Ben, Dan, Lily, and Honey, to find Papa sitting at the table with his head in his hands. In front of him is a small pile of paper, torn into small pieces. "Are you okay?"

He looks up and nods, then, with the side of one hand, he brushes the shreds off into the palm of the other. He rises, back bent like an old man, and carries them to the stove.

"What was that?"

"My membership card in the Last Man Club." His voice brims with sarcasm.

Hearing him say that feels like a jolt of static electricity. "Are you . . . giving up?" I don't know if I'm hopeful, as if *finally*, or angry that he'd consider leaving after all we've survived, all we've put into this place, and all we've lost.

There's a momentary spark of pride in Papa's eyes, then it's gone. He runs his fingers through his thinning, graying hair. "Do *you* want to call it quits?"

Without thinking about it a moment longer, I shake my head. "We can't give up now. We've held on too long. And where would we go? Mamie wrote that California is overrun with people like us. They're turning families back at the state line."

"I'd find work somewhere, enough to keep myself fed, and you kids could go stay with your mom."

Mama's voice pops into my head, "*See!*" She sounds vindicated.

For a moment, I try to imagine leaving Papa to live with Mama and realize it has always been easier to see us with him without her, than to imagine us with her without him. "No, Papa. It's going to rain again, and when it does, we'll be ready."

"Shouldn't we see how Owie and Gracie feel about it?"

"Gracie would never leave Honey, and you know Owie loves it here."

Papa's lips form a thin line and he nods. "Then we'll stay."

I go to the pitcher and pour water into the basin to wash my hands before starting supper. "If you're not giving up, why did you tear up your membership card?"

"John McCarty has taken a job in Amarillo."

"What?" I turn. Water from my wet hands drips and pocks the dust on the floor.

John McCarty is the editor of the *Dalhart Texan*, president of the Chamber of Commerce, and the damn fool—Mama's words—who started the club. McCarty always made a point of openly ridiculing every man who packed up his family and left.

51

1937

The radio is on in the mercantile, and everyone who comes in stops to listen. Amelia Earhart has just left Oakland, California, for her flight around the world. When I get home, I crank Gracie's farm radio and spend as much of the day as possible listening for updates until every station within range signs off for the night. The next morning, I turn it on first thing. She made it to Hawaii, but her Lockheed Electra had trouble with the right landing gear. She says she'll try again once the plane is repaired. When Papa goes to town for a meeting, he brings back the *Chicago Daily Tribune*. I cut out all the Earhart stories and add them to the wall above my bed.

On June 7, my wonderful father brings home yesterday's Sunday edition of the *Chicago Tribune*, which costs ten cents—eight cents more than the daily. Miss Earhart is making her second attempt to fly around the world. This time, because of the prevailing winds, she will travel from west to east. After the repairs were made to her Electra in Hawaii, she flew from Oakland, California to Miami, Florida. According to the paper, on June 1, she and her navigator, Mr. Fred Noonan, took off from Miami for the second try. By the time I find out she's on her way, she's already made it to Brazil and will cross the Atlantic from there to Africa. After that, there are no reports about her on the news for a few days until she leaves Africa on June 15, headed for India and Southeast Asia. I listen to the nightly news updates on her progress, but we don't own a map, so it's hard to picture the route.

On Sunday, July18, Papa buys another Sunday *Chicago Tribune*. When I come in with the basket of eggs, he has it open to a Correct Your

Nose! ad. A man is wearing an Anita Nose Adjuster with straps around his ears and another over the top of his head. Papa grins at me.

"I think your nose is perfect."

"What?"

I tap the picture.

He laughs and turns the page. In the top right-hand corner is a small map of Miss Earhart's route. I hug him.

I paste the map on the wall right beside my head so I'll be able to roll over and look at it each morning. The distance she's covered so far is a solid black line. June 18 has her in Calcutta, India. From there the line to Oakland is a series of dashes. I trace her flight, as the news comes in, with a purple crayon from the box Mr. Andersen gave Owie all those years ago.

It takes her fourteen days to reach Australia, which I remember from geography as an island almost as big as the United States, and one of world's seven continents. The radio news that night reports that, to lighten the load, she leaves behind some equipment she doesn't think she'll need, including their parachutes. By the time she leaves Lae, New Guinea, on July 2, she's flown 22,000 miles. Only 7000 more to go. This next leg is the longest—2,556 miles—and they say Howland Island is the tiniest target to find. She's scheduled to arrive at this dot in the middle of the Pacific Ocean on July 2.

Owie asks before I can, "How can she leave on the second, fly twenty-five hundred miles, and arrive on the same day?"

"She's crossing the International Date Line," Papa says.

"What does it look like?" Gracie's sick of eating beans, onion and potato soup again, and is whiny.

"It's an imaginary line in the Pacific. When she crosses it, she'll gain a day."

"How come we don't have one?"

"We have time zones," Papa says, "but the Date Line is where every new day starts."

On July 2, Papa puts the radio right in the middle of the kitchen table, then goes out on the porch to call Gracie and Owie in for supper. The weather is first: hot with a chance of dusters, same as yesterday, and the day before, and the whole summer.

"Come on. Come on." I coax.

"There has still been no word from Miss Earhart," the reporter says. "Her last radio broadcast was picked up at 8:43 a. m. by the *Itasca*, a ship in the vicinity of Howland Island.

"Miss Earhart reported they were low on fuel but believed they had reached Howland's charted position. She was apparently unable to hear the *Itasca*'s response or see the signal smoke they produced from their oil-fired boilers. Her failure to arrive has prompted the launch of an official search. This station will bring you updates as soon as we receive them. Farm news is next."

"They'll find her." Papa's at the screen.

Gracie runs up the steps and follows him in. When he hugs me, I start to cry and then I'm sobbing against his chest.

Gracie's eyes fill with tears. "Did Mama die?"

"Your mother is fine. Amelia Earhart is missing," Papa says.

"The lady-pilot on our walls?"

"How 'bout you finish feeding the chickens." Papa puts his hand on the top of her head and rotates her toward the door.

Gracie flaps her arms as she crosses the room to the door, then turns, runs back, and hugs me. "I'm sorry, Nona."

They don't find her. The days drag by until the official search is called off July 19. Her husband, the book publisher, Mr. Putnam, continues searching, but everyone else has given up.

I give up, too. I decide to face the truth. This is going to be my life. I'm a farmer's daughter, not a pilot. I tear down the stories pasted to my bedroom wall and feed them into the fire one at a time, stopping only once to read some lines I'd underlined. It's what Miss Earhart said when asked why she was trying to fly around the world. "I want to do it because I want to do it. Women must try to do things as men have tried. When they fail, their failure must be but a challenge to others."

I take the scissors from Mama's sewing basket, cut those words out, and put them in my tobacco tin with my other keepsakes from childhood: the buffalo nickel Mr. Fischer gave me, the pennies I found at the dump, and Mr. Andersen's 2 Kroner piece. Later that day, when I drive to town for supplies, I stop at the bank.

When I get home, Papa is in the barn. He looks up when I come in. "Whatcha got there?"

"Mr. Andersen's life savings."

"What?" Papa's brow creases. How did—?"

"He gave it to me the night before you took him to the hospital. He said I was to keep it for flying lessons and use what I earn as a pilot to help you and Owie with the farm, and help Gracie get an education."

He takes his hat off and wipes his face with his handkerchief. "You're letting this get the better of you, Nona. They may find Miss Earhart yet. Even if they don't, you've held on to your dream of flying since you were ten years old, and not all that long ago I saw you in the hayloft door, arms spread, eyes looking up. Nothing has changed."

"Everything has changed." My tone is unexpectedly angry. "I'm sorry." I touch his arm. "Flying was a childish dream. I need to grow up and accept that with Mama gone, I belong here and always will. Besides, there's no place around here to take lessons." I hand him Mr. Andersen's tobacco tin. "It's better that you have it."

Papa opens the lid, lifts out the bag of gold coins and weighs them in his hand. He closes his eyes for a moment, then puts the bag back in the tin, and shuts the lid. "Noel knew what he was doing when he gave this to you for safekeeping." He hands it back to me.

"I can't, Papa. It's not fair. Once the rains start again, you'll need seed and a new tractor." I stroke Lily's face. "And a younger cow."

"Nona, it wasn't my dream to be a failed farmer—"

"Don't say that. Who could have guessed what was going to happen?"

He shrugs. "I suppose. But if something sounds too good to be true, it usually is. And I still have to live with your mother blaming me for Katie's death—" He takes a deep breath. "But if I'd let her talk me out of trying to build us a life here, or quit when everything went to hell, I would still be wrapping chains around the legs of hogs and slitting their throats." He lifts my chin so I have to look him in the eye. "Don't push your dream away because one brave woman didn't make it. If she's dead, she died trying. I took a chance, hoping to give you and Owie a better life than growing up in that filthy Back of the Yards. Maybe learning to fly will work out or maybe it won't. Trying always trumps not trying." He pulls me into his arms and whispers against my hair. "One thing I know for sure, you weren't meant for this place. You were meant for a bigger life. I'm not going to take your money. Put that back where it was. We'll find a way."

52

1938

In the months following Miss Earhart's disappearance, nothing changed for us. The winter of 1937 was dry and cold, followed by a dry, windy spring. The only break from the monotony of another year of no rain was a yellow-dust blizzard two weeks after Gracie's ninth birthday, followed the next day by a black blizzard—dirt and dust—that blocked out the sun for three full days.

Then on July 11, 1938, the drought ended. President Roosevelt was giving a speech in Ellwood Park in Amarillo, eighty-five miles south of Dalhart. We were listening to it on the radio when we heard a clap of thunder and people in the crowd began to cheer.

"It's raining, folks. It's not just raining, it's pouring." The commentator's voice broke with emotion. "People are opening their arms and turning their faces to the sky. Oh my, the joy. The joy." Even through the crackling static, we heard the tears in his voice.

The article in the next day's *Texan* said nobody at the event had an umbrella, so Mr. Roosevelt smiled, stood in the rain, and continued his speech. He was still talking and we were still listening when the downpour reached Dalhart. We ran down the steps and out into the yard, laughed and danced, but what I remember most is Papa's forty-year-old face, turned up, wet with rain, looking almost young again.

Some folks, mostly Democrats, eventually credited Mr. Roosevelt with ending the drought. Of course, we didn't know that very minute it was really over and not a fluke. It just turned out that way.

In August, a few days before my twentieth birthday, Papa comes home from town with a flier advertising an air show this weekend at the Dalhart airport, which is really a landing strip built for crop dusters. The flier says they are going to let members of the public take a fifteen-minute ride for five dollars. He handed it to me and smiled. "Time to find out what you're made of, birthday girl."

The day of the air show, I take my tobacco tin from the shelf in my room and count out five dollars of the eleven I saved. For luck, I put Mr. Fischer's buffalo nickel and Mr. Andersen's 2 Kroner in my pocket.

I hand the bills to Papa to carry.

"What's this?" he says.

"The money I saved from cream and butter sales. I want to take a ride."

Papa stands for a moment looking at the money, puts his hand on the back of my head, and pulls me close. He wraps me in his arms and whispers, "I'm sorry."

"For what, Papa?" My voice is muffled against his shoulder.

"That you think I'd let you pay for your own birthday present. I've been saving, too."

I close my eyes and breathe in the smells of my father. In Chicago, he used to smell of blood, raw meat, and disappointment. Now he smells of sweat, dust, hay, and hope. I feel nine again, back in the boarding house, searching for the right words to tell Mr. Fischer about how important he is to me, and later to Mr. Andersen before he died. Then to Mama to make her stay. I look up at him. "Thank you."

We're in the car on our way to the airfield when I see my first plane overhead. It's flying upside down. My heart begins to thud.

Papa stops in the middle of the road and we watch the pilot make a giant loop in the sky. I watch the plane disappear into a cloud, and I'm suddenly full of doubt. What ever made me think I wanted to fly? I've never been farther off the ground than the hay doors. It was a childish whim, based on the excitement of Miss Earhart's flight, and a misunderstanding of where Papa told us we were going. Plains. Not planes. What did I know? I'll enjoy the show and that will be that.

The plane we saw flying upside down is landing as we park. It looks like the whole town has turned out. There's no way there will be time to take more than a few people up for a ride. I'm don't know whether to be relieved or disappointed.

The pilot steers to the end of the runway to enthusiastic applause and cheers which peter out as all eyes turn toward a second plane coming in from the south. It flies directly toward the crowd, so low off the ground, it stirs up the dust. When it looks like the pilot's going to lift the hats off every head, people start to scatter. I don't duck or run. I watch the underbelly pass right over me, blasting my face with grit. He pulls up and makes a giant loop. Everyone cheers, happy to still have our heads attached.

The second plane lands and taxis over to line up with the first, their wing tips practically touching. Together, they rev their engines, then start down the runway side by side. They take off in concert and bank in opposite directions.

Papa's standing behind me with his hands on my shoulders, as if holding me on the ground. My stomach flutters watching the two planes do a series of loops and spins, then fly past each other upside down. For the finale, they soar so high they nearly disappear before tipping nose-down and cutting their engines. There's only silence as they spiral toward the earth. The crowd gasps. A woman screams. Papa's fingers grip my shoulders so tightly it hurts. I take a breath and hold it. Blood whooshes in my ears. Some people look away, but I can't. When it seems like the planes can't possibly recover in time, their engines sputter to life, and they pull out of the dive. The audience cheers.

I tilt my head back and look up at Papa. "I've never been so scared."

"Me, either."

The first plane lands with the second one right behind it. They bounce toward the crowd, park, and cut their motors. The first pilot climbs out of the open cockpit and jumps to the ground. He's not much bigger than I am, and his face is black with soot. When he takes off his goggles there are white circles around his eyes. I'm pretty far away, and maybe it's the bomber jacket he's wearing, but it looks like he has breasts and a small waist. I touch Papa's arm, about to ask if he thinks that pilot's a woman, when she takes off her leather helmet and runs her fingers through short, curly, blonde hair. Her white scarf flutters as she walks toward the crowd. Papa smiles at me. "That's you one day."

The second pilot—a man—climbs down from the cockpit. The crowd surges forward surrounding them, trying to shake their hands. Others want to touch the plane.

It's a blazing hot day. There's a call for water, which is carried out in a bucket. The pilots take turns drinking from the ladle, then the male pours a ladle-full over his head, turns, and pretends he's going to pour another over the woman's. She laughs and ducks.

There's the squeal of a microphone, and someone announces that people who wish to take a ride should come forward. No one moves. Five dollars is a lot of money, or maybe, like me, they are thinking long and hard about leaving the ground.

I thought Papa was still standing behind me, but when I turn, he's not there. I see a man selling tickets, but he's not there either. Then I see him in the crowd around the woman pilot. She turns to look at him and at me when he points me out. She smiles and nods. Papa signals for me to come join them.

Gracie and a few friends she goes to school with are standing nearby, pretending to ignore the boys who tease them. Owie's inspecting the plane. I have no excuse. I can't talk about wanting to fly all these years, then not do it.

"This is Nancy Love," Papa says when I reach them.

"Happy to meet you." We shake hands. "Your father tells me you've wanted to be a pilot since you were ten years old."

"Yes ma'am." My whole body is trembling. Beads of sweat form on my upper lip.

Miss Love studies my face. "What made you think you wanted to be a pilot?" She doesn't say this unkindly.

"Miss Earhart's first flight across the Atlantic."

"Me, too. Until then, I was still dumb enough to believe women couldn't be pilots." She grins at me.

I laugh. "That's what Papa said when I first told him, but he never discouraged me after that." I look at my feet. "To be honest, 'til today, I've never seen a plane before."

"What did you think of the show?"

"I loved it, but . . . I'm not sure I'm brave enough—"

"Don't worry. I won't do anything to frighten you. You're going to love flying." She puts her leather helmet on. "And honestly, I was scared to death the first time. She never admitted it, but I think Amelia was too."

"You knew her?"

"Sure did. Met her at a meeting she organized to encourage women pilots. There were ninety-nine of us. We've been the Ninety-Nines ever since." She steps onto the lower of the two wings and holds a hand out to me.

"You'll sit here in the front cockpit. I'll control the flight from the rear one."

"What kind of plane is this?" I try to sound calm, like I'm simply curious.

I see a touch of amusement in her eyes. "A Boeing Stearman Kaydet biplane. One of the best."

My knees feel like rubber, but I take her hand and step onto the bottom wing.

53

There are eight dials on the dashboard of each of the two bucket-like cockpits. I'm so nervous, mine are a blur. There are two short, wooden planks on the floor like pedals, though I can't imagine what they do. In the center of the cockpit is what looks like a rake handle. I have to pull my skirt up and sit with a knee on either side it.

Miss Love tells me what each of the dials is for: air speed, altitude, how level the wings are, clock, oil pressure gauge, and fuel level. A second later, I can't remember which is which. The top and largest is obviously a compass. She leans in and points to the pedals. "It will help if you keep your feet off those when we come in to land." She wiggles the handle. "And make sure I've got plenty of play in the stick, okay? I use it to steer us in flight."

"Yes ma'am." My voice quivers.

She puts a hand on my shoulder. "You'll be fine."

I nod. My mouth feels full of dust.

"When we get up there, you can show me where you live."

"Okay."

She reaches into the front cockpit and hands me a pair of goggles, then climbs into the bucket seat behind me. "All clear," she calls—out of habit, I assume, since no one is near the plane. I glance over at Papa. He gives me a thumbs-up, and I give him a small, scared wave.

The engine, when it first turns over, sounds reluctant. It sputters, backfires, and blows a cloud of smoke. She revs it, causing the plane to shudder. There's a jerk, and we begin to roll. The wings dip and rise as we roll over the uneven, rutted ground until we are in position at the end of the strip. I grip the sides of the bucket I'm in and squeeze my eyes shut. Then I think, *don't be a fool,* and open them. I want to see everything.

As we bump along the ground, gaining speed, the two pedals on the floor move back and forth, under the control of Miss Love's feet. My hair whips my face. My stomach lifts as we bounce free of the earth, then sinks when we hit the ground again. I hold my breath. A moment later the rattling and bouncing ends and we're airborne. The dry, beige world falls away. Papa, Gracie, and Owie—all waving—grow smaller and smaller. The pedals are still, but the stick moves as if a ghost-hand controls it, though, of course, it's Miss Love. We keep climbing. There's a cloud above us, fluffy and white. She aims for it. When we fly into it, I feel a bump. I hadn't expected a cloud to have enough substance to jar us.

I let go of the grip I have on the sides of the plane and look down, trying to get my bearings. Every direction looks the same, flat and colorless. It's not until I spot the line of cottonwoods in our ravine that I know to point south. The stick bumps my right knee as the plane leans far to the right. It feels like only the seatbelt is holding me in. My heart bangs against my ribs. Miss Love levels the wings again. In a few moments, I see our weather-beaten house, the barn, and our windmill, and beyond, desolation in every direction, dusty fields all hopefully plowed. Tears fill my eyes. I lift the goggles and the tears blow into my ears. I can't stop them, and then I'm sobbing so hard it's hard to catch my breath. As much as I love Papa, Owie, and Gracie, I never want to come down. I want to keep flying west until the Rockies rise up to meet us, then on from there to the edge of the Pacific Ocean. I look left toward my beloved cottonwoods. They look like a green hedge from up here. Mr. Andersen is lying beneath them, with his son and Karlo, but I want very much to believe he's above me, watching and smiling.

Miss Love banks again until I am looking straight down on our house—the pitiful-looking place where we've been scratching out a living for nine and half years. We circle it twice, before she levels the wings, and we fly toward another cloud. Instead of going through it, she skims along the top, as if we might land, get out, and walk around. Our propeller dislodges puffy bits. So much cleaner looking than the little clouds that rise to coat our feet with each step across fresh dust. In the air, it looks and feels like we're crawling across the land, and when the sun casts our shadow on the ground, it too creeps.

She turns us back toward Dalhart and flies over our gray and brown town before banking to line up with the runway. When we land, I'll be back in my life and the reality of swirling dust. I can't stand the thought of waiting another day for rain, or carrying soapy dish and dirty bath water to the garden, or planting and losing another crop. I want more than anything to keep flying until I'm as far from here as I can get.

As we come in for a landing, the ground rises to meet us, and I can sense our speed. We bounce once, and the pedals near my feet move back and forth. I slip off my sandals and lightly touch them with my dusty, gritty bare feet.

Miss Love taxis over to where my family waits. Papa holds Gracie back until the prop quits turning, then she runs to the plane. When I climb out and jump to the ground, she wraps her arms around me. "I was so scared. Were you?"

I shake my head.

"Have you been crying?" Papa says.

Miss Love climbs down and stands beside me. I turn to thank her and she sees my red-rimmed eyes. "I'm sorry. Were you frightened?"

"It's not that. I loved it. I didn't know I would, but I do. A pilot *is* what I want to be. More than I ever imagined." I glance at Papa, then at my hands. "I'm crying because I'm afraid I will never be that happy again."

Papa pushes his hat back on his head and looks at me with those perpetually sad eyes. "I guess I should have expected that."

I turn to Miss Love. "Except there's no place around here to take lessons."

"We . . . she has the money," Papa says.

"Who flies that?" She nods toward the crop duster parked nearby.

"I don't know," Papa says. "I can ask in town."

She looks at me. "If you want, I can give you your first lesson right now."

"Will you?" I'm tempted to hug her but decide against it. "Yes, please."

Papa puts a restraining hand on my shoulder. "We didn't bring any more cash."

Miss Love smiles. "You can owe me."

Epilogue

1942

It's late and the night has been clear so far. There's no moon and the stars are as dense as grains of sand. I'm flying my favorite, the P 47 Thunderbolt, a single-seat, single-engine, low-wing fighter. I say I love every plane I fly, but I truly mean it about this one. The armored cockpit is roomy and the visibility is the best of any aircraft I've flown.

I picked up this one at the factory in Farmingdale, New York, and am ferrying it to a training airbase in Kearney, Nebraska, where a young man will be trained to fly it into battle against the Germans or Japanese. Papa and Zack were right when they said there would be another war with Germany, but the one with Japan came as a surprise.

Nancy Love gave me my first flying lesson that day four years ago, and Papa hired Doug Clarke, the man who owned the crop duster, to give me six more weeks of lessons until I logged the thirty-five hours I needed for my private pilot's license. We paid him two dollars and fifty cents an hour from the money Mr. Andersen left me.

For my solo cross-country, I flew to Carthage, Missouri, to visit Mama. On the way, I passed south of Texhoma, and thought of Mamie. Only a month before, Mamie sent me a picture postcard of a man standing inside a giant redwood tree. She and Mrs. Johnson have found work at the Kaiser shipyards in Richmond, California, across the bay from San Francisco, and she hopes one day to actually see a redwood. *Will write again when we're settled,* was written in the margin. There was no return address.

Mama, my aunt, and six cousins came to the airport to watch me land the old crop duster. I'll never forget the look on Mama's face when she saw me taxi in. She had a knuckle clamped in her teeth, and her other hand over her heart, a fist crushing the front of her dress. As soon as I cut the motor, she bolted out onto the tarmac, but stopped before reaching me. On purpose, I wore Mama's Farmerette coveralls. Our eyes met and I saw recognition. I did a pirouette then held out my arms. She ran into them.

By then, Mama had been gone three years. All her anger and resentment had faded, but they'd left their scars: a mouth permanently contorted by the bitter taste of life, and a fissure between her brows. When she smiled, I saw the tooth she'd lost had been replaced with one a bit too large and in a slightly lighter shade of enamel.

She asked about Gracie and Owie, about Dan and Honey, and finally about Papa. She took me to the dress shop she owned in town. Watching her lift one dress after another I realized that she, too, is living her dream, and is finally something that resembles, if not happy, at least content. I accepted that. Chasing one's dream comes with a cost.

I wasn't licensed to fly at night back then, so the visit had to be short. Mama watched me go through the pre-flight checklist. She looked proud of me. I was proud of myself. I hugged her goodbye and kissed her cheek, ready to climb into the cockpit.

"Wait." She reached into her coat pocket, took out and unfurled a lovely sky-blue scarf. I took off the worn white one Nancy Love had given me, and wrapped Mama's around my neck.

"Do you remember what you told me in Chicago—about when you were a Farmerette?"

"Which thing?"

"You said I couldn't imagine what it's like to be valuable and valued as a woman. Well, that's what I want, too, Mama. I don't know if the powers that be will ever let me fly more than a crop duster, but this is all I've ever wanted to do."

I don't know how to describe her expression: sadness, longing, but she only said, "I hope they do, too."

I watched her waving goodbye as I taxied away. As the plane gained speed, I remember thinking some people don't have it in them to be completely happy, but at that moment I was.

They did let me do a man's job. After Pearl Harbor, the Army had only 1800 pilots and needed millions. Nancy Love and I kept in touch, and in 1941, when she organized the WAFS, the Women's Auxiliary Ferrying Squadron, I joined her. She talked General "Hap" Arnold into letting women pilots ferry the aircraft being manufactured for the war effort to bases where the men—boys, really—were being trained. Later, she and Jackie Cochran formed the WASPs, the Women's Airforce Service Pilots. Twenty-five thousand women applied, 1900 were accepted, and 1074 of us graduated.

Our training base was at Avenger Field in Sweetwater, Texas. The other women complained about the heat, the dirt, the dust—all conditions I was used to. Wearing men's fur-lined flight suits, boots, and gloves did make it worse, but they kept us warm in the open cockpit planes.

Sara, my roommate, was one of thirty-eight trainees killed. She was flying in a three-plane formation when another plane's wing went through her canopy. We never knew if she was killed instantly or knocked unconscious. When her instructor couldn't raise her, he parachuted out of the crippled aircraft and she went down with the plane. I flew her remains to her home in upstate New York. We were civil service, without military benefits, so the Army wouldn't let the U.S. flag be placed on her coffin, which further broke her parents' hearts.

After we graduated, we were assigned to 120 different bases. My home base is Houston, close enough to get back to Dalhart when I have days off.

I went home for a few days after finishing WASP training. There were sunflowers as tall as Owie and the wheat fields waved as golden as I remember seeing them last in 1930. When the war started in 1941, we were afraid that before it was over, Owie might be drafted, but he not only has flat feet, turns out he's color blind to boot. He and Papa farm side by side. Gracie took over running the household and, at fourteen, has turned into a fine cook. She wants to be a teacher when she finishes high school.

I rode Dan out to visit Mr. Andersen's grave while I was home, and took new crosses for Henry's, and Karlo's. Long ago, in desperate times, we had used the old ones for firewood. I sat for a while in the shade of the cottonwoods and told Mr. Andersen how I used the money exactly the way he wanted me to.

Below, I see the lights of Chicago and ahead, lightning flashes through tall cumulonimbus clouds. There's a storm between me and my destination. I smile to myself. I'll have fun maneuvering this fighter between the towering clouds. It will be like flying through the canyons of New York high-rises chasing a Japanese Zero.

I remember the dreams I used to have. They were always in a color of dust: gray, beige, brown, black, and rust. It wasn't 'til I got away that they took on the colors of blue sky and sunlight.

When I'm up high like this, away from the lights of cities, the earth doesn't disclose its features. I can't tell forests from hills or from prairie. The darkness goes on forever. It's as alone as can be imagined, and for the hours aloft, I get to dwell in my head. Often my thoughts are of Papa and how brave he was to let go of an awful job for a chance at something better. To Mama, he was a failure. For a while, I thought he was, too. I lost faith in him. In the face of all that went wrong, I resented his optimism, and his refusal to change course. But he's not a failure. It was just a harder road. Now, when I picture him, he's standing at the edge of his heaven, and I know by farming, he found his life's meaning.

I feel Mama was just as brave. She may not have intended to stay gone, but I think she realized, to survive, she couldn't come back.

The lightning flashes get more frequent. I'm reminded of my first assignment after graduation. I towed targets so that young gunnery soldiers could practice their aim. They used live ammunition and the shells often burst unnervingly close. Women pilots were always sent to do the jobs they didn't want to waste a man on.

A cone of light forms off the nose of my plane and coats the wings with an eerie violet glow. I recognize it as St. Elmo's fire, but I've never seen it before. Seamen used to think it either brought good luck, a gift from the patron saint of sailors, or that it foretold bad weather. I hope, as it creeps across my windshield forming a spider web of light, it will mean this plane, and the young man who flies it into battle, will return unscathed. I hope he'll be able to pick up his dreams where he left off. I think of Mama again, relatively happy now, and Papa, Gracie, and Owie, all settled into the lives they want. And I send my love to Mr. Andersen, who made it possible for me to pursue my dream.

Historical Context

1928 June - Amelia Earhart becomes the first woman to fly across the Atlantic.

September – Amelia Earhart flies across North America

1929 Last of the Orphan Trains; This program began in 1853; 200,000 children were placed with families in the Midwest.

St. Valentine's Day massacre in Chicago. Al Capone's men kill Bugsy Moran's men.

October 29 – The Stock Market crash marks the beginning of the Great Depression

Amelia Earhart founds the Ninety-Nines, an organization of women pilots

1930 Unusual dry period begins in the Great Plains.
Amelia Earhart set a women's speed record of 181 mph

1931 October – Al Capone goes to prison.

1932 May 20-21 - Amelia Earhart flies solo across the Atlantic from Newfoundland to Ireland

1933 Hitler becomes Chancellor of Germany.

First of the dust storms hits the southern plains.

1934 Hitler becomes *Führer* of Germany

1935 Black Sunday, April 14;
The term *Dust Bowl* is coined by reporter, Robert E. Geiger

1937 March – First attempt by Earhart to fly around the world.
June – Earhart begins second attempt to fly around world
July 2 – Earhart disappears somewhere over the Pacific

1938 July – Rains return to the Texas panhandle

1939 Hitler invades Poland; World War II begins in Europe.
Fall – The drought ends when regular rainfall returns to the Great Plains

December 7 – Japanese bomb Pearl Harbor; America enters the war.

1942 September – Women pilots begin ferrying aircraft to U.S. airbases.

1943 August – Women pilots' groups merge to form the Women Airforce Service Pilots or WASPs.

Disclaimer

To keep up the pacing of the story, with the exception of Black Sunday, April 14, 1935, I approximated and /or condensed storm dates, the first rabbit hunt, and other notable incidents. Most of the characters are fictious, including the Williams family, Noel, Mamie, Kippy, and the Rydbergs. They are, however, named after people I love. Dalhart locals like Doc Dawson, Uncle Dick Coon, John McCarty, and Melt and Bam White, were quite real. Nancy Love was real, too, but probably never participated in an air show in Dalhart.

Acknowledgements

Nothing gets written without the help and guidance of my writers' group, the Mixed Pickles: Norma Watkins, Katherine Brown, Kate Erickson, Lynn Courtney, Virginia Reed, Amie McGee, and especially Nona Smith. I'm also indebted to Eric H. Bowen and Michael Lloyd for their expertise on trains. Thanks also to Robert A. Slayton, author of *The Back of the Yards*, for his helpful guidance, and to Nick Olson at the XIT Museum in Dalhart, Texas, for letting me hang out for days reading the memoirs of people who lived through these bleakest of years. Thanks also to Kathleen Scranton, curator of the Big Timbers Museum, Lamar, Colorado. And a special thanks to Judy Wilson at the Cimarron Heritage Museum, Boise City, Oklahoma. But most of all to Susan Bono's keen-eyed editing for making this more worthy of its readers, and to Nona Smith, Pat Dunbar and Mike Petherick, who between them, caught a million typos.

Author's Notes

This book was born out of regret that, when I had the chance, I lacked the curiosity to ask my parents about their young lives. After watching the Ken Burns' documentary about the Dust Bowl, I knew I wanted to write about that time from the point of view of a kid. My parents grew up in Iowa and Nebraska, not the dust bowl per se, but very close. I knew nothing about my father's people. My mother's family owned thousands of acres of farm land in those two states, and I remember she was always worried during a 'drouth' year. In addition, her father was a banker. I'm left to wonder how he might have acquired 3000 acres of Iowa and Nebraska farmland.

Nona's favorite recipe
Joan Gusweiler's Crackerflitters

2 sleeves stale saltines
Water, enough to cover crumbled crackers.
1 egg
1 teaspoon vanilla extract
1 – 3 tablespoons vegetable shortening
½ cup maple syrup (Nona's family had them with molasses.)

Place saltines in a large bowl; cover with water. Let stand 5 – 10 minutes. When saltines are soggy, squeeze out the water by hand. Combine drained saltines, one egg and vanilla. Stir well with a fork.

In a large skillet, melt 1 tablespoon. shortening over medium heat. When hot, drop spoonsful of cracker mixture into the skillet, shaping them into 5-inch pancakes. Fry until brown and crispy on each side (about 3 minutes). Add more shortening to skillet if necessary. Serve hot w/ maple syrup. Makes about 12 flitters.

Water Glassing Eggs

https://backyardpoultry.iamcountryside.com/eggs-meat/water-glassing-eggs-for-long-term-storage/

Liverice Sandwich

1 cup rice, 1/2 cup chopped cooked liver, 2 tablespoons butter, Parsley, mace, grated lemon rind. Boil the rice in plenty of hot water to which the salt, mace and a dash of grated lemon peel have been added. When tender, drain and add the chopped liver and butter. Pack in a glass jar and spread when cold on thin slices of bread.

Suggested Reading

Back of the Yards: The Making of a Local Democracy by Robert A. Slayton. "By 1910 the complex of yards, industries, banks and other structures—known collectively as The Yards—covered 500 acres, had 13,000 pens, 300 miles of railroad tracks, 25 miles of streets, 50 miles of sewers, 90 miles of pipes, and 10,000 hydrants. On a hot day, 7 million gallons of water fed the needs of the cattle, machines, and humans. . . In 1919, a boom year, the plants processed 14,903,487 animals, including 7,936,634 hogs and 2,331,233 cattle. On one day in 1920 alone, 122,748 pigs came to the yards. One Swift & Company factory had more than 11,000 employees."

The Worst Hard Time by Timothy Egan; don't miss this one.

The Dust Bowl, a documentary by Ken Burns. Visually stunning.

The Jungle by Upton Sinclair depicts the working condition at the Chicago Stock Yards, which eventually lead to the passage of the Pure Food and Drug Act, and the Meat Inspection Act in 1906.

Letters from the Dust Bowl by Caroline Henderson, a pioneer who settled in No Man's Land in the Oklahoma Panhandle by herself. This was a time when women still couldn't own property, but they could apply for land grants under the Homestead Act and own their own property.

Years of Dust: The Story of the Dust Bowl by Albert Marrin—for Young Adults

Dear America: Survival in the Storm: The Dust Bowl Diary of Grace Edwards.

http://www.npr.org/2010/03/09/123773525/female-wwii-pilots-the-original-fly-girls

http://www.ted.com/talks/allan_savory_how_to_green_the_world_s_deserts_and_reverse_climate_change.html?utm_source=newsletter_weekly_2013-03-09&utm_campaign=newsletter_weekly&utm_medium=email&utm_content=bottom_right_button

About the Author

Ginny Rorby is the author of six MG/YA novels: *How to Speak Dolphin; Lost in the River of Grass,* 2013 winner of the Sunshine State Young Readers Award; *Hurt Go Happy,* 2008 winner of the ALA's Schneider Family Book Award; *The Outside of a Horse; Dolphin Sky;* and *Freeing Finch,* the inspiring story of a transgender girl and a stray dog who overcome diversity to find love, a home, and a place to belong.

Note from the Author

Word-of-mouth is crucial for any author to succeed. If you enjoyed *Like Dust, I Rise*, please leave a review online—anywhere you are able. Even if it's just a sentence or two. It would make all the difference and would be very much appreciated.

Thanks!
Ginny Rorby

We hope you enjoyed reading this title from:

BLACK ROSE
writing™

www.blackrosewriting.com

Subscribe to our mailing list – *The Rosevine* – and receive **FREE** books, daily deals, and stay current with news about upcoming releases and our hottest authors.
Scan the QR code below to sign up.

Already a subscriber? Please accept a sincere thank you for being a fan of Black Rose Writing authors.

View other Black Rose Writing titles at www.blackrosewriting.com/books and use promo code **PRINT** to receive a **20% discount** when purchasing.

CPSIA information can be obtained
at www.ICGtesting.com
Printed in the USA
BVHW082128061221
623390BV00004B/171